FIERCE PROTECTOR

THE BIANCHI CHRONICLES
BOOK THREE

LAURA BENNETT

Paperback ISBN: 978-1-7384916-4-3

Hardback ISBN: 978-1-7384916-5-0

BLURB

DOCTOR KATERINA MANCINI IS A FORCE TO BE RECKONED WITH

Surgeon by day and mob doctor by night. There's almost nothing she can't handle. Except maybe the man who's been assigned to deal with her stalker. It was so much easier pretending her dad's best friend wasn't everything she'd ever wanted before he became her permanent shadow.
How dare he swoop in and rescue her!

STEFANO TIERO IS A MAN POSSESSED

He's spent years denying his feelings for Katerina, burying them under the weight of all the reasons he can't have her. Now she's in danger and he can't keep himself away from her. She's his. He'll keep her safe whether she likes it or not.

The more time they're forced to spend together, the harder it is to resist the inevitable.

BEFORE YOU BEGIN...

While this book is less dark than books one and two in *The Bianchi Chronicles*, the characters are still morally grey and it does touch on themes of medical trauma, unwanted attention, stalking, sociopathy, and organised crime.

Fierce Protector is an adult romance where our main characters gravitate towards bratting and caretaking. There will be elements of dominance, submission, praise, and mild impact play, though a specific dynamic is never explicitly discussed or defined.

This book is written in British English so remember we like *s* over *z*, *-our* over *-or* and we put two *ls* in words like levelling. There are some concessions for words that are specific to the characters' vocabulary like trash over bin, trunk over boot etc. However, if you find an error or issue and want to let me know, visit www.laurabennet tauthor.com/books and click on *Report Error*.

THE BIANCHI CHRONICLES SO FAR...

Fierce Protector is book three in the series and weaves in and out of the *Broken Princess* and *Brutal Queen* timeline. It can be read as a standalone but will contain spoilers for the first two books.

Read on if you want a refresher on the *Bianchiverse*.

The Syndicate is an alliance between the Bianchis and the De Lucas. Two rival mafia families who were at war until a truce was called and a marriage between Aurora Bianchi and Max De Luca was arranged to solidify a peace.

The Bianchi Chronicles begin when the De Lucas stage a coup—their plan being to annihilate anyone loyal to the Bianchis, murdering Don Mateo Bianchi and leaving his daughter, Aurora, for dead.

The *Broken and Brutal* duet follows Aurora as she avenges her father's death, forging an army and waging war against the De Lucas. She's supported by The Bianchi Bastards—Enzo, Sinclair, Nico, and Benedict—who sacrifice everything to help her.

Stefano and Katerina are featured in the first two books. He is the Bianchi consigliere, while she is a surgeon and mob doctor. Both are loyal to the Bianchis.

DON

AURORA
BIANCHI

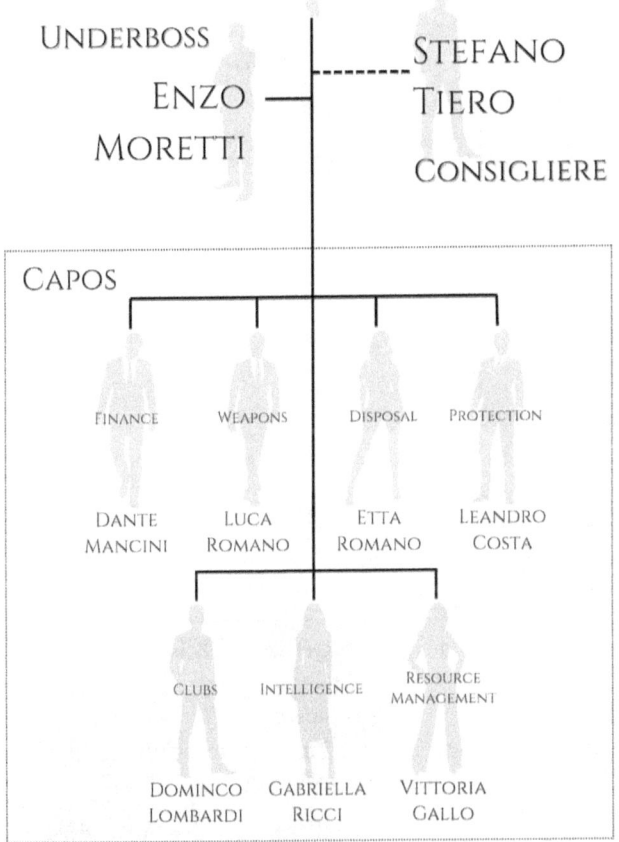

UNDERBOSS

ENZO
MORETTI

STEFANO
TIERO

CONSIGLIERE

CAPOS

FINANCE

WEAPONS

DISPOSAL

PROTECTION

DANTE
MANCINI

LUCA
ROMANO

ETTA
ROMANO

LEANDRO
COSTA

CLUBS

INTELLIGENCE

RESOURCE
MANAGEMENT

DOMINCO
LOMBARDI

GABRIELLA
RICCI

VITTORIA
GALLO

BEFORE YOU BEGIN...

THE MANCINI FAMILY

DANTE MANCINI — *estranged* — SARA MANCINI
BIANCHI CAPO

KATERINA MANCINI   MICHAEL MANCINI
DOCTOR   BIANCHI FOOT SOLDIER

THE TIERO BROTHERS

STEFANO TIERO   DAVIDE TIERO   ROMAN TIERO
CONSIGLIERE

THE BIANCHI FAMILY

MATEO BIANCHI — *married* — FRANCESCA BIANCHI
MURDERED   DECEASED

ISABELLA BIANCHI   AURORA BIANCHI *estranged*
MURDERED   BIANCHI DON

THE DE LUCA FAMILY

SALVATORE DE LUCA — *married* — EVANGELINE DE LUCA
DE LUCA DON   DECEASED

MASSIMO 'MAX' DE LUCA
DE LUCA HEIR

THE BIANCHI BASTARDS

ENZO MORETTI   NICOLO VERARDI   BRUNO SINCLAIR
UNDERBOSS   INTERROGATION   TECH SPECIALIST

THE ROMANO SIBLINGS

BENEDICT ROMANO   ETTA ROMANO   LUCA 'LUC' ROMANO
DEMOLITIONS   BIANCHI CAPO *twins* BIANCHI CAPO

X

For everyone who's waited long enough
for their happily ever after.

Not everyone wants a knight in shining armour,
but it's hard to say no to a stern brunch daddy!

CHAPTER ONE

KATERINA

FOUR YEARS AGO...

It's criminal how good that man looks in a suit. But in a tux? Stefano Tiero looks like a god. A very forbidden, completely off-limits, god. One with broad shoulders and the perfect amount of grey dusting his temples. I don't know when exactly I stopped looking at my father's best friend as 'Uncle Stefano', but all I know is every time I bump into him, I contemplate making very questionable life choices. I don't care that he's fourteen years my senior, and if I'm being entirely honest, that's part of his appeal. He's a man, not a man-child.

I swear, men my age go out of their way to make themselves as unattractive to the opposite sex as possible. I'm thirty years old and I've spent the better part of a decade working my ass off to get where I am. I don't have the time or inclination to waste any more of my life trying to find the exception to the general rule of mediocrity. Especially not when, as far as I'm concerned, I've found him already.

Trying not to look obvious, I sip my champagne and glance across the reception room at Stefano. He's chatting with my father on the other side of the dance floor and every time he takes a sip of his whiskey, and his lips touch the tumbler, I wish I was that glass. It's ridiculous really. I've been harbouring this crush for so long, I can't remember a time when I haven't pined after him like some kind of lovesick teenager. Wondering if one day he might see me as the woman I've become and not Dante Mancini's daughter.

I fantasise that he's the kind of man who'd appreciate me for what I really am; a strong, confident woman who needs a man who can match her, and not just be another insecure asshole intimidated by a woman's success.

A server cuts a path in front of me, momentarily blocking my view and breaking me out of my daydream. She's holding a tray full of lethal-looking shots and it only takes me a few seconds to make my first terrible decision of the evening. If I'm going to make it through this wedding reception, I'm going to need to be a hell of a lot more drunk than I am now. The ceremony was a farce of insincere vows and now I'm surrounded by people forced into a truce by marriage.

Half the room is filled with people I'd risk anything for—the Bianchis—and the other half I wouldn't trust as far as I could throw them. The marriage of Aurora Bianchi to Max De Luca might be our only shot at peace between the two Cosa Nostra families, but it feels more like a wake than a wedding reception.

Every time I catch a glimpse of the bride, I see the smile that doesn't reach her eyes, and I hate that she's the sacrifice for this ceasefire. This wedding is nothing more than a business deal, and Aurora is being used as collateral. I understand that it's necessary—the Bianchi's and the De Lucas have been at war for too long—there's just something about Max De Luca that makes my blood run cold. I catch a flourish of white lace in my peripheral vision and turn to see the groom spinning Aurora around the dancefloor for their first dance. The way he looks at her—dark and menacing—does nothing to assuage my fears for her.

"Do me a favour," I say, fishing a bundle of notes from my purse to slip the harried server a tip. "Keep these coming." Glancing down, she gives me a wry smile and a nod. I double-fist two of the shot glasses, downing them one after the other, gasping as the mix of alcohol and lime burns my throat. "Kamikazes? Really? This reception is going to get so messy."

"You're not wrong," she replies with a giggle, before dipping her head and continuing through the swathes of guests.

I turn and make a beeline for the buffet table, keen to line my stomach with something a little more substantial than the canapés I snaffled earlier. I'm distracted by the bruschetta and some delicious-looking arancini when I feel *his* presence behind me.

"Your father sent me over to find out why you're avoiding him, Katerina," Stefano whispers over my shoulder. As the warmth of his breath skips over my cheek, it's all I can do not to bite my bottom lip and let out a little moan. Instead, I roll back my shoulders and stiffen my spine before turning to face the most attractive man I know.

"I'm not avoiding Dad," I reply. *I'm avoiding you.* I'm avoiding that intoxicating smile. Stefano has many smiles, but there's only one that's truly genuine. It's the one where he cocks his head to the side and softens his expression just enough to let it reach his eyes. And don't get me started on that dimple. "Essentially, everyone we know is here; I've been busy catching up."

"I mean, sure. You looked like you had a lot to say to that wall I've watched you hugging for the last half hour," he says, leaning in conspiratorially. "Since when did the feistiest girl I know become a wallflower?" I wince at his choice of words. They cut me deeper than I expect them to. The idea that he thinks I'm dull is downright hurtful.

"Well, fuck you very much," I blurt out. His expression morphs into one of complete confusion. Of course, he's oblivious as to why insinuating I'm in some way plain or unremarkable might be insulting. *Jesus, this is unbearable.*

Throwing my plate down on the table, I wince at the loud clank of the crockery as it slides into the other platters of food, before I turn and storm off in the opposite direction.

I don't have a clue where I'm going, but I know I need

to be as far away from him as possible. I'm equal parts angry and mortified. I'm sure he was just trying to tease me, but nothing will punch you in the gut like the man you want to climb like a tree thinking you're a bland version of your former self.

Just fucking great.

"Katerina, wait," he calls out after me, but I don't look back. I'm halfway across the dance floor, heading towards the doors to the garden patio when he catches up to me. Stefano grabs my wrist in his palm and spins me to face him, hitting me with a reassuring yet pleading expression. I snake my wrist out of his grasp and continue on my way outside. The heat from his touch sends goosebumps up my arms and a shiver down my spine, but I shake it off, continuing my tantrum, running away from both him and the feelings he stirs within me.

"What's got into you? Where the fuck are you going?" His tone is laced with frustration, but it doesn't stop me.

"What's got into me? Nothing. Nothing's got *into* me, and that's exactly the fucking problem," I mutter under my breath, being careful to make sure he can't hear me over the din of the dancefloor. Somewhere in the back of my mind, I know exactly how counterproductive my attitude is, but what's the point if he's truly never going to see me for the woman I am?

I spot my waitress out of the corner of my eye and make a detour her way, grabbing another shot on my way to the exit. I slam it back in one and place the shot glass back on the tray, never slowing my pace.

The cold night air hits me almost as hard as the additional shot, but I still don't stop, stomping down the ornate stone staircase to the overly-manicured lawn. I instantly lose my heels into the soft ground, and just as I'm stepping out of them, bare feet on the dewy grass, Stefano's palms settle on my upper arms. He doesn't try and turn me, simply stands at my back and rests his hands gently against my skin like he's trying to settle a skittish animal, holding me gently to his chest.

My body appreciates the gesture, but my mind wants to tell him to go fuck himself.

"Are you going to tell me what's going on with you?" he asks softly.

"What's the point?" I reply petulantly, using every bit of willpower in my arsenal not to whimper as my body responds to his closeness. His body heat. His scent. Both conspiring to seduce me.

"Has someone upset you? I swear I'll have their balls on a platter if they have, Katerina." There's genuine concern in his voice, but that only makes it worse. He's so fucking unaware, he doesn't even know that it's him that's hurting me. Him that has never and will never see me how I want him to. A lone tear escapes from the corner of my eye, and I fail miserably to hide the sniffle that accompanies it. Traitorous body.

"Hey now, what's this?" Stefano says, pulling me tighter against his chest and wrapping me inside a bear hug that only makes it worse. I wriggle out of his grip and move away before turning to face him, losing myself in his midnight-blue eyes. It's either the worry etched on his face or the third kamikaze that has me opening my mouth and making my next terrible life choice of the evening.

I take the three paces needed to bring us toe to toe and wedge my hands firmly on my hips. "What do I have to do for you to notice me? How long do I have to wait, huh, Stefano?" I force out, my exasperation betraying emotions I've buried for years.

It cuts like a knife to my chest when his face morphs into one of complete and utter shock. He takes a step back, trying to put some distance between us, but I'm all out of self-respect, and I'm done pretending I don't want him. I move with him, matching each one of his retreating strides with an advancing one.

My hands find his cheeks and he freezes, our gazes colliding and a look I can't discern casting a shadow across his features.

"Don't," he commands with a dark tone he's never used with *me* before. I know all his tones. They tell me everything I need to know. This one sends a shiver down my spine, but does nothing to dissuade me.

Fuck It.

STEFANO

The second her lips touch mine, something almost primal spurs to life inside me. I've known Katerina her whole life. I've come to admire and respect the formidable woman she's grown into, but this feeling coursing through me right now is not that of a doting family friend. It's possessive, passionate, and undeniable.

She's a stunning woman who's as intelligent as she is beautiful. As gracious as she is petulant. She possesses the most unique collection of traits. They're an exquisite blend and while I've always recognised them in her, I've never been more tempted by them than I am now.

She's magnificent.

Her breath is hot against mine, and when her tongue sweeps against the seam of my lips, I have less than half a moment to decide between right and wrong. Do I stop this before it goes too far or do I, for once, listen to the parts of myself I keep buried? Do I ignore my head and obey my heart?

She lets out a tiny whimper and I'm done for.

The second I taste the citrus on her tongue, I know nothing will ever be the same between us again. She tastes like every pleasure I've ever denied myself, all wrapped up in a woman I can never have. Our kiss descends into something more desperate, frantic almost.

I want her. I need her, and it's going to destroy me giving her up. There's no way I can keep her. Her father would never forgive me.

I register the moment she realises the impact of what we're doing. She falters for a fraction of a second—her lips stilling against mine—but it's just long enough for sense and logic to make themselves known, and it steals our moment from us.

We pull back and stare in silence, letting the pregnant pause stretch out until it's almost unbearable. It doesn't matter that we're concealed by the darkness of the grounds, far away from the house. It still feels dangerous. Like we could be exposed at any moment by a stray guest. Both of us hesitant to speak, only able to pant as we steady our breaths. I know the minute I open my mouth, I'll ruin this moment.

"We can't." The words tumble out of my mouth. A twinge of regret lances through my chest, and it only gets worse when Katerina's expression falls.

She dips her chin, her eyelids shuttering closed, the sweep of her lashes wet with tears. "I know."

I reach out to brush my hand down her arm and she flinches. Before I can stop her, she's yanking her shoes out of the grass and running across the lawn. Away from the party; away from me.

It takes everything in me not to chase after her. Not to take her in my arms and finish the kiss we started. Not to pursue her just so that I know she's safe. I know she's perfectly capable of looking after herself, but the guest list for this wedding is a veritable den of vipers. I hold my ground, determined to give her space, while also watching to ensure that no one follows her.

I don't know what to do next. How to go back to how I felt five minutes ago—completely oblivious to how much I want that woman? All my walls have come crashing down, and I don't think I'll ever be able to build them back up. Not now I know what she tastes like. I'm forty-four years old and no one has ever made me feel like that. She's stirred a desire that can never become a reality.

I run my hands over my face and stare up at the night sky. I don't know how long I stand there, but when I see the flicker of a shooting star in the corner of the night sky, I close my eyes and wish.

Wish for what I know I can never have: my best friend's daughter.

CHAPTER TWO

KATERINA

PRESENT DAY...

Why, when you've spent hours saving a patient's life, do they try and fuck up all your hard work by crashing on you? Honestly, it's just plain rude. Especially when it's not related to the problem you've just fixed. I'd been seconds away from closing when the patient's blood pressure dropped through the floor, and he arrested.

Of course, the cardiologist on call has kept us waiting, which is why I'm now elbow-deep in my patient's chest cavity. I'm not averse to the exhilaration and thrill of dealing with complications, but I already saved this asshole once and I'm tired.

It's taking longer than I would like to get the

patient's vitals stabilised. I'm shouting for an extra hand to hold a clamp as the head of cardiology bursts into the operating room, finally deigning us with his presence.

"Nice of you to show up," I mutter into the back of my surgical mask. Hoping rather than knowing that I said it quietly enough for the fabric to muffle my words.

"Have something to say to me?" Doctor Jenkins says as the surgical nurse secures his gloves.

While we're technically peers, both heads of our departments, this prick goes out of his way to make sure everyone knows his seniority and specialty make him superior. I can't deny, he's a skilled doctor, but he's also a narcissist with a god complex. He scrubs up reasonably well when he has to impress the hospital board, concealing his heinous personality behind a veneer of charisma, but whenever I see his charm in action, I'm reminded that no matter how you try to present yourself, it doesn't change what you are. Even a waxed cunt is still a cunt.

I bite the inside of my cheek before I rattle off the chain of events that led to me cracking the patient's chest. After a back and forth on the best course, we work quickly to get the patient stabilised. I expect Doctor Jenkins to dismiss me as soon as the danger has passed, and I'm ready to start a fight over needing to stay to ensure the hours of work resecting this colon haven't been compromised. Instead, he surprises me by asking me to harvest the graft he needs for the bypass.

I can't tell whether it's because he rates me as a surgeon, or he just wants a captive audience to bask in his greatness. Either way, after waiting for the leg to be draped by the surgical nurses, I move into position to harvest his saphenous vein for graft. It doesn't take long and then I'm relegated to the position of Doctor Jenkins' surgical bitch, holding his clamps for the next three hours. There's an art to his technique, though, at times, I wonder if his skill is born from talent or obsession.

By the time I make it to my locker, my head is pounding, and every throb sends pulses into my neck and shoulders, doing nothing but highlighting how tight they are. All I want to do is collapse, but instead, I lean forward and rest my head against the door, closing my eyes. Maybe I should just sleep in the on-call room tonight. I'm back on in ten hours anyway.

Then I remember that Danny's on shift tonight, which means he'll be pestering me every thirty minutes with things only *I* could help him with. Don't get me wrong, he's a good nurse, but I swear if he doesn't get over this little crush soon, I'm going to end up in front of HR for punching him in his lost little puppy-dog face. We went on one date and it was a disaster. He needs to move on and stop holding out for more.

There's a loud buzzing and an offensively harsh vibration through the door of my locker, which makes me flinch and rub my temples. Opening the door, I reach straight for my phone, which lights up instantly with notifications. Fifteen missed calls and seven texts from Stefano Tiero. *Shit*. Something must be wrong. I scramble to call him without reading a single text.

He answers on the first ring, and before I can ask what the emergency is, he jumps in first. "What the fuck are you playing at, Katerina?" I wince as he shouts down the phone.

I can count on one hand the number of times I've heard him raise his voice to anyone. I straighten my back as much as my aching muscles will allow, as if trying to bolster my resolve and remind myself that while this may be one of the most powerful men I know, he has no business telling me off. "Why the fuck are you shouting at me?" I say through gritted teeth.

There's a pause, followed by a staccato cough as he clears his throat.

"Why didn't you tell me?" His voice is strained, but now at least it's quieter, and my heart breaks a little when I realise that he must have found out about Aurora.

"Oh, I don't know, *Uncle* Stefano... maybe because the son of a rival don had just killed his father-in-law as part of a fucking coup, left his wife for dead, and I was sworn to secrecy until she was safe. Until Aurora knew who she could trust, I had to keep my mouth shut. I couldn't even tell Dad, so why are you giving *me* shit?" I rasp, my voice barely above a whisper as my eyes dart around the locker room, double checking I'm alone in here.

There's another long pause and I'm baffled why, of all people, the Bianchi consigliere is contacting me about a situation as important as this one.

"That's not what I— never mind. I met with Aurora, Enzo, and Nico today, and we need to talk," he says, his voice more controlled but still sounding so very unlike him. "When do you finish your shift?"

"I'm heading home now," I say, unable to hide the weariness and letting out a half yawn.

"I'll meet you there." He hangs up before I can object.

It's been a long fucking day and the last thing I need is to face the man I've been avoiding being alone with for just over four years. I cringe when I remember how I embarrassed myself at Aurora's wedding. *I should never have had those kamikaze shots.*

Looking down at my blood-covered scrubs, I remember I still need to change. I reach to pull out my clothes, and a folded piece of notepaper flutters to the floor. I can't stop the roll of my eyes as I bend to pick up today's offering and unfurl it.

This day is going from bad to worse.

Did you know that the gold flecks in your irises are luminous under the OR lights? You come alive when you have a scalpel in your hand; it's scintillating to watch you work. You have a graceful elegance that few women possess.

I drag my hand over my face. I don't have time for my secret admirer today. He's persistent, I'll give him that, but I'm so over it now. It's not every day, and it's not like they're offensive, but they border on creepy and are just enough to give me pause every time I find one. I know it's just a locker, but it feels like an invasion of privacy to find them among my things. It's been going on for weeks now, and I'm rapidly running out of patience.

I shove the note back in my locker and head to the showers to wash the day off before I head home to face Stefano Tiero. As I step under the spray, I make a wish that the water will wash away the flush of heat that chases a path across my skin when I think of seeing him tonight. I've had a long time to try and quash my feelings for him, and evidently, the only success I've had has been in fooling myself.

CHAPTER THREE

STEFANO

Every minute I wait, the harder it is to maintain my composure. I check my watch for the hundredth time and realise that I've been sitting on the steps of Katerina's front porch for over an hour. *What the fuck is taking her so long?*

I know I'm being impatient, but I'm on edge after the clusterfuck of a meeting this afternoon. Of all the things the underboss and I suspected when we couldn't get hold of Don Bianchi, him being murdered by Max De Luca was not even on our list. To say that I'm in shock is an understatement. I'm fucking numb.

I've been Mateo Bianchi's consigliere, his right-hand man, for well over a decade. He's closer to me than my own brothers. I dip my head and swallow, trying to suppress the emotions that threaten to choke me. *Was* closer.

Listening and remaining calm while his daughter,

Aurora, told me how he died was the hardest thing I've ever done. The grief settled in my body at a cellular level. Then, when I found out what Max De Luca did to Aurora, I wanted to tear the skin from my body. Every member of the Bianchi family has failed her, and it feels like there's nothing I'll ever be able to do or say that will make it right.

What makes it worse is there's nothing I can do until we can uncover more information about who else sold their soul to the devil and betrayed Mateo. Betrayed us all.

That thought weighs on me so heavily, I feel helpless. I was close to losing it, struggling not to be overrun by the rage coursing through me, but the minute Nico mentioned Katerina, I snapped out of it.

He'd taken me aside, and with his usual disregard for details, told me 'Someone's bothering the doc'. In his defence, that's all I needed to know. The idea of there being any type of threat to Katerina has my stomach tied up in knots and my temper simmering somewhere close to rage.

I've spent years keeping my distance, but she's rarely been far from my thoughts since that night, hidden in the darkness of the wedding venue's grounds. I've tried to forget how she felt in my arms, how sweet she tasted, but honestly, sometimes it's all I can think about. The only thing that has stopped me from turning up on her doorstep before now is knowing I'm wrong for her. Even if her father wasn't my best friend, she's too good for me and I'm too old for her.

When her car pulls into the driveway, I stop staring

into the shine on my Oxfords and lift my gaze. She pulls up next to my town car but doesn't get out. I can see her hard glare through the windscreen, and if I know her half as well as I think I do, she's readying herself for an argument. A smile teases the corner of my mouth. I shouldn't enjoy getting a reaction out of her, but I do. *So very much.* If there's one thing that makes my day, it's seeing her quick wit and sharp tongue in action, even when I'm on the receiving end of it.

Doctor Katerina Mancini has always been a force to be reckoned with. She's never been the type of woman to accept help from anyone. Everything she has she's earned for herself, in spite of her upbringing and connections, not because of them. I respect the hell out of her for it. The minute she qualified, she could have left and worked anywhere, but she chose to stick by the family. Her only condition was that she reported to no one. She would get an independent life and career but would be on-call to the Bianchi family whenever she was needed. Her request was a no-brainer.

That doesn't mean she's alone, though. Her father being a capo means she's always been under our protection. At one point or another, she's dug a bullet out of or stitched up half the fucking foot soldiers. She's one of us and there's no way we'd tolerate a threat to her safety.

If she wants to fight over this stalker business, then so be it. But like fuck am I going to let her put herself at risk.

There's a soft snick as she pops the handle before she shoves the door open. The clack of her heels on the red bricks punctuates her irate march towards me. I grab the handrail and haul myself up. It's only my being on the first step that gives me a half a foot on her.

"Jesus, how do you work all day in those heels?" I say disapprovingly, but it morphs into something more admiring as my eyes start to wander up the length of her stocking-clad calves. I shake my head to snap myself out of it when her tight black pencil skirt obstructs my view.

Get it together, you lecherous asshole. She's Dante's daughter. Even if she wasn't fourteen years my junior, Dante would gut me if he caught me ogling his baby girl.

She folds her arms, cocks a hip, and taps the toe of her shiny black heels, drawing my attention to the ground again. "Yes, Stefano. I totter around the OR in my Jimmy Choo's, hoping that the litres of blood I'm often covered in won't splatter my Mary Janes." I don't need to look up to hear the eye roll in her tone. She tries to barge past me and looks almost disappointed when I step to the side to let her pass. It's as if she wanted to body-check me.

It shouldn't appeal to me when she acts like a brat, but my dick disagrees. It feels like she's been teasing my cock with her snark for years. Which is one of the many reasons I find it so difficult to be around her.

She's through the door and kicking her heels off before I get a chance to respond. She abandons her stuff in a crumpled heap and makes a beeline into the kitchen.

"I assume I'm not getting rid of you until you've said your piece, right?" she shouts over her shoulder as I close the front door. I can't help but add her shoes to the rack and hang up her coat on the hooks. "Whiskey or wine, old man?" she shouts.

"Whiskey, neat," I holler back, taking a second to stare at my reflection in her hallway mirror. I straighten my collar and spend a moment too long distracted by the dusting of grey at my temples. Cupboard doors bang and glasses clink from the kitchen. Throwing my shoulders back and fixing a stern glare on my face, I follow the sounds of her not-so-subtle strop to the kitchen. It seems she's not the only one that needs to prepare for battle.

I roll my eyes when I notice the ice she's added to my drink, but I refuse to let her rile me. I grab the glass off the counter and take a long draught, letting the rich amber liquid restore me as I swallow it down. Her eyes follow the motion and drop to my neck as if she's watching my Adam's apple bob with each gulp. I can't help but play up to her attention, loosening my tie and unbuttoning my collar, seeing how long I can keep her gaze on my body.

I smile when she bites into her plump bottom lip, but I'm left feeling disappointed when she snaps herself out of her little ogling session. Her eyes find mine and the hard glare returns. I place the glass down on the counter; rattling ice the only sound while I take a moment to gather my thoughts, running my hands over my face before pulling up a stool and leaning forwards on the countertop.

"I've had the worst fucking day, Katerina." My candour seems to take her by surprise and her expression softens. "I imagine as terrible a day as you had when Zo brought you in to treat Aurora."

"Yeah. I'm not going to lie. Having to treat the wounds Max inflicted on her was..." her voice is barely above a whisper, and she crumples, grabbing a stool and sinking into it, "difficult."

Difficult seems like such an inadequate word in this situation. The injuries I saw on Aurora this afternoon were far worse than I could have imagined. Over the years, I've seen my men succumb to far less. I dread to think what Aurora looked like a few days ago when Katerina first treated her.

"I know she looks bad, Stef, but why are you ready to tear me a new one for doing my job?"

Before answering, I grab my glass and toss the ice into the sink, reach for the bottle of whiskey, and pour myself another two fingers.

"I'm not here to shout at you for looking after her. You fucking saved her when it seems all anyone else has done is let her down." I pause, swallowing my whiskey in one large glug. I straighten up on the stool and turn to face her, attempting to channel a calmness I don't truly feel. "I'm here to find out why the fuck you're not taking a stalker fucking seriously? And why the fuck your father doesn't know about this. Because I know for damn sure if he did, he'd have already had me looking into this."

A glimmer of guilt washes over her features, but it's swiftly quashed when she matches her posture to mine and squares off against me.

"I see. You're here because Nico's been telling tales on me?"

Without giving me a chance to respond, she hops down from her stool and storms out of the kitchen, but I'm not letting her walk away from me. She needs to hear what I have to say because I won't have her putting herself at risk. I grasp her forearm, spinning her to face me, and march her back until she's pressed against the hallway wall. My pulse quickens as I grip her biceps and our gazes lock in a heated standoff, while her ragged breaths buffer against my cheek, making my cock stir. A groan of pleasure threatens to rumble in the back of my throat, but I swallow it down.

"Will you calm-the-fuck-down and talk to me, you infuriating woman?" I say with an exasperated rasp. Her expression hardens and her body tenses in my hold as her temper rises to meet mine, the air becoming heavy as our gazes smoulder.

"Fuck you, Stef. I'm a grown woman and I can handle a workplace crush without having to call in the cavalry."

"I am not the fucking cavalry. You're supposed to keep the *family* informed of any threat to your safety, and you know it. That's part of the deal. If you work for us, we protect you."

"Oh my god, you're being ridiculous. I didn't tell anyone because it's not a big deal. It's nothing. It's a crush and a few notes left in my locker. It's basically high school level nonsense." She rails against me, her body writhing and drawing every urge I've tried to suppress to the surface. I force myself to loosen my grip, but I don't move away. I stay pressed up against her, drawn to her like I'm snared by a siren's song.

"If it's so harmless, why does Nico, of all the heartless bastards we know, think it's important enough to tell me about it, Katerina?"

"Because apparently, he's as much of an old woman as you. Now let me the fuck go. Right now." Planting her palms on my chest, she shoves me. From the frown that clouds her expression, it's obvious she was expecting to be able to escape easily. Not fucking likely. I may be forty-eight, but that doesn't mean I'm not built like a brick wall.

Most men in my position rely on their men and their guns to protect them and tend to slack off when it comes to staying on form. Half the capos couldn't fight their way out of a paper bag. It's embarrassing really.

Not me though, and she's mistaken if she thinks she can overpower me. The idea of it draws a smirk to my lips, which is swiftly followed by a gasp of pain when she scratches long gouges into my neck.

I jump backwards, more out of shock than anything, but I doubt she's done any lasting damage to anything other than my pride.

"Easy now, *micetta*. There's no need to get your claws out," I tease in a low rumble.

"Then back the fuck off, Stef." Her shoulders rise and fall in time with the soft pants escaping her parted lips. "This is getting out of hand."

"I couldn't agree more." She has no idea how much I agree. My heart thumps like it's trying to beat out of my chest. She hasn't been this close to me since that kiss and my body wants nothing more than to taste her again. My mind though, knows that if I did, it would be my undoing.

I straighten my collar and run my fingertips over her scratches, hoping the motion will soothe the sting and bring me back to my senses. Right now, it's taking everything in me not to throw her back against the wall and remind myself just how soft those lips feel against mine. *Fuck*. What is it about the way this woman rails against me that makes me want to conquer her?

Her rich chestnut eyes lock on to mine and as always, they simmer with unspoken words. The silence forces an air of awkwardness between us.

After flicking her gaze away, clocking the neatly stacked shoes by the front door, she smiles and lets out a resigned sigh. "I will concede that there is a guy at work who got in my way while I was trying to source supplies to treat Aurora. However, when I told Nico about it, I was venting. I needed to get back to the safe house, and Danny was slowing me down."

"Okay, but why does Nico think he's a stalker?" I ask, knowing she's not telling me everything.

"He's not a stalker. We went on one date and the chemistry wasn't there, so we decided to stay friends. It's just that his idea of friends involves a lot more day-to-day interaction than I'm used to. You know I'm an introvert at heart."

"Give me an example of what he's doing?" I stand a little straighter and cross my arms over my chest, refusing to drop this.

"He keeps swapping his shifts with other nurses to get on my rotation."

"And?" I push. A sheepish expression blossoms across her features, and I struggle to maintain my rigid composure. As she softens before me, I worry how much she's not saying. What if she's more worried than she's letting on and she doesn't trust me enough to tell me?

"On to my service."

"And?" I simply arch a brow with my last prompt.

Kat shakes her head before rolling her eyes, cocking her hip, and folding her arms across her body defensively. "And posts notes into my locker every day."

My body has moved before my brain has fully engaged. I slowly dip my head to hers and fix an unforgiving glower at her. "And you can't see why maybe that's a little unsafe? A man you rejected is inserting himself into your life. As you told me earlier, you're a grown ass woman, Katerina. How are you not seeing that this is problematic?"

"Well... when you put it like that. I guess I can see you have a point." Her voice is softer now, the cadence betraying the doubt that seems to be seeping into her thoughts. "But it's not your place to do anything about it. This is my life, Stefano. And it has the potential to impact my career."

Our foreheads are nearly touching, eyes entirely focused on each other, while our breaths ricochet off each other's cheeks. Every part of me is desperate to close what little distance is still left between us, but I know I can't. She can't be mine. "And why is that?"

"Because his father is on the hospital's board of directors, and I don't want to end up on the board's radar for the wrong reasons."

Of course, now it makes sense. "That's how he changed his shifts so easily. So, you need to get rid of him without pissing off the hospital administration?"

"Exactly. So, you see why you kneecapping him for wanting a second date is out of the question?" The thought of her dating leaves a bitter taste in my mouth.

Even if this asshole was good enough for her, I'd still detest him for simply being able to date her. When you add in not taking no for an answer, I'd gladly kneecap him.

"I can see your point, but I don't like that he hasn't got the message." I nod at her reasoning, but honestly, I'm too busy trying not to inhale whatever intoxicating scent is wafting off of her hair. I shouldn't be this close to her. If I stay here much longer, I'm likely to do something stupid. I swallow hard, the scruff of stubble scraping against my collar.

Katerina snaps my focus back to her with a gentle cough. "There is another option."

"I'm listening." *I think I'm listening.* It's tough to focus when her tongue flicks over her plump bottom lip.

"The quickest way for Danny to get the message would be to start seeing someone else."

Her words don't register right away, but when they do, I shake my head, forcing myself back to reality while taking a swift step away from her.

"What did you just say?" I ask, unable to hide the surprise in my voice. My mouth is suddenly as dry as The Sahara. *Is she saying what I think she's saying?*

"If he thought I was seeing someone else, he'd probably back off." There's a smile teasing the corners of her mouth and her familiar brand of impertinence is eking its way back into her tone. "I guess I could ask one of Dad's men to do me a solid and show up a few times at the hospital."

"The fuck you will," I growl, my hand shooting out and gripping her jaw tightly. "If you think I'm letting anyone else handle this little weasel, you have another thing coming, Katerina."

"You're too easy, Stefano," she says with a wicked grin, and I'm so far beyond screwed.

I release my grip and drop my hand, closing my eyes tightly. *Thou shalt not discipline your best friend's bratty daughter.* "And you're too tempting, Katerina. There's only so far you can push me before I break." I may have walked away from this temptation before, but I don't know if I can keep doing it. My thoughts oscillate between right and wrong, and for the first time, I wonder if my friendship with her father is worth the sacrifice I keep making by not making Katerina mine.

She taps her palm on my cheek before saying, "I'm counting on it."

I turn away from her, desperate to get out of this house, stalking out of the front door, slamming it as I go. My heart races, doing nothing to ease the yearning ache that's been caged there for so long.

Katerina Mancini doesn't realise what she's started.

CHAPTER FOUR

KATERINA

I 'm not entirely sure what line we just crossed, but I know we crossed one and I pushed us over it. I did not have 'suggest fake dating to my dad's oldest friend' on my bingo card for this year. *Shit. What have I done?*

I've wanted this man for longer than I care to admit, and he's never shown the slightest hint of attraction since *that* night. In return, I've done a spectacular job of avoiding him for the past few years. The last time we spent more than thirty minutes in each other's company was at Aurora's wedding, and look how that ended.

I close my eyes tight, trying to block out the memories of my spectacularly poor life choices that evening. Just a few of the many reasons I avoid Stefano... and kamikaze shooters. In my defence, he kissed me back... before rejecting me, leaving me devastated and fleeing the scene of my humiliation. That's a hangover I'm still recovering from four years later, and just his presence is bringing every detail of that ravenous kiss flooding back.

A kiss he's never even mentioned since. He's made it perfectly clear that I'm nothing more than Dante's daughter. A member of the family. An obligation.

So why the fuck was he acting like a possessive alphahole from the minute he stepped through my front door tonight? His behaviour is like an earthquake, shifting the ground beneath my feet, making it impossible to know what's real.

Technically, this is all his fault. As soon as I felt his hands on me, something in my physiology rewrote itself, and I knew I'd do anything to keep his eyes on mine. He looked like he wanted to devour me. The heat of his gaze, his touch, his overwhelming presence, sent flurries of goosebumps roaming across my skin. It was as torturous as it was hot as hell.

I wander back towards the kitchen and tidy away our glasses into the dishwasher, pausing to enjoy the scent of the amber liquid in his glass. It's an oaky aged malt with undertones of ginger that warm my nose as I inhale the remnants. It's been in my drinks cabinet for years. I maintain it's for when my dad visits, but deep down I've always known it's a lie. It's as much Stefano's favourite as it is my father's. However, keeping a $400 bottle of whiskey stocked for a man who, until now, had never stepped foot in my house would be crazy.

I grab my glass, pour myself a finger of it and head up the stairs.

When I reach my bedroom, I put my drink down and strip, tossing my clothes at the hamper and missing. I leave them where they fall and wonder if Stefano was here would he straighten them up like he did my hallway? I didn't miss that he'd put away my shoes and hung up my bag. It should irk me that he felt the need to tidy *my* things in *my* house, but it doesn't.

I've never wanted or needed anyone to take care of me, but when I think about Stefano taking care of me, it wouldn't be something I minded. *At all.*

Sitting at my dresser, I start my skincare routine. I'm not one to waste my time with endless lotions and potions, but as a woman in my thirties, not using the basics is foolish. Not to mention, these are the few moments each day where I get to look after myself. This and when I manage to grab some time in my home gym. What with my shifts at the hospital and my second job patching up the Cosa Nostra's stab wounds and bullet holes, it feels like I don't get a moment to myself these days.

When I'm finished with the face cream, I take a swig of my drink, enjoying the sensation as the whiskey warms me from the inside out. Then, reaching for the rose quartz gua sha, I revel in the contrasting temperature as I run its cool surface over my skin, massaging out the tension of the day. I have no idea what I'm doing or if there's any benefit to it, but I just enjoy how it feels, and it's become part of my nightly ritual.

I have to be back at the hospital in eight hours, so I set the four hideously loud alarms I'll need to coax me out of my pit in the morning before crawling under the covers. I down the dregs of the whiskey and wonder if it would taste even better on Stefano's lips. My heart sinks a little, knowing I'll never find out.

It's been a long shift, and while Danny's persistent attentions worked out great for my patients—he's a phenomenal nurse—he's been tapdancing on my last fucking nerve as he seems to be everywhere, constantly needing my input on charts or approvals for fuck-knows-what.

Thank God I have residents I can offload him onto. In order to get some peace, I've set them a challenge. Whoever keeps Danny out of my hair for the longest, gets to scrub in on the next massive abdominal trauma. It's not like it's a huge sacrifice on my part. All of them are perfectly capable—I wouldn't have them on my service if they weren't—but at least this way, I'm killing two birds with one stone. Danny and my residents have been AWOL for the last hour.

There's a series of aggressive beeps from my pager that have me rummaging around in the deep pocket of my doctor's coat till I find it. Glancing at the screen, it seems I've been summoned to the nurse's station on four.

Fuck. I knew my luck would run out sooner or later.

It doesn't take more than five minutes to make my way back up to the surgical floor. I'm approaching the nurse's station when an arm wraps around my waist and turns me towards a tall, warm body. My hackles rise, ready to give whoever has the audacity to touch me a piece of my mind, only to notice the arm in question is wrapped in a bespoke charcoal grey suit. I'm overwhelmed with a rich scent of oud and bergamot, which has me relaxing into his hold. I know who it is before our eyes meet.

Stefano.

"Sorry, darling, I just couldn't wait to see you." His lips are pressed to mine before I can register his words. The kiss is soft and delicate, his lips muffling but not silencing my squeal of surprise, and there's no concealing the satisfied moan that slips out from my lips. My mind is clouded with need and ignites every feeling I've long suppressed for this man.

In the second it takes for reality to sink in, he steals the weight of his lips from mine. I almost stamp my foot in annoyance. Not because he kissed me, but because I didn't have time to enjoy it. What's more, I'm speechless. Which is very unlike me.

"I... uh..." Words aren't wording right now.

Shaking my head, I attempt to pull myself together, but it's difficult when every romantic thought I've ever had about Stefano is rampaging through my mind like a stampede of wild horses. I'm pulled out of my fantasy world by the nurses chattering and the bitch who always screws up my charts muttering 'old enough to be her father'. I'm ready to tell her where she can shove her opinion when Stefano rests a hand on my lower back and drags my focus back to him.

"I know you weren't expecting me, but I thought I could surprise you and take you for a coffee." Stefano pauses and gestures towards someone behind me.

"Nurse Costello here was just telling me that the cart out front has the best coffee in the hospital. Isn't that right, Danny?"

There's an awkward pause as I pivot to face him. "Hi, Danny." My voice is thin and painfully awkward. I feel like a teenager who's just been busted trying to sneak her boyfriend up to her room.

What's worse is Danny looks devastated, like a puppy who's lost his favourite chew toy. Why I ever agreed to go on a date with him escapes me as I look into his sad eyes. All he needs is a quivering lip, and I'll truly feel like the villain in his story. He was never going to compare to what I want in a man. I'm ruined for anyone who's not gruff, dominant, and able to handle my attitude. Preferably someone in a tailor-made suit and carrying a gun.

"Err… yeah. Enjoy your coffee," he replies, his voice meek and his face crestfallen. He grabs a chart from the rack, turns, and retreats down the corridor without another word.

Great. Now I'm the bitch who humiliated him in front of all his co-workers. My hands are firmly on my hips and my toe is already tapping by the time I turn back to face Stefano. The arrogant smirk plastered across his face makes me want to slap it clean off of him.

He leans into me again, taking my elbow in his palm and steering me along the hallway. His low rumble drags itself across the shell of my ear as he whispers, "Not here, Katerina. You can unleash your vicious tongue once we're fully caffeinated."

Biting the inside of my cheek does nothing to stifle

my growl of frustration, but it does stop the tirade of words I want to hurl at him. I force what I'm hoping is a convincing smile, and follow along, if only to escape the shocked expressions of my colleagues. Not once in the years I've worked here has anyone I've dated visited at the hospital.

I'm aware that most of them think I'm a heartless bitch. Well, the other surgeons don't because they're almost all built to exude the same cold detachment necessary to carve people open on a daily basis. For male doctors, that makes them strong, stoic, and dependable. As a female surgeon, that same professionalism makes me a callous narcissist, incapable of enticing any man. At least that's the sentiment of the hospital grapevine.

If that's how they want to view me, so be it. I've never been one to get hung up on people's opinions of me. Unless you're feeding, financing, or fucking me, why should I? Plus, it's been a long time since I've needed anyone to take responsibility for any of those things. My side hustle for the Cosa Nostra pays handsomely and has wiped out the debt I amassed at med school. I'm yet to find a man who cooks better than my local takeout restaurants, and I have a drawer in my bedside table that, when paired with my rather vivid imagination, keeps me in orgasms.

Sure, I've dated over the years. There was the professor who thought the belly button was an erogenous zone, the stockbroker who thought the size of his portfolio offset his stunningly dull personality and the architect who had entirely too many opinions on why Bella should have picked Jacob. The problem with working pretty much every waking hour is that you mostly only bump into people in the line getting your morning coffee, and this back catalogue of mediocrity is why I've bought my own coffee machine.

It doesn't take long to navigate our way through the maze of corridors out into the afternoon sun. I look up and bathe in the warmth of it. Stefano walks us towards a bench off to the side of the courtyard and finally meets my eyes. He has the gall to smirk at my glare.

"Who the fuck do you think you are?" I grind out, but he simply shakes his head before pushing my shoulder lightly, encouraging me to sit down.

"Sit. First coffee, then shouting," he says with a smile.

His words do nothing to bring my boiling rage to a simmer, but what surprises me more than the fact I obey him, is that I *want* to obey him. There's something about the way he speaks to me that has my core clenching and my nipples peaking. A note of authority that for once, I don't want to rebel against quite so much.

I perch myself on the bench and turn to catch the first softening rays of the setting sun. I can't remember the last time I spent any time outside the hospital walls mid-shift. Sure, we have breaks, but I normally use them to grab a shower or catch up on charting with a snack from the cafeteria. Hospital, work, home, sleep, occasional *family* emergency, repeat. This is the most Vitamin D I've been exposed to in what feels like forever.

The changing colours in the sky lull me into a far more reasonable mood. Completely against my will. I glance back towards the kiosk and see Stefano at the counter, adding sugar to my coffee. It shouldn't make me happy that he knows how I take it because he's been in my life for as long as I can remember, but our history is also why this is a terrible idea, and what's worse is that it was *my* terrible idea.

Why did I open my big mouth? I'm a masochist, that's why.

I only said it to shock him. To get him to drop this ridiculous interest in a situation I'm perfectly capable of handling myself. Admittedly, he was right. I do need to take it more seriously, which is why I was going to have a word with Danny today. Deal with it myself, but oh no, Stefano's decided to entangle himself in a career I've managed to keep entirely separate from the family for years.

Heavy-handed, sexy-as-fuck, pig-headed, salt-n-pepper fox.

I'm so confused right now. I can't tell if I'm angry or turned on or both.

"So let me have it, then." His words snap me out of my trip down memory lane. He takes a seat next to me and hands me my coffee. His posture is relaxed, and that pisses me off even more.

"You can't just waltz into my hospital and make a unilateral decision that affects my career. What the hell are you playing at? Publicly marking your territory in front of the whole damn floor. You might as well have pissed on me for how subtle you were."

"In my defence—"

He's holding up a palm as if he's trying to calm a wild animal, which only serves to wind me up further. "There is no defence for this, Stefano. How dare you insert your-self into my life. You have no right."

"I think you'll find it was your idea," he says with a small, mischievous little shrug. This man is so fucking confusing. I can't tell if I want to fight him or fuck him. It's maddening.

"I wasn't serious. And I sure as shit didn't think you'd rock up the next day and run with it. This is ridiculous. You couldn't—I don't know—discuss it with me first?"

He drops his gaze to his coffee, looking oddly embar-rassed all of a sudden. I swear there's colour flushing his cheeks. I don't think I can remember a single time where I've seen a sheepish expression on his face. I mouth off and he smirks. It's our routine. We have it down pat. It catches me off guard and I find myself lost for words, letting the pause grow into an awkward silence.

"You have a point."

"Of course I have a point. Exactly how am I supposed to explain this to my dad? What if it gets back to him?"

He grimaces and I shouldn't find it endearing, but I do. He looks genuinely uncomfortable at the prospect of explaining this to my dad.

"You're a pain in my ass, Tiero," I say, trying to lighten the mood a little. A smile warms his features, and it diffuses my temper. A little.

"You want the truth?" he asks, running the tip of his index finger around the lid of his coffee cup.

"Always."

"I didn't plan it. I came to check him out, heard him talking about you with another nurse and—"

"Lost your mind?"

"Maybe. But I needed to do something. Everything is so out of control right now. I'm a consigliere with no don to serve. We're on the verge of a war, and we don't know who we'll be fighting. My hands are tied until we know more. There's nothing I can do. But this, this I can do something about. I know you think I'm being ridiculous, but just for a moment, can you humour an 'old man' as you so kindly put it?"

I choke a little on my coffee. "Well, when you put it like that..." I reach out a hand to his forearm and squeeze, trying to reassure him that I understand where he's coming from. Our gazes collide and the space between us feels heavy with a million things I want to say, but know I shouldn't. It's not my place to soothe him, even if all I want to do is hug him right now. Instead, with as much lightness as I can inject into my tone, I say, "Hey, you may be a bossy, overbearing pain in my ass, but you're not old, Stefano."

"I'm closer to your father's age than yours," he says, arching a brow.

"It would be great if you didn't mention that, as you had your lips on mine ten minutes ago. That's just creepy." I fake a little shudder to hammer home my point.

"Fair," he says with a chuckle, and I light up inside, feeling a little smug that I was able to coax out that sexy-as-fuck dimple.

"So, we're really trying this? Fake dating?" I ask. There's a slight tremble in my voice, not because I wouldn't love spending more time with him, but because I worry I'll love it too much.

"Well, you won't let me kneecap him," he responds, dimple still activated and playful smirk with it. That dimple is going to be the key to my ruin. "It's not like we need to do a lot. I'll swing by every now and again, and you just start telling everyone about your hot new boyfriend."

"My, we're full of ourselves, aren't we?"

"You could do worse, Doctor Mancini." I can't help but laugh at this side of him he's showing me. I've missed this. The gentle, teasing, and playful conversation. A pang of sadness creeps into my chest, reminding me how I wish my feelings didn't make it so hard to be near him.

"True," I concede. "But if I agree to this, you can't just rock up whenever you feel like it." I try and fail to tamp down the hint of unease in my tone. It's not that I object to him turning up, it's more that I've gone to great lengths to keep my career separate from anything remotely Cosa Nostra, and it unnerves me to have the two coming together so suddenly.

"I'll text you. I won't surprise you again, but the frequency of my visits will depend on how quickly Danny-boy takes the hint."

"I can work with that. Hopefully it won't be too long. I wouldn't want to distract you from your day job." I swear I catch a hint of disappointment in his expression. Which would be crazy because he's the one who rejected me after our kiss at Aurora's wedding. Burying that thought, I take a sip of my coffee and continue, "Are we telling Dad about this arrangement? I'd rather not split his focus. When the don's death becomes public knowledge, he's going to have enough on his plate. His men are not going to take it well. Plus, you've seen Danny now. He's a minor inconvenience at worst. I don't need the full wrath of the Cosa Nostra being unleashed on him, which is exactly what my dad will demand if he finds out."

He considers my words before nodding. "We'll keep it between us for now. I'll admit, he looks about as dangerous as a marshmallow knife."

The snort that erupts from my nose takes both of us by surprise. Well, that was the least sexy noise I've ever made and only serves to make me feel inadequate compared to Stefano Tiero. He always exudes a power that feels like it's ingrained in his DNA. *And it's quite possibly one of his sexiest qualities.*

He's a man who radiates the biggest of big dick energies. He could end a man with the flick of his wrist... but also *finish* a woman with the same.

Thankfully, he ignores my graceless reaction and continues. "We'll try it your way. For now. You make sure everyone knows how happy you are with your new boyfriend, and I'll keep an eye on Danny—" I try to interrupt and protest the need for surveillance, however light, but he steamrollers over me. "That part is non-negotiable. I'll be keeping tabs on him if I feel it's necessary. Besides, Aurora needs you on call for the foreseeable future and the last time you were needed, he delayed you with his bullshit. He's paying far too close attention to you, and we can't afford any civilian loose ends entangling themselves in our business."

Well, that told me.

"Don't fight me on this. You won't win, Katerina." His

voice is deep and rich, edged with an authoritative rasp and stern tone that has me wanting to clench my thighs together. There's a part of me that's revelling in the idea that a man like Stefano is making my safety a priority. But I'm not going to admit that to him.

"Doesn't sound like I have much of a choice, does it now?" I say, doing my best impression of a petulant teenager.

"No, you don't." He takes my cup and tosses it in the trash along with his own before reaching for my hand and pulling me up. "Now go back to work. I'll see you soon."

Leaning into me, he lays a gentle peck on my cheek and heads off towards the town car I didn't notice idling in the drop-off zone.

"I never knew you were this bossy, Stefano," I shout after him.

"Yes, you did," he calls, turning to glance back over his shoulder and hitting me with a wry smile. "And you love it."

CHAPTER FIVE

KATERINA

I understand why Stefano came to the hospital, really, I do. The Cosa Nostra protect their own, and I've had thirty-four years to adjust to their way of doing things. Right now, anyone inserting themselves into my life is a problem. The Syndicate is about to tear itself in two. Lines will be drawn, and people are going to be hurt. I need to be able to fly under the radar, not be under constant watch by some misguided crush.

It's only been two days, and Danny has already backed off. I haven't seen hide nor hair of him on my last shift. I feel a little bad, but I'm not a people person, and having to be consistently professional while he was refusing to take the hint was grating on my last nerve.

I wish he'd cut it out with the notes though. It's unsettling knowing he's been creeping into the doctor's lounge to slip them through the vents in my locker every day. It's beginning to feel more and more like a violation. Today's was a bit much, even for him.

I'm disappointed in you, Doctor Mancini. He's not good enough for you.

I crumple the paper and throw it in the trash, fighting off a shiver at the tone. The difference between sweet and unnerving is persistence in the face of rejection. The last thing I need is for Stefano to see this. I'll admit the notes are crossing a line, but if I show it to Stefano, he'll overreact. I can't have him hospitalising James Costello's son.

I'm doubting myself, because I really thought Danny had got the message when I said no to a second date, but that can't be the case if he's still sending me these notes. How did I read him so wrong?

I'm just changing out of my scrubs when my phone echoes in my locker. When I check the notifications, the bottom drops out of my stomach. I have six missed calls from Sinclair and no voicemails. Members of criminal organisations tend not to leave messages when the contents could get them put away for years. The volume of calls doesn't bode well, so I call him back immediately, and he picks up on the first ring.

"We need you," Sinclair shouts down the line. His voice is urgent and strained as he goes on to give me the details of where I'm needed. It sounds like an absolute clusterfuck of a situation and there's no way I'm not dropping everything to help them. It's an all-out siege between the Bianchis and the De Lucas. I gasp when he drops the bomb that the De Lucas have captured Aurora. I worked my ass off to save her when her psycho husband left her for dead and I'll be damned if I let them finish the job.

"*Shit*, I'm on my way. Where?"

"Stefano is on his way to you. We have basic med-kits. Bring anything else you think we might need for triaging an all-out assault."

"Got it." Hanging up, I throw the phone down on the bench and grab a fresh set of scrubs. I don't have anything else with me that would be appropriate. Digging out my sneakers and pulling them on, I tie my hair back before grabbing a hoodie from the long-neglected gym kit at the bottom of my locker. I turf out everything else in the bag, then grab my phone and slam my locker shut, turning and nearly jumping out of my skin when I discover Danny standing in the doorway.

"You scared the shit out of me, Danny. What are you doing in here?" I snap. It's late, and even though I told Stefano he's not a real threat, catching him watching me is more than a little unsettling.

"Sorry, Doctor Mancini. Is everything okay?" he asks, his voice laced with a little too much concern, so much it sets my teeth on edge. He doesn't move out of my way as I head towards the door and despite his over-familiarity, he does look genuinely concerned, but I really don't have time for whatever this is right now.

"Family emergency," I say, and I barge him out of the way. As I head down the hallway towards the supply cupboard, I can hear the squeak of his thick-soled running shoes following me. Acutely aware that I'm under a time crunch, I opt for ignoring him and hoping he doesn't get in my way. I shoulder open the door, stepping into the room, and grabbing anything I think will be useful. Should I be using the hospital as my personal dispensary? No, but I don't think the kits I designed for our teams to carry with them will be enough. I have a stockpile of supplies at home that I can grab later if necessary, but you can never have enough gauze or suture kits when you're launching an assault on a rival family. I start cherry-picking a few smaller items when the door behind me opens.

"You going to tell me what's going on?" Danny presses. His brow is drawn in what looks like worry as opposed to judgment. I deserve judgment. I'm stealing from the hospital after all.

I turn, cocking a hip and resting the holdall on it, checking what I've already got. "Wasn't planning to."

"You keep a lot of secrets," he says. It's a statement and not a question, and I have no doubt that he's also referring to the recent revelation of my new *boyfriend* as well as the fact I'm about to walk off shift with a bag full of stolen supplies.

"Ones I'm not going to elaborate on, Danny. I have to go." I zip up the bag, throw it over my shoulder, and elbow my way past him. "I'm sorry. If I *could* tell you... I still probably wouldn't." When I look back, my apology appears to have softened his expression, and he nods before turning and letting me go without uttering another word.

STEFANO IS quiet as he drives us across town. With every passing minute, the tension grows, leaving me worrying my lip and picking at my cuticles. This is not how I saw today going. I'm only called in after the action, never before it.

"You're to stay out of harm's way, in a van with your father's men. Any injuries will be brought to you, and when we find Aurora and Nico, you'll get them to safety. You're not to be within a quarter mile of the compound. Do I make myself clear?"

"Yes, sir." I fail abysmally to hide the 'fuck you' in my tone. I want to be doing more than just hanging back and picking up the pieces. Doesn't he realise this whole situation hurts me just as much as it hurts him?

We've been betrayed. Sold out to Salvatore De Luca. I may not be a foot soldier, but I was born and raised in this life and there's no way I'm standing by and letting monsters like the De Lucas slaughter us.

"What about Dad?" I try to hide the tremor in my words and fail, my voice breaking.

"We're hitting the De Lucas with a rapid response and reduced numbers. Your father is coordinating back up from Zo's safe house."

"Does he know I'm on the ground too?"

Stefano doesn't reply immediately. "He knows you'll be on the perimeter." He turns his head briefly and raises an eyebrow. "Don't make a liar out of me."

"Don't start with me, old man."

There's a barely audible growl from the driver's seat, though I don't know if it's because I'm arguing with him or because I called him old. I'm nervous and taking it out on him, so I feel a little bad about both.

"Sorry," I say meekly. "I didn't mean to snap. I know you're only trying to protect me."

When I cast my gaze his way, he dips his head, acknowledging my words, but as I turn back to look out the window, I swear I hear him whisper, "Always."

The buildings whizz by the window so fast and yet our pace feels glacial. When Stefano finally pulls the car to a stop, we find ourselves in the middle of a makeshift command centre. There are multiple panel vans and SUVs parked up with men congregating, ready for their orders. From memory, we're not far out from the De Luca compound.

I head towards Sin—Enzo's tech specialist—who's already reiterating Stefano's orders as I stop in front of him. "No fucking way you're going in with us."

"Of course not, you prick. I'm here to triage any casualties and help when you get Aurora and Nico out of there."

He gives me a 'I'll believe it when I see it' face, and I hold up my hands. "Scouts honour. I'll be in the van with my father's crew backing me up. Besides, this fucking guard dog you sicked on me is making it really hard to have any fun at the moment." I cock my head sideways at Stefano, who ignores my teasing.

"Less talk, more getting in the van, Katerina," Stefano instructs.

I shake my head and make a move towards the vehicle. "That's Doctor Mancini to you, old man."

Sinclair mutters quietly to Stefano under his breath, "So, she's glad of the protection, then?"

"I'm not above shooting you, Sinclair," I threaten. I don't hear Sin's response, but I don't need to. I have other things to be getting on with. I start sorting through the med kits and checking what I'm working with.

Leo, my father's right-hand man, hands me an earpiece so I can listen in on the action, before he closes the doors and moves us into position on the perimeter.

We're waiting for what feels like forever, and every time Stefano's voice rings out over the comms, updating his location, my heart beats a little more evenly. I've never been in the field like this before, but then, there's not been an assault like this in my lifetime. It's unprecedented.

Chatter erupts, and I heave out a sigh of relief when someone announces that they've found Nico and are bringing him to me. I start readying myself, laying out what I can for triaging trauma patients, but as I listen, I hear exactly what I don't want to hear. *"Fuck, Zo, we're sitting ducks out here!"*

I look up at Leo as we process the back and forth between Enzo and Sinclair.

"They're pinned down. We need to get in there," I plead.

"No way, Doc. I have my orders and you're staying put. Your father would have me shot," he says, shaking his head.

I pull myself forward between the front seats and lean close so the rest of the team can't hear. "Don't test me, Leo, or I'll tell my father about the time I caught you fucking my aunt in the guest room at his fiftieth birthday party." I lean back, crossing my arms over my chest and daring him to test me. "Your call."

"She came on to me," he mumbles before turning the engine over and putting it in gear. "You will stay in the fucking van." He guns it in the direction of the compound and pulls up in an alley at the rear. It's chaos in the courtyard. Even with the windows closed my ears are assaulted with a cacophony of gunfire and breaking glass. As I look out of the windscreen, Enzo bursts through a window on the second floor onto a flat roof, dropping low and focusing his weapon on taking out any unfriendlies. It probably takes less than a few minutes for him to neutralise the threats, but my heart is in my throat the whole time. There is a thunder of boots on the ground heading towards us before we see Sin, and his team hauling a pale-looking Nico our way. They throw open the rear doors and I blanch under Sin's glare.

"Thank fuck you're here, but you're on your own when Stefano finds out you went rogue." He looks exhausted and more than a little concerned to see me so close to the action, but I can also see that he's relieved to see me.

"Fucking coward," I say with a wink. Trying to reassure them all in some way with my usual attitude. I glance down at Nico and bang on the side of the van. "Close it up and get moving. I need to get him out of here. Now."

He's pale and despite the field tourniquet on his leg, it's obvious he's lost a lot of blood. I cut his pant leg open to get a better look, finding that the culprit is a gunshot wound above his knee. It's a through-and-through and appears to have missed the artery, but it's made a mess.

"Get me back to Zo's safe house. They have what I need to treat him there. I can't take him to the hospital. The city will be crawling with police looking for any injured stragglers they can pin this clusterfuck on," I bark out over my shoulder as I pack the wound with gauze.

"On it, Doc," Leo replies, his voice steady and even. Every one of my father's men are calm under pressure, which I appreciate now more than ever.

The further we move away from the compound, the weaker the signal in the earpiece gets. The last thing I hear before it cuts out is Stefano. *"Ground floor front room. Lay down cover fire. Aurora is the priority. Enzo is do—"*

"WHAT IS it about you lot? Always fucking up my masterpieces. Every time I patch you up, you go and break yourselves all over again." I'm talking to myself since my patient had to be sedated when we got back to the safe-house, so I startle when I get a response.

"We don't mean to, and in this case, the De Lucas started it." I smile at the familiar rich tenor of my father's voice, and when he crosses the room to stand behind me, I lean back into him and let his arms wrap me in a hug. "How are you doing, my brave girl?"

There's nothing like a parent's love and support to smash through your carefully crafted defences. I open my mouth to dismiss him and insist I'm fine, but all that falls out is a cascade of gentle sobs. I don't know where the surplus emotions have come from, but they wash over me like a river bursting its banks.

"Sh-sh-shhh. It's okay. I came down to tell you they're on their way back."

I turn in my seat and look up at him hopefully, but as soon as I meet his eyes, I know there's bad news. "Tell me. Please Dad, just tell me," I plead softly.

"They got Aurora out, but Enzo didn't make it." My father's words hit me with a force that drags the air from my lungs in a raw and strangled gasp. He squeezes me tight before dropping into a crouch by my side.

Dead? That can't be. He can't be gone. Enzo's one of the best of us. An ache settles in my bones, and it feels like it won't ever let go of its grip on me. I've known Enzo my entire life. We grew up together and grew even closer when his brother fell in love with my best friend. That feels like a lifetime ago now.

He's family.

Was family.

He's gone.

A wave of nausea rolls over me and I struggle to suppress the sadness that's threatening to pull me under.

"What about everyone else?" *Please let everyone else be okay,* I beg silently. *Please let my bossy-as-fuck fake boyfriend be okay.*

"Sinclair is on his way back now with Aurora, Benny, and Stefano. They'll be able to fill us in more when they return." My dad rubs my shoulder and hesitates before adding, "I'm not going to push this, you're an adult and you're a part of this world, but if you put yourself in danger like that again you're going to give your old man a heart attack."

I can't help but smile at his tone. It's as warm and loving as it is stern. "You know I had to, Dad. I couldn't not help." He arches an eyebrow, obviously not satisfied with my answer, prompting me to continue, "I'll be careful, Dad. I promise."

He shakes his head and smiles, standing back up and then kissing my forehead. "I guess that's all I can hope for. I need to head out, but I want you at home for the next family dinner. Your brother will be there. He's going to need proof of life when he finds out about everything that went down today. And it's been too long since you've joined us."

I start to protest but when I register the implacable expression on my father's face I nod. "I'll be there, Dad."

It's not that I don't want to see them, but half the time, family dinner includes my father's best friend. It was easier to make an excuse that I was called into surgery than to torture myself spending time with a man I can't have. I don't imagine it's going to be any less awkward sitting through family dinner now that I'm secretly fake dating Stefano. Either way, I'll still be wishing he was mine, and knowing he can't be.

"No excuses, Katerina," he mutters as he heads back out the med-room door.

I continue with my sutures, each stitch lulling me into a sort of trance as I focus on only what's in front of me. When I finish the last one, worry seeps back into my consciousness. Even though I know they're on their way back, I don't think this feeling of dread will fade until I see them with my own eyes.

Until I see Stefano.

I'M aware of Stefano's presence at my back, the anxiety that's taken up residence in my chest beginning to ebb.

"We need to debrief, and then I'm taking you home." His warm breath skates along the slope of my neck while he rests a hand on my shoulder. It's a small gesture, but it's everything I need right now. It quashes the undercurrent of unease rippling through me and makes me feel more grounded. Protected. Supported. Whatever is going on around us, Stefano always knows just how to handle me.

The next hour passes in a blur. I listen to Aurora as she addresses the room. It's a rousing speech, but it's not meant for me. She's taking control of her father's organisation. Practically daring anyone present to challenge her while honouring the memories of those we've lost today.

It's hard to fathom the implications of what she's saying. Salvatore De Luca is dead, his son still lives, and we are declaring war on the De Luca family.

Today has changed everything. I started the day on shift at the hospital and I'm ending it witnessing the ascension of the first female don.

CHAPTER SIX

As I drive Katerina home, the tension is almost palpable and does nothing to suppress the unsettling feelings today's events have stirred up. Everyone who lives this life knows the risks associated with it. We go into every confrontation knowing we might not come out of it but at the same time, assuming we're the ones who'll beat the odds. We're not untouchable though. Sometimes we lose people who deserved to cheat death.

Enzo is one of those people. *Was* one of those people.

Taking my eyes off the road, I glance at Katerina. She's subdued, lost in thought, staring out of the passenger side window. I catch the slightest tremble of her lip, which is the only indication that she's struggling. I'm not used to seeing her walls crack.

I haven't seen her fall apart since Isa's funeral. Years back, our don lost his eldest daughter. Both he and

Aurora were devastated, but Katerina... she lost her best friend and she's never been the same since. Isa brought out her playfulness and joy and when she was murdered, a part of Katerina died with her.

Seeing her mournful expression reflected back at me on the darkened window, I know exactly where I'm taking her and it's not back to her place. She's not going to like it, but after the day she's had, she needs someone to take care of her. She's so lost in thought she doesn't notice when I don't take the turn towards her neighbourhood. In fact, she doesn't figure it out until I pull into my driveway.

"What are we doing here?" Her tone is lacking its usual bite. Like the fight has left her.

I don't answer, and she doesn't force the issue. I'm not sure what I'd say if she did, but I don't want to leave her alone. Today has been a long and terrible day. Neither of us deserves to be alone tonight.

We're across the drive and into the house without saying a word. I don't miss the look of surprise on her face as she studies her surroundings. I can't remember the last time she was here, but a lot has changed.

When I first bought the place, it was a time capsule of all the worst decorating trends of the 70s. Every wall was panelled with hideous orange pine, while the floors were covered in a muted rainbow of discoloured shag carpets. Dante said I was crazy, buying the place, but it had always been my intention to buy a project. I needed something I could lose myself in after the worst of days. A place where the only thing I had to focus on was the task in front of me.

Therapy would have been cheaper.

This house is a money pit, but it's worth every penny. Most of the ground floor is open plan with double height ceilings in the living room that are flooded with light by the folding glass doors that open out to the deck. There's a brick fireplace housing a cast iron wood burning stove I salvaged from a scrap yard and reconditioned myself.

In fact, barring the sofa, I've scavenged most of the furniture in the house from antique stores or salvage yards. Even made a few pieces. Admittedly, the aesthetic is still largely influenced by wood but it's much more oak and leather sanctuary these days, than tangerine pine ski chalet.

"Take a seat. I'll grab you a drink and something you can sleep in." I say, waving towards the large leather sectional.

"Drink first, please. Red wine if you have one open," she says quietly before she flops down on the sofa and relaxes back into the cushions, closing her eyes.

"Who do you think you're talking to? Of course there's one open." I cross the room to a small bar and drinks cabinet in the corner, grabbing the bottle I opened last night. I pour out a large glass and place it on the table in front of her. "Be right back."

I find myself almost bounding up the stairs, eager to get back to her. Having Katerina in my home is sending a warm tingle through my body and making the hairs on the back of my neck tingle. Like the feeling you get when ASMR tickles your senses. Everything about having her in my home feels right. After years of denying how much I want her, it's like my heart has decided to overrule my head and is basking in any and all time I spend with her.

Whether she realises it or not, her presence has lifted me in a way I hadn't expected it to. I've spent years building this home, but honestly, tonight is the first time it's actually felt like one. What's the use of a home without someone to share it with?

I'm a man who's been ruled by logic for so long. I make the hard choices. I do what's right. But there's a little voice in the centre of my chest whispering that she is what's right, and without her, everything else feels wrong.

When I get to my room, I head to the walk-in and pull out some sweats and a T-shirt for Katerina to wear before catching a glimpse of myself in the mirror. I'm wearing my usual tailored charcoal-grey suit; one I have multiples of with only the occasional variation. I switch up the look with the odd feint pinstripe, but mostly this is my uniform. The only time I wear anything else is at the gym.

I strip before throwing on a pair of dark wash jeans I'm not sure have seen the light of day before, and a henley. *Do people even wear henleys these days?* I'm probably showing my age right now, but my suit is covered in blood, so I have to change. As I fold the suit, I notice it's singed. My dry cleaner is talented, but there's fuck all he can do with burn marks.

I ball it up and throw it into the trash, cursing Benny and his flair for explosives.

"It's not his fault you don't dress for combat."

I jump halfway out of my skin as Katerina appears in

the doorway. She looks less withdrawn and there's a hint of a smile dancing across her face.

"Jesus H Christ, woman. Are you trying to give me a heart attack?" My pulse races and I rest my hand across my chest. The movement only serves to highlight I haven't actually put the henley on yet and she tries to hide her smile, but her pink cheeks betray her with a subtle blush. I wrestle the shirt over my head and then pick up the clothes I got for her. "I thought I told you to relax and wait downstairs. Can't you ever do as you're told?"

She shrugs and crosses the threshold. "Rarely. Besides, I was intrigued. You were taking too long, and this place is unrecognisable since I last saw it. I wanted to see what else you changed. That and ask you who your contractor was." With her wine glass in one hand, she wanders through to the bathroom continuing her inspection.

"No contractor. Aside from some electrical and water work that needed certifying, this is all me." I chuckle when she pops her head around the doorframe with her eyebrows somewhere around her hairline and her mouth agape.

"Who are you, and what have you done with Stefano?" She squints theatrically as I laugh at the way her mockery is lightening the mood.

"Don't be so dramatic. This place was a relic in dire need of modernisation. I've only recently finished the bulk of it. There are still a few rooms that need finishing off though."

"It's impressive. Didn't know you had it in you."

"I'll give you a tour," I say, reaching for her elbow and steering her out of my bathroom.

"Lead the way, *Uncle* Stefano."

It's impossible not to wince every time she throws that word at me. "Stop calling me that. You never did when you were younger, so it makes no sense now."

She shrugs and does what she always does—completely ignores me. "If you say so, Uncle Stef."

Clenching my teeth, I swallow down the tension building inside me. "You're a brat sometimes, Katerina." I come to a stop in the hallway and she bumps into me arching her back, almost savouring the connection.

"Only sometimes?" As I turn back to face her, she quirks a slender brow. I've never met anyone who can say so much with the slant of an eyebrow. More often than not, hers are telling the nearest person to go fuck themselves. Right now, they're baiting me.

"It's been a long day. Don't test my resolve, Katerina." A shadow falls across her face, and it's impossible to miss the moment she retreats back into herself. Her smile pales and her shoulders drop. "Here," I say, pointing towards the door closest to us and handing her the clothes. "This is my guest room. Go grab a shower and get changed, then come downstairs and I'll have another glass of wine waiting for you, and I'll give you the full tour if you like."

She gently nods her head as she hesitates for a second before retreating into the room. I stare at the closed door, wondering what it would be like if she was mine and I could follow after her, before snapping myself out of it and forcing myself to walk away, back down to the living room.

Grabbing the open bottle of red, I carry it through to the kitchen and pour two glasses of wine before assuming a perch on a stool at the island. I take a moment to check my phone and see that all my team leads have checked in. All is safe at the Bianchi house and from the updates it looks like Dante dealt with the skirmishes at the clubs. It looks like both sides are taking time to organise and regroup. The repercussions of today will be felt for years to come.

Reaching for one of the glasses, I palm the base to warm it as I swirl my favourite red. I don't know how long I sit here, contemplating everything that's happened and is likely to be coming our way when there's a padding of feet on the tile floor and I look up to see Katerina making her way towards me. I lift the glass to my lips and take a large sip of my wine to mask my reaction to her. The second I caught a glimpse of her bundled up in my clothes, with her rich mahogany waves framing her face, I started salivating.

While the sweats are far too big for her, the T-shirt hangs in a way that's not tight yet somehow manages to highlight every curve, from the swell of her breasts to the flare of her hips.

It'll be a miracle if I manage to keep my hands off her.

"Your guest bathroom is insane. That shower is my new best friend. It's like the jets washed off years of stress." She reaches for the other glass and takes a sip while using her free hand to run her fingers through her hair, wafting her freshly showered scent through the air.

I have to bite the inside of my cheek to stop myself from groaning at her being saturated in the fragrance of my shower gel. She doesn't just smell like me; she smells like *mine*.

This woman is going to be the death of me.

I distract myself by taking her on a tour of the house. As I show her around, her smile slowly returns. Every time I point out something I've made myself she teases me a little but goes on to ask me more and more questions. She seems genuinely interested, and it fills me with a sense of pride. Aside from the odd delivery from my people and the rare occasion Dante has picked me up, I haven't had many people come here, let alone come inside long enough for me to wax lyrical about my obsession with dovetail joints.

When I've shown her everything, we find ourselves hovering in the hallway between my room and the guest bedroom. She stifles a yawn, and it's hard not to notice the adorable way her nose crinkles with it. Closing the distance between us, I lean in and take the glass from her hand. I'm close enough to appreciate the spark of interest in her eyes, like she wants me to kiss her. Our breaths mingle and it takes a mammoth amount of willpower to deny myself her taste. I turn my head and reach behind her for the door handle, pushing the door open for her.

"You need some rest. Go to bed, Katerina," I say, taking a step backwards. My cock twitches like it's objecting to my shutting whatever this is down.

I don't miss the shocked little gasp, and when I look at her face, I half expect to see outrage, but I've missed whatever expression it was and instead, she looks relaxed. Like she's relieved to have the decision made for her.

The idea that she enjoys giving up even a little control to me has my cock protesting even more and my zipper straining against my now fully hard length.

For a moment, I worry that I'm reading too much into things and then she smiles. It's sultry; the kind that hints at so much and promises everything. Turning and walking into the room, she speaks without looking back. "Goodnight, Uncle Stefano."

For fuck's sake.

CHAPTER SEVEN

SIX WEEKS LATER...

The next time I see Stefano Tiero, I'm going to punch him square in the face. I glance down at my clenched fists and decide that's a terrible idea. I need to protect my hands if I want to be able to do my job. Maybe violence is not the answer, but honestly, I'm at the end of my rope. He's at the hospital every damn day, and keeping up this charade is becoming increasingly difficult. Especially now.

Two weeks ago, I got a call I never expected to receive. Enzo was alive—barely—and I had to do everything in my power to bring him back to us. My worlds collided that day, but it didn't matter. My only task was to save him. For Aurora. For the Bianchi Bastards. For all of us.

It took every ounce of my skill, but when he pulled through, I don't think I've felt relief like it. I've done everything I can for Enzo throughout his recovery. Pulled every string and called in every favour to make sure that he has the best care on the most secure ward we have.

Given my position, there's very little the hospital administration would refuse me, but by leveraging my influence for a patient so clearly involved in criminal activities, my colleagues have started asking more questions than they ever had before. Then you throw in that my 'boyfriend' is obviously connected with our new VIP patient, it's getting harder and harder to keep prying eyes out of my business.

It's like I'm being watched by everyone. There are prying eyes around every corner and it's nearly impossible to maintain this façade of dating Stefano Tiero. This was supposed to be an easy fix to chase off an idiot with a mild infatuation, and while it's working and the notes have stopped, I'm now sneaking around my hospital making sure that the staff see me with Stefano while simultaneously avoiding anyone connected to the Bianchi's.

It's exhausting.

I'll be so relieved when Enzo is discharged, and everything can go back to normal. Well, norma-lish. Fuck knows when this fake relationship is going to end and some of the nurses are getting a little too attached to Stefano.

Speak of the devil.

I glance around the hospital corridor and see a congregation of scrub nurses watching him as he makes his way towards me. I beckon him towards the nearest door so we can speak in private. I'm fed up with the perpetual audience I seem to have these days. As I open the door, I'm just about to drag Stefano inside with me when a strained cry of *"Occupied"* rings out from what I can only describe as a well-fucked Benedict Romano. He's holding on to a metal shelf above his head that looks like it's buckled under his weight, while Nico has his face buried in Benny's neck. He's rutting into Benny like a wild animal, holding him off the ground, legs spread with Benny's knees hooked over his forearms.

There's an animalistic snarl before Nico turns his head and glares at us. There's no need for words. The "fuck off" is loud enough without them. The last thing I was expecting to see today was Nico Verardi buried to the hilt in Benny's ass. That wasn't on my bingo card, and it knocks the wind out of my sails.

Stefano reaches in front of me and closes the door. It doesn't take more than a moment for me to remember that I'm pissed off at him, however now I'm pissed off and more than a little turned on. I'm not saying I want to head back into that room and join Nico and Benny—hell, no—but oh my god, seeing the absolutely feral look in Nico's eye and the expression of bliss on Benny's face has reminded me how dire my own sex life is. How I'd love to be railed with the same kind of reckless abandon.

It wasn't too long ago that I thought Stefano was going to be the man to rail me, however, since that night at his place, he's completely shut down on me. He made it clear when he sent me to bed. He's not interested in me.

"You need to have a word with them," I hiss. "I know Enzo needs protection while he's recovering, but you all need to keep a lower profile around here."

"You want me to tell Nico Verardi he can't blow off a little steam?"

"He can *blow* Benny at home," I whisper shout. It's hard not to smile back at him when he lets out an unexpected chuckle at my words. There's something about how Stefano's eyes light up when he smiles that has butterflies fluttering in my belly. I shake off my symptoms of unrequited infatuation and steel myself to scold him. "It's not fucking funny, Stefano. My colleagues are asking too many questions about my *boyfriend's* friend and his many visitors, and need for round-the-clock security. It's getting harder to explain the longer you're all here."

His smile drops and he nods. "Sorry Katerina, I'll have a word with everyone. The last thing we want to do is risk your reputation, and we appreciate the strings you pulled to keep the hospital from reporting Enzo's injuries to the authorities."

It's really difficult to rant at someone with conviction when they're agreeing with you.

He leans in and kisses my forehead, and I sigh. I can't figure out if he genuinely wants to comfort me or if he's simply putting on a show for our audience. I turn to check if we're still being watched and my heart sinks when I clock the gaggle of nurses still looking our way.

"Well, then. See that you do. I have a consult to get to," I say, but just as I'm about to leave, Doctor Jenkins approaches us. Fighting the urge to roll my eyes at having to deal with him, I conjure up my best adoring girlfriend smile and lean in to kiss Stefano's cheek. "I'll see you later, darling."

Stefano's eyes close, and I let myself believe for a second that he's savouring my closeness and not putting on a show.

I really have to stop letting my emotions trick me into thinking he wants more. This is a ruse and nothing more. Whatever I thought was happening all those weeks ago at his house were nothing more than heightened emotions after a bad day, and I'm an idiot if I keep hoping for more. I'm too old to be clinging to dreams I should have forgotten long ago.

"If it isn't the happy couple," Doctor Jenkins says with a sneer. There's very little you can find appealing about Dylan Jenkins, and his perpetual look of disgust only makes him less attractive. Some doctors have a way of carrying their god complex with an air of confidence that can almost make you forgive their complete lack of personality or compassion. Doctor Jenkins has no such talent. "Anyone would think he didn't trust you, Doctor Mancini, bearing in mind how frequently we see him here these days."

"He's here visiting a family friend," I reply. My words are polite enough, but his blatant disrespect for Stefano has my hackles up and ensures my tone is laced with as much disdain as I can get away with. It makes my skin crawl that a man so obnoxious sees himself as better than Stefano Tiero. Like his overblown ego in any way compares to the power the Bianchi consigliere wields. Stefano could destroy him. Literally and figuratively. The idea of Stefano crushing him shouldn't turn me on, but we've already established my feelings for him are less than healthy.

A satisfied smile takes over me and I lean into Stefano, wrapping my hands around his waist possessively. "Seeing him every day only reminds me how lucky I am to have him."

"Since you're inseparable, I assume I'll be seeing you both at the charity gala next month," he retorts with a slight curl in his lip, doing nothing to hide his disapproval. I can't tell if he's judging us because of the age gap, or because he's judged Stefano as somehow beneath him. Either way I don't like it, and I can feel my blood starting to boil. *Who does this sanctimonious prick think he is?*

As if he can sense my slow burning rage, Stefano steps in. "Of course. I wouldn't miss an opportunity to spend an evening with my Katerina."

The glint in his eyes tells me that Stefano is enjoying baiting him and I revel when I catch the flare of anger bloom in Doctor Jenkins' expression. His eyes darken as the smug expression slips from his features and is replaced by a scornful glare. He quickly recovers, his uncomfortable smile returning as he shifts his focus back to me. "How... romantic. I must say, he brings out qualities in you no one here thought you were capable of."

Every word out of his mouth makes me want to ram my fist so far into his face he'll be swallowing teeth. I'm about to tell him where he can shove his observations of my character when there's a firm squeeze on my hip and the warmth of Stefano's palm centres me.

"Anyone who claims to know a woman based on the way she presents herself in a professional setting is a fool. The only person who truly knows a woman is the one she gives her heart to."

My eyebrows end up somewhere around my hairline at Stefano's words and Doctor Jenkins lets out a sound like a cat choking on a hairball. My shoulders give away the giggle I'm trying to silence, which only angers him further.

"If you'll excuse us, Doctor Jenkins," I say, before turning and pulling Stefano away with me.

When he's out of earshot, I mutter, "Narcissistic twat."

"Of the highest order," Stefano adds.

"Sorry about that. He's not normally so blatant in his assholery."

"Katerina, don't apologise for the shortcomings of men." His words once again take me aback, and I don't miss the satisfied smirk on his face, like he enjoyed ruffling Doctor Jenkin's feathers. I nod my agreement as he bends to kiss my cheek goodbye. "I need to head up to speak with Aurora."

I'm trying desperately to ignore the blush flourishing across my face from the heated gazes of the nurses. I know they're not watching me anymore though. They're doing exactly the same as me. Watching Stefano's fine ass as it saunters away towards the elevators.

Snapping myself out of it, I turn in time to catch them all looking and raise a judgemental brow at them. They avert their eyes when they realise they've been busted ogling 'my man' and scatter, waddling off like startled geese.

I can't suppress my smile and head towards the OR for my next surgery. The sooner I'm in scrubs and focussed on scalpels and sutures, the better. I need a healthy dose of reality to combat my Stefano-related daydreams.

AFTER FOUR HOURS in the OR and then nearly as many reviewing charts, it's almost midnight when I pull into my driveway. I'm dead on my feet, and so distracted scrambling around in the bottom of my bag for my keys that I nearly trip over the long white box wrapped in a matching satin ribbon.

I gaze down at the box, confused, since I haven't ordered anything and I rarely have things delivered to my home anyway because of the hours I work. I turn to open my door, throw what I'm carrying in a heap just inside, and bend to retrieve the gift. The box is ridiculously oversized, so I have to cock my hip to shut the front door and balance somewhat precariously while I kick off my shoes. I head straight for the kitchen, and lay it out on the countertop and stare down at the gift.

I don't like the look of it at all. It's pristine and stark and its size makes it mildly disconcerting. It screams ostentatious twat. There's a dull ache in the pit of my stomach and it takes a moment for me to admit to myself that it's dread.

It's been quiet for weeks on the old unwanted attention front. The notes in my lockers stopped, and for the most part, swapping my shifts around has limited my contact with Danny. He got the hint—or so I thought.

I really don't like the idea that he's now sending me things to my house. It feels like far more of an invasion of privacy. I'm not sure exactly why, but homebody Katerina is very different from general surgeon Doctor Mancini, or mob doctor Doc Em, and she likes to hang up her work life at the door.

I take a step back from the counter and find myself talking out loud, "If I have to deal with this, there's no way I'm doing it without wine."

After digging out my favourite glass from the dishwasher, I head to the pantry to dig out a bottle. I settle on an Argentinian Malbec taking it back through to the kitchen.

I glare at the gift-box, wishing it would just disappear. I consider ignoring it and heading straight up to bed, but the sooner I know what this is, the sooner I can toss it in the trash.

Opening the bottle, I pour out a more than generous glass and take a long sip, savouring the bold flavour. It's one of my favourite little rituals, especially after a stretch of back-to-back shifts. Although usually I would be curling up on my sofa under a blanket with a book by now.

There's a disturbingly loud chink at the base of my glass taps down against my granite countertop. I thread the tail of the satin bow through my fingers and pull it open, using my free hand to flick the lid off the box as the ribbon falls away. I realise as I'm doing it, I must look ridiculous. Treating the box like something might jump out at me.

Nothing does.

I stare down at the contents and I'm speechless. Inside are at least two dozen long-stemmed white roses, bound together with yet more white ribbon. They're stunning, but I'm more than a little confused. This doesn't feel like a nice gesture. It feels oppressive in its ostentatiousness.

I search the box for a card and quickly find a small white envelope the size of a business card. I pick up the wine glass and take a larger glug before ripping it open.

Reading the message, my heart sinks, and my pulse races.

Your heart is mine, D

Well, that's not at all unsettling. Goosebumps break out across my forearms, and I fold in on myself, rubbing my arms to try and chase away the chill. What the actual fuck? Is it a love letter? Is it a threat? Who can tell.

Grabbing my wine glass, I am ready to swallow the lot to steady my nerves when there's a loud banging at the door. I jump halfway out of my skin at the noise and the glass slips from my grip and shatters at my feet.

Fuck.

"Katerina, open up," comes Stefano's strained voice through the door.

The relief that washes over me is palpable. I thought it was Danny. *Is he watching me now he knows where I live?*

"What was that noise? Are you alright?"

I'm barefoot, surrounded by glass, and trapped in place. "Hang on, I smashed a glass," I shout back, looking around for my best route to freedom. However, I'm obviously not quick enough as there's a sudden thud against my front door from what I assume is Stefano's shoulder as he tries to force it open. "For fuck's sake, cut it out, you lunatic. I'm coming."

The glass is everywhere. My only escape is over the kitchen island. Pushing the box to the side, I hop up on the counter just as the second bang hits and the hinges of my door give way. Stefano falls through, tripping on the shoes and bag I left in a heap there.

"You absolute fucking moron," I shout as I scramble across the island and drop down on the other side. "What the fuck do you think you're doing?"

Careful to watch out for any stray shards of glass, I pad down the hallway as Stefano rolls onto his back and reaches for his shoulder. Looks like he came down pretty hard on it, but I have zero sympathy.

"I thought I heard something." He groans as he pokes and prods at his collarbone.

"You did. I smashed a wine glass," I snap at him, as I kneel at his side and bat his hand out of the way, feeling his shoulder and checking for any serious damage. "Why the hell are you here anyway?"

His eyes flick to mine and I know I'm not going to like what he's about to say.

"Stefano. Why are you here?" My tone is firm and to hammer home the point, I extend my index finger and use it to poke him hard in centre of his chest.

"I was informed that a suspicious package had been delivered to you."

"Informed by who?" My finger pushes harder into his sternum, and he winces.

"The team I have assigned to you."

I'm speechless at his admission and from the confused expression on his face, Stefano can't tell if I'm furious at the invasion of privacy or flattered that he's protecting me. I'm not sure I know myself, for that matter. He has people watching me? The thought that he's wasting Bianchi resources should have me spitting feathers, but I'm struggling to muster any anger.

Stefano sits up and rolls his shoulder which snaps me out of my thoughts. "Come on," I say, standing and reaching out to help him up. "You can ice your shoulder and explain yourself while I clear up."

CHAPTER EIGHT

KATERINA

Having relieved him of his suit jacket and settled him at the island with a bag of frozen peas to ice his shoulder, I'm distancing myself from Stefano and busying myself with the dustpan and brush. Trying to pretend it wasn't insanely hot to see him burst through the door to come to my rescue. And seriously, does he own anything other than tailored shirts that fit him like they're a second skin? "So, what you're saying is you only have people on me to and from the hospital?" I'm trying my best to sound irritated that he's in some way encroached on my independence, but it's tricky when I'm flattered. I hate arriving home alone in the dark. Despite my fierce commitment to the idea that I don't need a man to protect me, that doesn't alter the fact that no woman feels safe on her own at night. It's an inescapable fact.

"When they followed you home, they saw you bring

something into the house, and I don't know about you, but oversized boxes left on porches seem awfully suspicious, given we're currently at war with the De Lucas." He shifts uncomfortably on his stool, moving the makeshift icepack to a different part of his shoulder while I sink into a pit of mortification, because he's entirely right. I know better than to trust this package was safe. I'd blame it on my insanely long day, but that's really no excuse for my stupidity.

I'm not sure I'm ready to confess that to Stefano though.

I don't say anything and continue to sweep up the floor, keeping my eyes cast down. Avoiding the giant white box on the counter, he's been glaring at it since he sat down.

"Are we going to discuss this?" he pushes, flicking the side of the box, and I shrug. "Come on, Katerina. You told me he'd stopped."

"And he had. This is new," I say quietly. He's not going to like this next bit, so instead of explaining, I fish the card out of the box and hand it to him. His face turns puce, and his neck flushes with rage. I mentally chastise my body for the reaction it has to his unhinged level of fury.

He doesn't say a word to me, just pulls out his phone and starts barking through gritted teeth. "I need you to pick up a Danny Castello and deliver him to one of Etta's 'guest suites'." There's a brief pause before Stefano snaps, "This. Is. Your. Priority."

He hangs up on what I assume is Marcus, his number

two, and shoves his phone back in his pocket before steadying himself against the counter.

"Don't you think you're overreacting?" I whisper, refusing to look up from the dustpan that's resting, still full of glass, on the counter.

He moves around the island. "Stand up, Katerina." I swallow hard at the tone of his voice. It's commanding and indisputable and sends a flurry of need coursing through my body. I gasp when the soft pad of his index finger hooks under my jaw and demands I meet his gaze.

His irises are flecked with a kaleidoscope of blues that glimmer and shift under the muted lighting. It's unfair how easily I can be trapped in his gaze. Any time I stare too long, it's like I'm being pulled in by some kind of magnetic force.

"We did this your way. Now we're going to do it mine." His voice is so low I can feel the authority of his words vibrating in the air between us. "He needs to back the fuck off."

I shift my weight as I clench my thighs together. For a moment I say nothing, but when his brow arches, it compels me to respond. I whisper, "Yes, Stefano."

There's a guttural rumble of approval that grates in the back of his throat as he savours my words. "Say that again."

My body lights up. Revelling in the reaction I'm drawing from him. A smile pulls at my cheeks as I lean in, close enough to feel his breath feather across my face. "Yes, Stefano."

I lean back, catching his pupils dilate, and I know I'm

done for. His now dark orbs bore into mine, and it's like I'm being claimed from the inside out.

Oh, I am so screwed.

Every cell in my body is screaming at me to throw caution to the wind and climb this man like a tree. I'm still arguing the pros and cons in my head when he moves.

His lips descend and there's no stopping the desperate moan that escapes me as his tongue tangles with mine and we fight to steal the air from each other's lungs. It's wanton and passionate and about goddamn time.

He breaks the kiss, leaving me panting while he takes in our surroundings. He glares at the box of roses before letting out a little roar of frustration and hurls them off the counter to the floor. Wrapping his arms around my waist, drawing out a gasp of shock as he manhandles me on to the cold granite worktop. I let my legs fall open, eager to touch him as he steps forward, advancing on me like a predator.

The energy between us is electric. His hands grip my hips while mine claw at his chest, trying to burrow under his shirt. I lose myself in the rhythm of his tongue as it glides against mine. He tastes better than I remember, and as I struggle not to lose myself in the flavour of him, I'm overwhelmed by his scent. He smells of oak and amber and whiskey, and it seduces my senses. This is reckless and will only come back to bite me in the ass, and I couldn't give a flying fuck.

Stefano's hand traces a meandering path upwards.

The pressure is faint, but every featherlight touch ignites a fire within me that flows through my veins and flourishes in my core. I moan when his fingers dance across my waist and trace the swell of my breasts. He doesn't stop until his palm is firmly on the side of my neck, tilting my head until I'm at the angle he demands. It allows him to deepen the kiss, and I feel almost ravaged as his lips take what they need from me. The only thoughts in my head are 'yes' and 'more' and 'this is everything I've ever wanted'.

I stutter a little groan, both loving and hating how desperate his touches are making me feel. I flex my fingers and drag my nails down his back, which has the opposite effect to the one I want when he pulls back and I whine at the loss.

Stefano quirks a devilish smile at me as he lifts his arms and starts to unbutton his shirt. "If you're going to use me as your personal scratch post, *micetta*, I might as well give you unrestricted access."

Kitten. The nickname should make me bristle. It should feel like a bucket of cold water being thrown over me, dowsing any ember of arousal, but instead, I'm almost giddy.

"So thoughtful, Uncle Stef."

The minute the words leave my mouth, his expression darkens. He reaches forwards and threads his fingers through the hair at the base of my scalp, gripping tightly, his eyes boring into mine. "Don't ever call me that again. I'm not your fucking uncle."

Despite how tightly he's gripping my hair, there's nothing aggressive about it. I don't feel threatened in any way. I feel protected. I feel cherished. "What do you want me to call you?"

His face softens, and he leans down, brushing his lips along the slope of my neck in delicate kisses, his warm and reverent attentions chasing shivers across my skin. "You can call me anything but that."

"I don't think giving me that kind of leeway is a good idea, *vecchietto*."

He growls. "You're playing with fire, *micetta*. Call me 'old man' again. I dare you."

"So grouchy."

"Keep pushing me and you'll end up over my knee."

"Do that and I'll call you daddy while you spank me," I practically purr. He flinches and I wonder if I've pushed my teasing too far, but then his mouth is on mine again and I'm overwhelmed by the hunger in his kiss. His cock presses against my core, and I resent every item of clothing I'm wearing.

He drags me off the counter, letting me drop to my feet before spinning me roughly. I let out a startled squeal, but it quickly turns into a moan when a firm hand at my back pushes me down onto the worktop. The marble surface is cold against my cheek and a sharp contrast to the heat radiating through my core. I couldn't find the words to complain even if I wanted to. I've drawn out a side of Stefano I want to see so much more of.

I yelp when the full weight of his palm cracks across my ass.

"I warned you, kitten."

"Fuck," I mutter, drawing it out into a long and

reverent whimper. Whether it's how he's manhandling me or the way the sharp sting is petering out into a blissful tingle, I already feel like I'm floating on a cloud of pleasure. Like this is what my body has been craving all along.

Leaning over me, Stefano strokes a slow trail up my spine before wrapping his hand over my collarbone and dragging me up against him. I instinctively turn to lace my arms around his neck and we meld together like I was always made to fit with him. He cups my ass and I jump up, wrapping my legs around him like a koala clinging to a tree. I'm a tall woman, and while I'm slim in the waist, no one could call me skinny. Any concerns I have that he won't be able to carry me evaporate when he starts striding towards the stairs with ease.

I tilt my head into the crook of his neck and inhale the scent that has tortured me for years. His aftershave is heady and evokes images of wood panelled rooms and rich smoky bourbons. The latter enticing me to pull at his collar and nip at the column of his throat. I'm ravenous for him. We've denied each other for far too long.

"Keep that up and we're not going to make it up the stairs."

"I don't fucking care," I snarl. "I've wanted you for too long to give you a chance to change your mind."

He stalls, and in a feat of strength, it's hard not to be impressed as one hand leaves my ass and wraps around my throat, forcing me to pull back and look at him. "There's no stopping this."

I unfurl my legs, and he dips to let my feet touch the

ground before walking me back against the wall, tipping my chin up to lock eyes with him.

"I'm done denying myself what I want above anything else."

"Tell me. Say it out loud. I need to hear you say it." My voice trembles and tears threaten to flood my lashes.

"I need you, Katerina," he says, while running a thumb along my cheek. "Tell me you'll let me have you?"

It's on the tip of my tongue to ask him for how long, but there's a corner of my heart that's terrified I won't like the answer. What if one night is all he can give me? I've spent years trying to bury the feeling I have for him and I think it would hurt more never to have him than to have to let him go. If I only get to have him tonight, then so be it.

"I'm yours." The words escape from my lips before I can stop them. I take his hand in mine and lead him along the hallway to my room.

Whatever happens tomorrow, tonight he's mine.

CHAPTER NINE

STEFANO

There are so many reasons why I shouldn't be walking into Katerina's bedroom right now, but as she slinks elegantly towards the bed, I couldn't give a flying fuck what they are.

She leans down and flicks on the bedside lamp before untucking her shirt and slowly unbuttoning it. An involuntary moan slips out as the silk fabric drapes open, exposing the lace cups of her bra. Her breasts rise and fall as her breathing grows heavier. I can see a thousand emotions flutter across her features, but the ones that shine out the strongest are excitement and anticipation. She bites her bottom lip and cocks her head to the side. Challenging me to follow her example.

My pulse thrums in my ears and I suddenly feel a little nervous. This woman is stunning, but she's a hell of a lot younger than me. I quash any thoughts that threaten the mood. From the way she's teasing her fingertips along her collarbone and down her chest, she doesn't care about the greying hair at my temples or the lines etched on my face. She looks like she's ready to pounce. I return her sinful smile as I toss the shirt over the chaise at the foot of her bed.

Katerina unzips her pants and lets them drop to the floor. Stepping out of them, she prowls towards me and rests her hands over mine where I'm opening my belt. "Let me unwrap my present."

If I could speak, I would. Instead, I nod and cast my eyes to the ceiling in silent appreciation to whatever gods have conspired to have Katerina Mancini sinking to her knees before me.

I chuckle when she pulls off my socks first. *Nothing quite so unsexy as a naked man in socks.* My gaze returns to her as she unbuckles my belt and hooks her fingers into the waistband of my boxer briefs. Her focus shifts and her pupils blow wide when she takes in the exceptionally hard cock bobbing in front of her pouty lips.

"Well, well, well, *vecchietto.* Is this all for me?" she purrs. It might be because she's saying it affectionately in Italian, or it might be because her mouth is so close to my cock I can feel the warmth of her exhales dust over my crown, either way, I don't mind her calling me an old man. Not if I'm her old man.

I reach out and run my fingers through her hair before gripping tightly and pulling her closer. The soft lighting highlights the strands of burnished copper as they tangle in my grasp. We both let out a groan when she parts her lips wider, and the wet heat of her mouth envelops me. My body comes alive, ripples of pleasure chase themselves along my spine, and for a second I think my legs will buckle.

Holy fuck. It's not just the sight of her on her knees before me. It's the hum of pleasure, the flutter of her lashes, and the way she rolls her tongue along the underside of my shaft as she bobs on my dick. Just when I think I've got my rapidly building orgasm under control she seals her lips around the head of my cock and hollows her cheeks.

SHE'S MAGNIFICENT.

"*Micetta*, if you don't want me to flood your throat with cum, you're going to need to save some of your tricks for later."

Sitting back on her knees, Katerina looks up at me with a coquettish smirk. "But I want to play with my new toy. It's so responsive." Her eyes brim with desire, and I bite my bottom lip as my gaze roams over her curves. From the swell of her breast to the flare of her hips, she's exquisite. Everything I've ever wanted and more than I ever imagined.

She returns her attention to my straining hard-on only this time, when she swallows me down, she relaxes her throat and takes me fully. I cry out, half in frustration, half in ecstasy.

I pull her off me. "I know you've never liked doing as you're told, but if you deny me the pleasure of coming inside you, there will be consequences, *micetta*."

She lifts a hand and I take it, helping her to her feet. "You keep threatening me with a good time, *vecchietto*."

I don't give her time to think, sweeping her up in my arms and carrying her to bed, laying her down like an offering on an altar. Her hair fans out over the sage green covers and glistens against them with rich mahogany hues, her strands shimmering like spun silk. I'm awed by her beauty. Wrapping my palms around her ankles, spreading her legs, I pull her towards me with a swift tug. I'm on my knees and throwing her legs over my shoulders in an instant. Her thighs quiver as I hook a finger into her panties and pull them aside. I can't wait a second longer. Something snaps at the sight of her glistening cunt. I groan, my tongue swiping from pussy to clit.

I couldn't tell you if it's her moans of pleasure, her nails raking through my hair or the taste of her on my tongue, but I lose all conscious thought. Right now, I have only one purpose and that's to make this woman come so hard she loses time.

"Stefano—"

I pull back, replacing my tongue on her clit with the pad of my thumb. "If you can still speak, I'm not doing my job."

"Holy fuck, what are you doing to me?" she whimpers.

"Giving you what you need, *micetta*." I don't waste time on more words, lowering my mouth to feast on her, thrusting my tongue inside her pussy. She tastes like *mine*. Threading a hand around her thigh, I reach up, flattening my palm against her belly, pinning her firmly down. She moans as I lap at her; savouring her.

I swap, moving my mouth to her swollen clit and my

fingers to gently circle her entrance. When I tease the swollen bundle of nerves with my teeth, she strains against the hold I have on her.

"Too much, it's too much," she cries.

Lifting my head to lock eyes with her, I slide my middle fingers into her dripping cunt and curl them, making sure to tease her G-spot as I thrust mercilessly. She shatters as I reply, "This isn't too much, Katerina. It's exactly what you need."

The way she writhes under my tongue has me moaning along with her and my cock dripping pre-cum. I'd love to bury myself in her tight cunt and feel her ripping my orgasm from me, but this first one, her first orgasm at my mercy, I want to taste it. Savour it.

I keep my thrusts deep and hard, drawing out her orgasm for as long as I can. When I finally steady my hand, it takes her a few minutes to come back to herself. When she seems more lucid, I drop my head and return my attention to her clit, blowing a cool breeze over the sensitive nub, revelling in the way she rolls her hips in response.

I draw my hand back, dragging my fingers out gently and smiling as her pussy clenches around them, as if she's objecting to the loss of them. She'll have to wait a moment though, because I want to lick them clean.

"Eyes on me," I grind out and the moment our gazes lock, I plunge my fingers between my lips, lapping at her cum like a feral beast. I'm not even touching her, yet her ragged breaths and groans tell me how much she's enjoying my little show. When there's nothing left for me to taste, I drop my hand to her thigh and slowly massage up to her apex.

"You can give me another, baby girl." I smile when she whimpers in response, shaking her head from side to side, muttering half-hearted denials.

I dive forward, nibbling and sucking, drawing out more moans as she clamps her legs around my head and another orgasm barrels towards her. Her cum coats my tongue, showing me exactly how much I'm affecting her.

Katerina's hips rock and her thighs quiver, but the thing that has me moaning with her is the way her pussy grips me. My fingers are buried inside her, stroking against her overstimulated G-spot, but I want to give her more so I pull back just enough to slide in a third finger.

"Fuck, yes. Oh, my god." Her voice is laced with a delirious, frantic edge as she comes for me again.

Every flutter of her pussy has me desperate to bury myself inside her, but I wait. Torturing myself exquisitely as she slowly returns to herself. I rise to stand before leaning down to cage her between my arms, resting on my elbows so I'm close enough to feel her contented sigh against my cheek. I can't help but preen at the effect I've had on her. She looks like she's boneless, like she's drifted into a haze of post-orgasmic bliss.

"You're exquisite, Katerina," I whisper as I feather slow kisses along her jaw. She mumbles and gasps with every brush of my lips against her molten skin. Pulling her into the centre of the mattress, I settle my hips between her thighs and I groan when the head of my cock nestles at her core. "This is probably a bit late to be asking, but please tell me you have condoms."

Her eyebrows dart upwards in what looks like surprise. "Oh shit. No." She pauses for a moment before asking, "I take it that you don't either?"

I'm forty-eight. I'm an experienced man. Yet at this moment, I feel like an unprepared teenager. I shake my head and then run a hand over my face, feeling slightly embarrassed at what I'm about to say. "I never carry them because, well... it's been a long time."

Her disappointed expression morphs to one that is a little more playful and a lot more inquisitive. "How long?"

Arching an eyebrow, I try my best to look disapproving of her gentle mocking. "Four years."

"Four years?"

"Yes."

"Well, isn't that interesting," she says, her voice light and her smile bright.

I close my eyes tight for a moment before confessing. "I haven't so much as touched another woman since the night you kissed me at Aurora's wedding."

There's an audible gasp and I push myself up, sitting back on my haunches and lowering my gaze. She follows me up and rises to her knees, but I daren't look at her. It feels like such a strange admission. Nothing else happened between us that night, but ever since then, I've not been able to stand the thought of another woman's lips on mine.

Silence hangs in the air until Katerina clears her throat. "That's one hell of a lot of pressure to put on a girl. What if I'd been terrible in bed?"

I laugh loudly at her attempt to break the tension.

"Now I've tasted you, I'm ruined for anyone else, Katerina."

"You're going to have to stop saying the right thing all the time. Otherwise, I'm going to get used to it, and you'll have set an unreasonable bar for yourself."

"Fair," I say, before leaning in and stealing a kiss from her lips. "But what it means is that I'm clean since I was last tested."

"Funny you should say that. So am I," she replies as she trails a path up one arm and down my chest, scratching her nails through my mostly not-grey smattering of chest hair, reminding me once again where my nickname for her came from. Every flex of her fingers sends a current of electricity burning through me. "That and I have an IUD," she adds with a smile.

The thought of fucking her bare shouldn't turn me on as much as it does. But it's that which has me wrapping my arms around her and rolling her back underneath me. Has me spreading her legs and guiding my cock to her core and filling her to the hilt.

Her cry is louder than mine, but not by much. I don't move, immobilised by the vice-like grip her eager pussy has on me.

"I'm going to need you and your impressive dick to fuck me, and fuck me hard." I smile down at her, amused that while her words are one hundred per cent Katerina Mancini, her tone is like nothing I've ever heard from her before. They're strained and broken with a hint of desperation.

She's begging me.

Not once in her life has Katerina begged for anything. But right now, she's begging for me to fuck her, and that triggers a primal response that will not be denied. I rock my hips before setting a punishingly slow pace. Each thrust is brutal. As my orgasm builds, our moans complement each other in a symphony of bliss. My breathing becomes ragged, and my balls tighten in anticipation.

Our gazes collide as I stare down at her caged beneath me. She's close but I don't want close, I want devastated. I pause and she whines in protest. Still buried inside her, I kneel back, grabbing one thigh, and straddling the other while I roll her on her side. Her expression morphs back to one of sheer pleasure when the change in position hits. With her leg held tightly against my chest, I rock my hips before thrusting and fucking her deeply enough to force the air from her lungs.

"You're going to take what I give you, *micetta*," I say as I find her clit with my free hand. Her reaction is instantaneous, pushing her to new heights of pleasure and making her shriek in ecstasy. I can't help but smile proudly as I say, "That's my girl."

I'm sure she thinks she's using her words right now, but all that tumbles out of her is a string of incomprehensible nonsense as her orgasm peaks and she pulls me over the precipice with her. My cock pulses and I come harder than I ever have before. Glancing down, I pull out, causing my cum to cascade out, coating her pussy. The sight does something to me, and I can't help but run my fingers through the mess I've made of her. She groans when I slip them inside, pushing my release back into her.

"Anyone would think you have a thing for cum play," she teases.

"When it comes to you, there's not much I wouldn't try. But right now, I'm just enjoying seeing you well fucked and full." Her eyes roll back in her head as I circle her clit with my thumb.

"You're trying to kill me," Katerina says softly before she's overcome by an insistent yawn.

"I'm trying to unravel you," I say as I lean over her, wrap my arms around her waist, and roll on to my back, pulling her with me. I settle her over my chest and in her exhaustion, she melds herself for me like a blanket. I can see that she's struggling to keep her eyes open, so I reach for the comforter, pull it over her, and stroke back the curtain of hair that falls across her face.

She's beginning to lose the battle with consciousness, her eyelids drooping. I run my hands down her spine and over her body in a gentle caress, memorising every dip and curve. For so long, I've denied myself what I've craved above all. Her. There's an undeniable sense of rightness that's settled in my chest. An intimacy, a peaceful contentedness, and it's as if the ache and longing I've become so familiar with have evaporated into the ether and been replaced with hope.

I need a future where I get to experience moments like this with her. She's a masterpiece I want to appreciate forever. Katerina mumbles a soft, contented hum against my chest that makes my heart feel full.

"Sleep now, *micetta*."

"Promise you'll be here when I wake up?" she whispers. It's so quiet I'm not sure if she meant for me to hear her plea.

"I'll be here, sweetheart," I reply. When her breathing evens out and I start to hear a purr that I'll never describe as a snore, I say, "I'm not going anywhere. Now that I've got you, I'm never letting you go."

CHAPTER TEN

KATERINA

I don't want to open my eyes. If I do, I'm worried I'll discover last night was a dream and that the warmth against my cheek isn't Stefano. That I'm not curled up in a nook, with his chest for a pillow and his arm wrapped around me, gently stroking my hip.

"I can tell you're awake, *micetta*."

I crack open my eyes, trying not to smile, and failing as I try to scold him. "I don't think I ever officially agreed to that nickname."

"You don't get to choose my pet name for you," he says, with a broad smile on his unnaturally handsome face. His greying temples only amplifying his attractiveness.

"I suppose that's true," I say, pausing for dramatic effect before sarcastically adding, "*Vecchietto*." He rolls his eyes, but it's obvious from the gleam in them that it doesn't bother him. At least nowhere near as much as 'Uncle Stefano'.

I turn on to my back, trapping his arm underneath me as I stretch. The last thing I remember is falling asleep in his arms; naked, exhausted, and satiated. More content than I've ever felt. "What time is it?"

"Nearly ten."

I whip my head around and stare at him, my mouth open wide. "I haven't slept this late in years, even on my days off."

"Well, you were more than a little tired," he says with a grin, giving me a hint of the dimple in his left cheek. "And so was I." I adore that dimple. Even more now that I'm the one who's lured it out of hiding.

"Remind me why we've waited so long to do this?" I say, sighing with a contented smile. The words slip out before I can stop them, and I regret them instantly. The last thing I want to do is burst our perfect little bubble. A bubble I'm perfectly happy existing in for the foreseeable future and hopefully mostly naked.

"Are you looking for another answer other than my best friend will beat me to within an inch of my life when he finds out I've tongue fucked his daughter?" he says, and it's obvious from his tone that while he's half-joking, he's also half-not.

"Yeah, aside from that." I wince, retreating in on myself at the thought of having to explain to my father that I slept with his best friend. Only as I think about it, that's not what I'd say to my father, were I forced to explain myself.

Suddenly, I'm having images of *The Little Mermaid*

when King Triton barges into her sanctuary with Ariel's cry of 'But Daddy, I love him' playing on a loop in my head.

Nope. Hell no. No matter how long I've wanted this man, there's no way I'm stupid enough to confuse mind-blowing sex with love.

You're thirty-four years old, for Christ's sake. Snap out of it, woman.

I give myself a mental slap and say, "My father is the last person I talk to about who I'm..." *Fuck*, I don't know how to finish that sentence. *Fucking? Dating? Madly in l—*

"Dating." Stefano's response is firm, and the tension leeches out of my body as soon as he says it. I'm a confident woman, but with the torrent of emotions that are threatening to overwhelm me, I don't think I could have taken the rejection if this was just a one-night thing for him.

"We're dating?" I say, unable to hide my smile. Stefano's arms wrap around me and hold me tight.

"I couldn't let you go if I tried, Katerina," he whispers against my forehead. I'm lost for words. If I could think of what to say, I don't know if I would ever be able to convey how he makes me feel. There's no one who makes me feel as free to be myself, feel so seen. When I tip my chin to reply, I'm transfixed, captured by the adoration beaming back at me. Placing my hand across his collarbone, I slide my palm to cup his cheek before stretching to lay a gentle kiss against his lips.

My pulse flutters in response when he kisses me back. We lose ourselves in a playful caress, where our tongues tussle and his teeth nip and draw out little groans I'm not sure I've heard myself make before.

When we pull apart, soft and desire-laden pants filling the air, I smirk. "I call not telling my father."

He frowns, but the chuckle and gentle tickle at my waist reassures me he's not actually annoyed by my teasing. I giggle as I writhe against his poking and prodding.

Although, I'm deadly serious. There's no way I'm going to be the one to tell my father. We have a wonderful relationship. It's not that I think he'll be mad at me, but Stefano is his closest friend. If he's not the one to tell him, my father will never forgive him. They need to hash it out between them.

Ceasing his attack, he lets out a contented sigh. "I'll speak with him." I smile as a sense of relief washes over me.

We sink into a haze of kisses and wandering hands—both his and mine. I'm just about to curl my palm around his mouth-wateringly hard cock when his phone assaults my ears with its outrageously loud ring.

"What the fuck is that? I know you're not so old you need the ringer on that volume," I protest, rolling off him and covering my ears.

"Rude," he admonishes. "That's one."

"One what? Stop talking to me and answer the damn phone, *vecchietto*."

He shuffles off the bed and rifles through the pile of crumpled clothes on the floor. Pulling out the offensively loud device, he answers, his tone and cadence returning to one of absolute authority. Not a hint of the warmth and affection it held seconds ago.

His expression gives nothing away as he listens to whoever is interrupting us. He wanders around the bed, so I take the opportunity to take in what I was too blissed out to appreciate last night. He's hiding a sinful body under his pristine suits. There's a smattering of chest hair doing a damn fine job of highlighting the understated ripple of muscle. It's obvious he looks after himself, and I find my mind wandering as I try to imagine what weight machines I'd find him sweating over if I were to see him in the gym.

I'm bombarded by images of hip thrusts and leg presses and sweat running down his beautifully defined abs and disappearing into his happy trail. He turns to pace in the other direction and I bite my bottom lip when I get my first glimpse of his naked ass in the light of day.

I sink back into the embrace of my pillows and cover my eyes with my forearm. I'd quite happily take a bite out of that peach. I chastise myself because never before have I thought that about a man, but holy fuck, there's a reason his ass looks good in a suit and that's because it's spectacular out of one.

"You inform me the minute he returns," Stefano commands. His tone is low, and while he's not threatening the person he's speaking with, it brooks no dissent. He ends the call and tosses the phone on the bedside table, taking a moment to run a hand over his face, like he's trying to wipe away the frustration written there.

He looks down at me and smiles, but it doesn't quite reach his eyes. "It would appear that Danny Costello is out of town. Has been since yesterday morning."

I furrow my brow. "But there wasn't a delivery notice on that box?"

"He could easily have paid someone to drop it off for him," Stefano responds.

"I still think you're overreacting."

He raises a brow and leans over me, settling on the bed and caging me in. My heart stutters when his hardening cock presses against the apex of my thighs.

"Not that I don't relish our little disagreements, but on this one, you're not going to win." He drops a trail of tender kisses along my jawline and I whimper. If I could muster enough fucks-to-give I'd be disappointed in myself for folding under the weight of his alpha male tenancies but while his breath is heating my skin and his cock is hardening between my thighs, he can call the shots when it comes to my not-so-secret admirer.

"Fine, you win. Have it your way," I say.

"I intend to," he growls as he lowers himself down my body, lavishing every inch with his attention. He kisses his way down my chest, stopping to take each of my peaked nipples between his teeth, gently tugging until I'm writhing against the weight of his body. He continues his descent down my navel and feathering his touch over my hips until his tongue is gliding over my clit.

He lifts his head, sliding two fingers into my aching heat, making me arch off the bed and forcing my gaze to his.

"Make no mistake, sweetheart. Now I finally have you, I won't allow anyone else to lay claim to you. You're mine." His words are everything I want to hear and soothe my soul, only adding to the bliss he's drawing out of me.

His head dips and my eyes roll back as his tongue sweeps along the length of me before finding my clit. He's ruthless in his ministrations, pushing me closer and closer to my release with every flick and curl.

When I shatter beneath him, I lose myself, drifting into a haze of pleasure that, punctuated with a feeling of security, I've never felt with a man before.

CHAPTER ELEVEN

STEFANO

I snuck downstairs to prepare Katerina breakfast after she'd drifted back off to sleep. When I'd seen the crumpled box of flowers on the floor, where I'd hurled them the night before, my blood pressure rose. I hated the idea that anyone so inferior thought they held any claim on the heart of a woman as breathtaking as Katerina. It made my blood boil. I'd snatched it up and stormed outside to find a trash can. It had seemed like a good idea until I'd found myself freezing my ass off in my boxers and button-down, bare feet like blocks of ice against the cold stone driveway. As I'd stuffed the box in the trash, the handwritten card had fluttered to the ground. Picking it up, I slipped it into my shirt pocket and headed back inside to start on breakfast.

The pan gives a gentle hiss as the scrambled eggs cook through. Taking them off the heat, I plate them up with some toasted bagels, but as I turn to search for a tray, a telltale creak lets me know she's coming downstairs.

"Smells amazing. I could get used to this kind of treatment," she says playfully as she rounds the bottom of the staircase. My heart soars. This is the Katerina I've been wishing for. She's wearing silk sleep shorts and an off the shoulder gym shirt, hair piled on top of her head in a messy bun. She looks contented and completely at ease.

She has none of her usual armour on. Not the surgical scrubs, not the doctor's coat, and definitely not the reserve she's forced to project when she's dealing with life and death situations. She's always had a reputation as a cold-hearted ballbuster, but I've known for years that couldn't be further from the truth. Any man in her profession would be praised for their ability to compartmentalise. Celebrated for their focus.

The fact that she performs her job as well as she does, in addition to being at the family's beck and call, only goes to show how accomplished she is.

Anyone who takes the time to look beneath the veneer of professionalism will find one of the most caring women they'll ever meet. It killed me to see how affected she was by treating Aurora and Enzo. I'm relieved that she's off shift for the next few days. The woman needs a break.

"Funny you should say that. I'd like to make a suggestion." I keep my tone even, knowing I'll have to phrase the next part well if I want her to go for it.

"What type of suggestion?" she says, eyeing me with suspicion as she takes the coffee mug I'm holding out to her. She takes a sip and smiles, inhaling the wafts of steam rising over the brim.

I slide the plate and cutlery across the island and motion for her to sit.

"If you're taking the trouble of bribing me with caffeine and home-cooked food, I get the feeling I'm not going to like this." Her tone is sceptical, but hunger must win out because she takes the offering, perches herself on the stool, and digs in. "Ohmagod, what did you put in these eggs?"

Smiling, I say, "More butter than a doctor would probably recommend and some cream cheese with chives."

"I had chives?" she says, looking up in astonishment.

"You have an herb garden on the porch," I say incredulously.

"Correction, my gardener has an herb garden on my porch. I have no idea what most of it is." I take a seat next to her and make a start on my plate. "Come on then. Hit me. What am I not going to like?"

"I'm going to start by saying this is not because I don't think you can take care of yourself." She picks up her bagel, loading it with eggs, and uses her fork to gesture to go on. "I want to add some security measures to your house, so I'd like to have one of my crews fit out the place with security cameras and an alarm system."

"I mean, so far I'm not hearing the unreasonable part," she says, her expression morphing into one of suspicion.

I clear my throat before continuing. "I'd like to stay here with you. At least until I'm sure there's no real threat." I look down at my plate, ignoring the glare burning into the side of my face.

"You, a man I've just started dating, want to move into my house? Because I got sent a bunch of flowers?" I don't need to look up to know that she's talking through gritted teeth.

I reach across the counter for a napkin, wiping my hands before throwing it down again. Turning slowly, I don't miss the subtle little shift in her seat or the nervous swallow.

"I want the woman I'm dating to be protected in her home, whether it's from the idiot harassing her, or from Max De Luca who is looking for any excuse to hurt anyone who's aligned themselves against him. I am the consigliere. You are our primary medical care." Her eyes widen, and I grimace at the bluntness of my words, hating that I've scared her. "You've always been a target; we've just guarded you from the shadows. If you're in this. If you really want to see where we go, then I need to know that you're protected."

"This is a lot, Stefano. Don't you think you're moving just a little too fast?"

I pull her stool to me, sliding her so her knees are bracketed by mine. "I've wanted you for years. If we go much slower, the ice caps will melt before I can tell everyone you're mine."

She remains quiet for longer than I'd like, stretching it out into something uncomfortable that makes the hairs on the back of my neck twitch nervously.

"You're very territorial for a man I've only seen naked in the last twelve hours." Her familiar wry smile returns, and I huff out a sigh of relief that she appears to be conceding to me. I thought this would be a bigger battle. Katerina Mancini has never liked being told what to do.

"I'm territorial for a man who doesn't want to see you get hurt."

She nods, and her pupils flare wide when I reach for her hands, holding them together in mine. "I'll do you a deal."

"I'm listening."

"You let me turn your house into Fort Knox and I'll be the one who tells your father about us?"

"You already agreed to that," she says, raising her voice in mock outrage.

"Alright then. Name your price."

She cants her head to the side as she considers her demands. "No taking Danny to one of Etta's interrogation rooms. Don't think I'm going to let you terrorise a co-worker, let alone the son of a board member. Are you trying to get me fired?" I try to object, but she pulls out a hand and covers my mouth. "No interrupting, *vecchietto*." I furrow my brow in protest, but she continues, "This is my career. You don't get to control every aspect of my life."

Dragging her hand away from my mouth, I growl in frustration. She cocks her brow and huffs at my frustration. She's right. "Fine. I won't do anything that jeopardises your job."

She smiles broadly, taking the win and adding, "Just promise you won't make me feel like some incapable damsel in distress."

"I promise," I reply, crossing my hand over my heart and returning her smile.

Whatever she needs for me to be close to her, I will make it happen.

I SHOULD HAVE EXPECTED her to push back against me moving in. If it's one thing my Katerina hates, it's men making decisions for her. That was a rookie mistake on my part. In my defence though, I'd woken up with her nestled into me, arms draped across my chest, hair cascading around her shoulders, and I wanted nothing more than to wake up like that every morning.

My chest warms and my pulse races at the thought of having her close to me, even if it's only for a short while. I bite my cheek at the thought of her padding about the place in those tiny silk shorts and realise my mistake as soon as my cock hardens behind my zipper. I'm flooded with vivid memories of how she tasted on my tongue and the mewls that escaped her lips as I made her come. Not to mention how my legs buckled at the sight of her on her knees for me.

If the only way to achieve that was to stay with her, so be it.

There is no way I'm leaving her unprotected. I don't care whether she thinks it's overkill. I hate the idea that anyone was lurking around on her property. Even if it turns out it was just a delivery driver. My second, Marcus, discovered through Danny-boy's very public socials that he was out of town visiting his family's estate, a few hours north of the city, for a family wedding.

It doesn't reassure me any, though. The escalation to home deliveries pisses me off no end. As far as he's concerned, Katerina is seeing someone, so where does he get off sending her roses? I may have promised not to take him to an interrogation room, but I'm going to make sure he knows exactly who he's dealing with when the weaselly little twat returns. Gripping the steering wheel, my knuckles blanch white, and the leather creaks in my palms.

I left a few hours ago to head home. It should concern me how much the distance from her affects me. It feels like my body is rioting at a cellular level. My heart thumps in my chest, chasing the blood around my veins so fast it feels like I could hear it whooshing if I listened closely enough. It feels wrong to be away from her for any length of time. Not only because I'm overwhelmed by the urge to keep her safe, but because now that she's mine I'm loathed to be apart.

There was no avoiding it though; I have a job to do and Aurora is keeping me busy—as any don should. Having kept me as her consigliere, it's my responsibility to get the new capos up to scratch. I've been holed up in my office, going through the updates from yesterday.

I run my hands along the stubble on my jawline absentmindedly, my fingertips grazing through the growth, reminding me how late in the day it is.

I'm about to head upstairs to pack a bag when my phone buzzes in my jacket pocket. The screen lights up with a familiar name and I pause. I can't not answer it, but when my best friend greets me over the speaker, waves of guilt wash over me almost instantly.

"*Fratello*, did you get the breakdown of the accounts I sent across this morning?" Dante says. *Brother*. That's not what you want to hear when you spent the previous night fucking the man's daughter. While I agreed I'd be the one to tell her father, over the phone is not the time. "Are you there, Stef?"

Shaking off my conscience, I reply before I let the pause multiply into an awkward silence. "I'm here, just walking and talking."

"You never were great at multitasking," he replies. To anyone else, his tone would sound brusque, but I've known him long enough to hear the hint of humour he's infused it with.

"Fuck right off."

"Right back at you, you grumpy asshole." There's a little chuckle before he gets back to business. "You got any questions about the numbers?"

"Nah, looks like putting Lombardi in charge of the clubs was a good call. The changes he's testing at Inferno seem to be making a big difference if the numbers are anything to go by."

"Yeah, his vision appears to be what the clubs need. Clever, eager to prove himself, and young enough to stay awake till closing." We both laugh at that one. "Aurora was right to promote him."

I'm nodding as I say, "She was. We need profitable, legitimate businesses if we're going to fund this war."

Don't get me wrong, we're by no means pure as the driven snow. We trade in a lot of illegal merchandise, from weapons to stolen goods, but we draw a line. Trafficking of people or drugs is a no-go. It turns my stomach, knowing the types of people we aligned ourselves with. Never again.

"So, are we going to see you at family dinner again soon?" Dante adds as we're wrapping up the call.

What am I going to say? No? That would be unusual, but it also feels strange saying yes now. Like I should talk to Katerina first. "Er—"

"None of that 'I'm too busy' bullshit. We're all too busy and it's been far too long. You're coming to the next family dinner. And tell Katerina she needs to be there too."

I stutter, unsure of what to say, but I heave a huge sigh of relief when Dante adds, "You know. Next time you're at the hospital visiting Enzo. Word is from the security detail you practically live there these days."

My shoulders drop, forcing me to recognise just how much tension was bubbling below the surface of this phone call. I hate this. I feel like I'm lying to my best friend. Who am I kidding? I am lying to my best friend.

I just hope he forgives me when the time comes.

CHAPTER TWELVE

KATERINA

I am regretting my life choices. I should never have agreed to this. Now I'm stuck here witnessing the destruction of my personal bubble. There are people in my house, drilling holes in walls and installing little boxes of electronics, trailing wires all over the place, and leaving dust and footprints everywhere.

It's not like I'm obsessively tidy. I'm what I would describe as 'chaotic good' when it comes to housework. Everything is mostly tidy and then I do one big clean every time I'm off shift. And truthfully, 'mostly tidy' means all mess is coordinated into piles, drawers, or baskets of organised disorder. But the dust and the noise and the people are too much.

Having changed into my gym kit, I storm into my kitchen and grab a water bottle from the fridge before turning and heading towards the garage. I have a home gym set up in there and I need to burn off the excess frustration. When I open the internal door from the utility to the garage, I stop still at the sight before me. I'm both furious and also struggling to contain my laughter.

I have many pieces of equipment spread out in here. I haven't managed to make a massive mark on my home since I moved in, but this space is one I took the time to put together. It's my sanctuary. When I'm off shift, I turn into a complete homebody and the last thing I want to do is leave the comfort of my home in order to sweat in front of strangers.

None of those pieces of equipment are why I'm giggling though. Before me are two of the workmen. One is laughing at his friend while he tries—and fails—to hold himself with any dignity on the shiny spinning pole in the centre of the garage. I vaguely recognise them. They're young, so I'm sure they're the son or nephew of someone I know well, but right now I can't place them. They definitely look similar enough to be brothers though.

The one on the pole is off the ground, straddling it and holding tight with one arm. I'm about to tell him not to let go when he does just that and throws his head back. I can't stop the snort of laughter that erupts from me as he's left gripping the pole with only his trouser-clad thighs, which lose all traction against the shiny surface, causing him to slide with great speed towards the floor. He lands on his ass with an undignified grunt, crushing his left shoulder. I flinch as he hits the ground, remembering how painful it was when I was learning.

"Having fun, boys?"

They whip their heads around, visibly blanching when they see me.

"It's not as easy as it looks, is it, gentlemen?" I admonish, forcing a stern tone into my voice and arching a brow at them. I'm really not mad, but I'm enjoying fucking with them.

They don't move, dropping their mouths open like fish out of water, seemingly having forgotten how to speak. I make my way over to them as the man who made the valiant attempt at the pole rights himself and starts dusting off his trousers.

"Is there a reason why you're in here playing with my pole, gentlemen?" I feel a little bad when they blush before suddenly becoming enormously interested in staring at their feet. I decide not to let them off so easily. "Well?"

"Sorry, Doc," they reply in unison. It's impossible to keep a straight face at their complete mortification. The cackle I let out does nothing to reduce their awkwardness. As I step further into the room, they scurry towards the door, giving me a wide berth, like getting too close will somehow magnify their embarrassment.

"What exactly were you working on in here before you decided to ride my pole, boys?" I'm probably being a little mean now, but the looks on their faces make it too tempting not to tease them.

"W-we were putting up sensors on the window and garage door for the alarm. Sorry, Doc," says the spectator. They both pause at the door like they're waiting to be excused, but I can tell from their pained expressions they'd rather be anywhere but here.

I finally let my face fall into a warm smile, and I can see their relief when they grasp that I'm not actually mad. "I'm just fucking with you. Although if you want to play with the pole in future, you need to lose the trousers."

I take a step towards it, stretching up high with one hand and taking a firm grip. I push off, lifting my legs off the ground, and start the pole in a slow spin before wrapping them around it, holding myself in a seated position as it rotates at a leisurely pace.

"You'll never get the grip you need to hold the position with pants on," I say with a grin before letting go with my hands and throwing my head back, leaving me hanging upside down, the pole in a tight grip between my thighs. I'm wearing a sports bra and my pole shorts. They're slightly longer than booty shorts, but not by much, and they're necessary for pole work.

As I spin around, I now realise that perhaps it wasn't just the falling that caused their red faces, because right now they don't know where to look. Every time they come into view as I turn, they look more and more flustered, doing everything they can not to look at me. On the next rotation, there's a shadow in the doorway, and as I come back around, Stefano steps into view—face like thunder and anger rolling off him in waves.

"Get the fuck out right now," he roars at his men, and I can't help but giggle as the guys flee like startled cattle. They're their own two-man stampede.

I loosen the grip my thighs have on the pole, sliding down and laying my hands on the floor, kicking back into a handstand before standing. Stefano slams the door to the garage and storms towards me, his expression rigid and his jaw clenched tight. He looks like a bull charging a matador. I hold up my palm as he reaches me, stopping him dead in his tracks.

"Don't you fucking start with me, Tiero. I came in here to work out and found your men playing on my pole—"

"What do you mean playing on your pole?" he growls, and I snigger. "Don't laugh at me. This isn't fucking funny. Why the hell were my men standing here ogling my-my... you, wearing next to nothing on a stripper pole?"

Any humour I was experiencing is sucked out of me, replaced with an irritation at his tone that festers around me, hanging in and gearing us up for what's about to be our first official fight as a couple. *Wait, does dating for twenty-four hours make us a couple?* Who the fuck knows.

"Where the hell do you get off coming into my house and judging me for how I choose to exercise?"

"Th-That's not what I mea—" he stutters, clearly realising his mistake. He's poked the bear and now he's ripe for a mauling.

"How fucking dare you judge me for what I do and what I wear," I screech, stepping into his space only for him to take a step back to escape.

"That's not why I—"

"I don't care why you're acting like a fucking cave-man, Tiero. I came in here and found them dicking about on my 'stripper' pole, as you so eloquently put it. So, I decided to teach them a lesson. Quite literally, and they were mortified. You think the minute you turn your back, I'm in here putting on some kind of show for anyone who'll watch. You think I'd do that to you?" My chest is heaving with each sentence I spit at him. "And if you think you have any say in what I do with my body, you've got another thing coming. What the fuck do you thi—"

He bats away the finger I'm using to repeatedly stab him with and steps towards me, placing his hands around my waist and hoisting me up against him. My traitorous legs wrap around him to balance as he walks me back against the wall of mirrors. I flinch when my bare skin hits the cold surface.

"What the fuck are you doing? We're fighting," I grind out. My breathing is ragged and strained as he leans in closer.

"We're not fighting," he fires back at me.

"I beg your pardon. Yes, we fucking are," I snap. My arms encircle his neck but I unfurl one just long enough to slap at his shoulder. He loosens his grip on me and drops me down, startling a yelp out of me as my feet find the floor. His hands dart for my wrists, dragging my arms over my head and pressing them firmly against the cool glass. "What the fuck is your prob—"

Pinning both my wrists beneath one of his broad palms, his free hand darts for my throat, cutting me off mid-irate sentence.

"Enough," he roars, before crashing his lips to mine and stealing the head of steam I'd built up straight from my lungs. I gasp and let out a little whimper when he shifts his stance, pressing against me with his hips, and showing me just how much he likes having me at his mercy. The corner of my mouth curves in a smile when I calm down long enough to recognise that this reaction isn't down to mistrust. There's a torrent of emotions drifting across his features, but the one I can see gleaming in his eyes is jealousy. He's jealous. Jealous that anyone other than him got to see... what's his.

"Goddammit, why do you have to make it so difficult to apologise? You're a fucking menace sometimes." His tone is gruff and strained. We're so close our breaths mingle and tussle with each other.

"Are you saying you can't handle a woman like me, *vecchietto*?" I say with a sarcastic lilt to my voice. Throwing down the gauntlet, trying to see how far I can push him. The tips of his fingers flex, just enough to elicit a half-feral moan as the pressure around my neck fluctuates.

"You know what I think, *micetta*?" he teases, his mouth curling into a lopsided smirk and letting his dimple come out to play. "You need a firm hand or a hard fuck, don't you, baby girl?"

"Why not both?" I say with a dramatic pout.

He releases my wrists and throat, and I instantly miss the sense of possession they gave me. I need his hands on me. I crave them and my body seems to come alive under his touch.

He looks like a beast about to tear me limb from limb. I'm so exposed, so vulnerable, and so fucking turned on. A low rumble in his chest is the only warning I get before he grabs my arm and drags me with him as he stalks across the room.

The more roughly he handles me, the more my core heats and my arousal builds. "What are you going to do to me?" I ask, not really caring what the answer is, but desperate to hear his gruff voice again.

"What do you want me to do to you? What will make you understand who you belong to?" he says, his timbre so full of gravel I swear I can feel it vibrating in my molten core.

"I've been yours for years. You just never claimed me," I whine, hating every second his hands are not on my body.

"Is that what you want? To be owned?"

"Yes. But only by you, Daddy," I whisper, but I may as well have shouted for the reaction my words elicit. Stefano's expression darkens and one hand darts back to collar my throat before squeezing just enough for my pulse to hammer against his fingertips.

"On. Your. Knees," he commands. With his other hand, he wrenches open his belt and unbuttons his pants. "Take out my dick and show me how good you can be for me."

He cups my jaw firmly, pulling me forwards, and I instinctively open my mouth as I scramble to tug down his clothes, eager to feel him fill my throat. My pussy is throbbing almost as hard as my heart is pounding. I'd love to feel his cock in my cunt right now, but I want him to punish me more. His erection springs free as I drag the waistband of his boxers to his taut thighs and smile with satisfaction as I take in his swollen length.

It's magnificent. Thick and long, with a vein that snakes from the base to the flare of his crown. I don't hesitate to lean in and trace it with the tip of my tongue, moaning in harmony with him as he obviously savours the sensation.

Cupping the back of my head, he starts a slow and unforgiving thrust, not stopping when I gag a little. Pushing deeper until I'm forced to swallow around him. My hands fly to the backs of his thighs, gripping them tightly as I brace myself against him, eager for him to take me exactly how he wants to.

I've never felt like this before, but the more he takes what he needs, the more turned on I am. I want him to own me. *I need it.*

Just when I start to think about my dwindling air supply, he pulls back enough for me to heave in my next breath. But he doesn't give me a chance to take a second. He sets a slow and brutal pace, eking out both his pleasure and mine. It's savage, yet at the same time, loving.

Our eyes are locked, and his gaze is fierce.

Dragging me off his cock, he growls, "Who do you belong to?"

"You."

"Damn fucking right," he roars, before plunging back between my lips and sheathing himself in my throat. Saliva pools under my tongue, coating his dick and dribbling out of the corner of my mouth. The sounds of half-chokes and hollow cheeked sucks fill the room as he picks up the pace, and I don't know whether it's his groans of pleasure or the pre-cum he's coating my throat with, but they're pushing me into a state of arousal I've never experienced before. I'm overwhelmed with a sensation of complete ownership while feeling entirely cherished at the same time.

His hips stutter a moment before his cum erupts on my tongue and paints my throat in hot, salty ropes. I struggle to swallow, smiling as he pulls out, dripping the last of his release across the swell of my breasts.

He leans down, running his hand through his masterpiece, massaging it in, branding me. When I start to moan, he stops, teasing me.

"Uh-uh-uh, baby girl. You'll get your release when I say so. Right now you can get dressed and finish the workout you came down here for, covered in my cum."

I whimper in response, but I can't deny how much the idea turns me on. Doesn't mean I'm not going to protest. "But you can't do that."

"You're lucky I granted you the privilege of choking on my dick."

He zips up his pants and fastens his belt as he stalks over to the door and then slips out of the room without another word, leaving me speechless and eager for his touch.

I don't know where this version of Stefano has been hiding, but *fuck me,* I'm desperate for him. If any other man used me like that—like his personal fuck toy—I'd kick them out quicker than they could unzip their pants, but when Stefano tells me to get on my knees? Then I want to fall to the ground and suck his cock like it's my favourite lollypop.

He's left me desperate and horny and despite my pussy's fluttering protests, the rest of my body is at peace. Happy to have been so thoroughly owned by him.

As I lean into the first stretch of my workout, I smile, happy to do as I'm told, and switch my brain off for the next hour, focussed on only one thought.

He makes me feel like I'm his.

CHAPTER THIRTEEN

STEFANO

My team left a few hours ago, and I did a mostly stellar job of not punishing the Vitale brothers. Somehow, I managed to avoid beating them to within an inch of their lives for lusting after what's mine. However, unhinged, jealous boyfriend is not a good look outside of the bedroom. Especially not if you're the Bianchi consigliere. There are times, very rare occurrences, when my position limits my preferred course of action. I'm the trusted advisor to the Don; I can't be seen to be making irrational decisions.

Gouging the Vitale's eyes out would probably be considered rash.

Instead of physical violence, I found a way to sate my need to discipline them. Right now, they're on a four-day stakeout in the ass end of nowhere. I figured it couldn't hurt to have eyes on Danny, and I know within twelve hours they'll be driving each other crazy. If it's one thing you can count on, it's that Thing 1 and Thing 2 can't spend more than a few hours in each other's company without bickering. I usually go out of my way to give them separate assignments, but today I'm not feeling too generous. They can be each other's punishment.

Earlier, I left Katerina to work out in peace while I supervised the team. They managed to install everything, but there's wet paint everywhere from where they righted any damage, which is evident from the streak of it across the sleeve of my suit.

I make my way upstairs to her bedroom, hauling the last case with me, finding Katerina coming out of the bathroom wrapped in a fluffy white robe and tousling her hair with a towel. Her eyes are practically on stalks when she catches the suitcase.

"Jesus. How long are you planning on staying? I've never seen a man bring so much luggage. You sure as hell don't travel light, do you?"

"Suits. Weapons. Electronics," I say, pointing at each case in turn.

She nods. "That makes sense, but what about the two in the kitchen and the one in the bathroom?"

"Toiletries and food," I reply, slightly confused by her surprise.

"If that case in there is just toiletries, you're going to need to get a team in here to remodel my bathroom."

I shrug. "You seem to like a man who takes care of himself."

She blushes, crossing to the dresser and spraying

something on her hair before brushing it. It's too long for her to reach the ends, so she drags it over her shoulder. I move to stand behind her and point at the chair. "Sit down. Let me."

"You don't have to, I've got it." Her brow furrows, and I hate that she's resistant to even the smallest gesture of care. I love how strong and independent she is, but behind closed doors, I'd love for her to feel safe enough to allow those who love her to look after her. It's not just me. She's the same with her family. Never asks her dad or brother for help, yet she'll drop everything to be there for anyone who needs her.

I don't move, my hand still pointing at the seat. We're in a standoff of stubbornness.

Eventually, she rolls her eyes and concedes defeat, handing over the brush before sitting down and folding her arms across her chest with a huff.

"If I'm not allowed to have an alpha male tantrum, I really don't think it's fair for you to act like a stroppy teenager?"

She glares at me in the reflection of the mirror, her open mouth poised to tear me a new one, but instead, I reach my free hand up the nape of her neck, squeezing firmly before pulling her back into my chest.

"Sit still, keep quiet, and let me brush your hair." The timbre of my voice slips into an octave I'm not sure I've ever reached before. It's deep and commanding and I smile when she unfolds her arms and drops her hands in her lap. I can see any desire to argue with me seep out of her when I squeeze tighter and her eyes close involuntarily.

I release my grip and start alternating between the soft bristled brush and raking my fingers through the rich strands. Now it's damp, the colour has phased from the familiar rich mahogany to closer to molten chocolate, laced with filaments of deep copper.

When I'm quite sure I've unfurled every tangle, I reach for the hairdryer neatly stored in a cradle under the desk.

"You don't need—"

I sweep my free hand across her shoulders and under her hair, rotating my wrist, wrapping her tresses around my arm like a twist of rope, then gently tugging. "I said, sit still, and keep quiet."

Releasing her, I fluff out her hair and turn on the hairdryer. I have no goddamn idea what I'm doing, but from the contented look on her face, I'm not sure Katerina cares. I take my time and make sure every strand is dry before switching it off, and returning the dryer to its cradle.

Her reflection shows how flushed her skin is, like she's embarrassed by this level of intimacy. I don't think I've ever seen her look so bashful.

"Anything else I can do for you?" My voice betrays me. I loved being able to give her the attention she deserves.

"As much as I enjoy your hands on me, I think I draw the line at you doing my skincare routine," she says with a giggle.

"In that case, I'll unpack some stuff and then head downstairs and start on dinner." Her eyebrows end up somewhere near her hairline.

"You're going to cook for me?"

"What did you think the bags in the kitchen were for? I can't survive on cereal and bagels, woman."

"Breakfast for dinner is a valid meal choice."

"Not while I'm staying here," I reply, my voice stern but laced with a light-heartedness I haven't indulged in for years.

"All you have to do is add a 'young lady' and you'd sound like my father."

For the first time in years, the mention of her father doesn't make me flinch. I know we'll have a tough time explaining what this is between us when the time comes, but I don't see her as my best friend's daughter. I see her as a strong, confident woman who deserves a man brave enough to love her the way she needs.

"Such a brat, *micetta*."

I'm gifted with a playful eye roll that somehow makes my pulse thrum, pulling a broad smile at the ease of domesticity that flows between us. I head to the bathroom and leave her to her lotions and potions so that I can find a place for some of my things.

While there's a part of me that misses the comfort of my own home, I'm happy that she feels comfortable enough having me stay with her. Although, I do see her point as I start to unpack my bag. I've brought a lot with me for a man she only slept with for the first time yesterday.

Shit, has it only been a day? It feels like so much longer, especially when I've wanted her for what feels like an eternity.

The bathroom is smaller than mine, but I smile when I note that her tub is large enough for both of us. The shower would be a bit of a tight squeeze, but we can probably make it work. She's decorated with rich green tiles and jade-coloured walls. It's serene and relaxing, although every time I turn around I'm bumping into an overgrown plant that's trying to escape its pot. Honestly, I didn't have her pegged as a plant person.

When I've found space for everything, I head back to her room. "What's with the rainforest in there?"

"Honestly, patients keep giving me the damn things and it's the only room in the house that they survive in."

A loud, boisterous laugh bursts out of me. "Well, that certainly makes a lot more sense."

She brings a hand to her chest in faux offense. "Are you accusing me of being a terrible plant mother?"

"I would never," I say, holding my palms up in surrender.

"I'll have you know I only killed the first ten or so before I figured out that they're more likely to survive in there," she says, gesturing towards the bathroom before returning her attention to massaging a new product into her skin.

"How many moisturisers does one person need?" I ask, gesturing towards the collection of bottles in front of her.

"I don't do this because of some need to look young or live forever, *vecchietto*. I do this to unwind. It's my little ritual, and it's for me and no one else." She reaches for a flat pink stone and starts to drag it along her collarbone.

I have no clue what it's for, and as she so rightly pointed out, it's for her benefit, not mine, therefore none of my damn business. She moves the stone leisurely across her skin, the tension melting away from her body and a sense of calm settling over her.

Walking over, I bend and kiss her forehead. "As long as you know, I think you're stunning either way."

She lets out a contented sigh, that same blush blossoming up her neck and into her cheeks. "Thank you."

I press my lips to hers, careful not to disturb whatever products she's applied, and leave her in peace.

I head downstairs to unpack what I brought with me and start on dinner, getting lost in my own ritual. I'm by no means a master chef but I remember every recipe my mother taught me, and cooking brings me peace. I'm making a simple ragu with pappardelle pasta, but I'm cheating a little. Digging through the cooler, I find the container I need. Working for a criminal organisation means I'm rarely able to predict when I'll be home. It's not like we work regular business hours, so I've been known to batch cook.

Who am I kidding? My freezer is full of food. If anyone ever needed to hide a body in a chest freezer, mine would never be the one to use. It's full to the brim.

After grabbing a saucepan, I turf out the slow-cooked beef ragu, setting it on a low heat to defrost and cook through. I ready the oversized pasta pot, letting it simmer gently with the lid on, ready to throw in the fresh pasta when Katerina comes down.

I finish emptying what is only a fraction of my pantry stores into her barren cupboards. When she's on shift, I know she frequents the canteen most days. It's one of the places we added to our rotation of public dates in order to keep tongues wagging about us. From the sheer volume of menus in the junk drawer, it would seem she survives on a variety of local takeout restaurants.

"What's that amazing smell? And how is it coming from my kitchen?"

I look up to find her leaning against the doorjamb, one leg crossed over the other at the ankles, emphasising her insanely long legs. She's changed into a loose-fitting loungewear set and she's wrangled the haphazard hair I undoubtedly left her with into a set of thick braids.

Is she trying to kill me? She looks adorable and simultaneously sexy as fuck. There's a glint of desire in her eyes as she watches me stirring the ragu and I'm sure I'm reflecting the same expression right back at her.

"It's just something I had at home. Beef ragu and pappardelle," I say as I throw the pasta in to boil. We spend the next few minutes dancing around each other in the kitchen. She fetches the plates and cutlery while I drain the pasta and start serving.

"Can we eat in the lounge?" she asks a little sheepishly. "I know you've cooked this wonderful meal, but I'd love to kick back and relax on the sofa. This looks like the perfect comfort food."

I'm nodding and picking up the pasta bowls before she's even finished. However she wants to eat is fine by me. As long as she's well fed, well fucked and well looked after, that's all that matters. Fuck standing on ceremony.

As I follow her into the living room, I smile when she shuffles back into a mountain of cushions in the corner of the couch. Pulling her legs up, she sits cross-legged before hauling one of the cushions out of the pile and placing it on top of her legs like a makeshift table.

She's snatching the bowl with grabby hands before I know what's happening and gesturing for me to sit down beside her. There's a selection of remotes on the side table and within a few moments, she's dimmed the lights and queued up something to watch.

Katerina turns her head and eyes me warily. "This is where I find out if you have a sense of humour or not."

"So, this is a test? I see. Press play then and let's see if I pass."

I'm worried when I don't recognise the title. Honestly, you're more likely to find me reading a book and listening to music than you are watching television, but it doesn't take long for me to get into it and concede that it's hilarious.

"What is this?" I ask between mouthfuls, softly nudging her arm.

"*Schitt's Creek*. It's hilarious and quite frankly if you hadn't liked it, it would have called this whole 'real dating' thing into question. I have no qualms fake dating a Schitt's Creek hater, but being with one for real, it could never be me."

I chuckle and glance at her expecting to see her giggling right back at me, but she's side eyeing me. "I'm not joking, *vecchietto*."

She nearly has me fooled until she bursts into fits of giggles. "Seriously, though, I would have judged you. This is my comfort watch."

"In that case, I'm glad I haven't disappointed you," I say, leaning over and kissing her temple.

"It would be hard to disappoint me, Stefano. Especially with cooking like this. How did I not know you were this talented?" she asks between large, twirled forkfuls of pasta.

I place my cutlery down and reach over, wiping the splash of sauce on her chin with my thumb. That sexy little blush flourishes back to life when I hold it in front of her. I give her a moment for her to decide what she'll do, and I groan when she wraps her plump lips around my thumb and sucks the sauce right off before releasing it with a satisfying pop.

That simple little interaction shouldn't have turned me on as much as it did, but my cock has ideas of his own. The zipper of these pants does nothing to suppress my now-growing erection. The only thing that's keeping it in check is the pasta bowl in my lap.

It doesn't take long for us to devour the rest of the pasta, so I decide to make a discreet getaway to adjust myself and clear away the dinner. I grab a bottle of wine and some glasses and bring them back through, placing them down on the coffee table.

The rest of the evening passes in a sort of haze of relaxed domesticity. She moves me to the pillow mountain in the corner and curls up into my side, laying her head on my chest and trailing her fingers up and down the buttons of my shirt in a never-ending pattern. Like I'm her personal fidget toy. I have no complaints but every time the pads of her fingers veer too close to my belt buckle, my cock twitches in anticipation, desperate to recreate the night before.

I have no idea how much longer I can hold out for before I pull her on to my lap and make her grind and ride me till we both come in our pants like horny teenagers.

Fuck it.

CHAPTER FOURTEEN

I let out an undignified squeal as Stefano hauls me on to his lap without warning. Any confusion I might have evaporates when he grips my hips firmly and pulls me down against his rigid cock. I let out a feral whimper when his hard length grinds against me from clit to cunt.

I lay my hands on his shoulders, steadying myself against his broad chest. I claw at the fabric, irritated to have anything separating me from him. His dimple appears when he finally comprehends how much his clothes are frustrating me and he releases my hips to unbutton his shirt. His shirt parts wider and I take the opportunity to slide my fingers under the fabric, dusting my touch across his chest as I snake my hips, rubbing my pussy against his impossibly hard cock.

When he reaches the last button, he pulls out the shirt from his waistband and lets it fall wide open. He's a glorious blend of lean muscle adorned with soft accents of hair that only make his physique more enticing. I don't even try to hide how much the sight of him bared to me turns me on. I lick my bottom lip before pulling myself closer, running gentle kisses down the slope of his neck and nuzzling under his collar to nip and bite at his collarbone.

There's something about his scent that drives me wild. It's so rich and warm and welcoming. He smells like home. Safe, secure, and somehow sinful along with it. I let out a moan as I exhale, scraping my nails hard against the muscle across his shoulders.

"Be a good girl and take what you need from me, *micetta*. Careful of those claws," he says with a wicked grin. "Unless, of course, you enjoy marking what's yours." His hands glide along my outer thighs, stopping when they reach the curve of my ass. He massages my cheeks before suddenly pulling one hand back and spanking me with just enough force to leave a delicious sting heating my skin. "I know I do."

"Do that again," I whisper so quietly that I'm not sure he's heard me. I gasp in surprise when I hear the next strike a fraction of a second before the same warmth blooms on the other side. My eyelids drift shut as I sink into the sensation, revelling in the heat that radiates up my spine and through my core. My body takes control, seeking more sensation and rocking against him.

This hunger for Stefano Tiero feels urgent, like there's no time and I'm so far gone for him that I've lost all reason. I don't care that I'm still fully clothed. I just need to feel his hard body beneath me, giving me everything I need to fall apart. Every grind of my hips brings me closer to detonating. My breaths become ragged, laced with desperate pants and wanton moans.

That wicked dimple pops on his cheek as I brush the head of his cock against my clit. "I can feel your hot little pussy teasing my dick. Keep this up and you'll make me come so hard, sweetheart." There's a smile on his lips and a sweet agony in his tone. He's almost as lost to this as I am.

"That sounds like a challenge," I purr, my hips never stopping their unrelenting pace against him. Every motion brings me closer to the edge of orgasm, and from the pleasure etched on his face it's obvious the same is true for him.

I don't know how we got here, but clothes-on-rutting is turning out to be one of the most erotic things I've experienced and doesn't hold a candle to the desperate fumbles I had as a teenager. Perhaps you need the experience of age to know exactly how you can torture your partner with understated intimacies.

The moment the first groan passes his lips, I'm done for. There's nothing hotter than hearing how much your man is enjoying you. The low growls and husky grunts as he attempts to stave off his orgasm and hold himself still are my undoing. As I increase the tempo against his cock, his jaw clenches and neck strains, and I know I've succeeded in making him come first. It's the last piece of the puzzle and exactly what I need to tumble over the edge of my climax. My body seizes in ecstasy and a flourish of stars dance behind my eyelids as I collapse against Stefano's heaving chest.

His arms wrap around me in a tight embrace, and I nuzzle into his neck, resting my cheek against the rhythmic drumming of his pulse.

I'm unaware as I drift off to sleep, but I wake a little while later in my bed, wrapped around his warm, freshly showered body—the scent of his shower gel, heady and soothing. He's naked underneath me and I revel in the heat of his skin as it warms my cheek. I have no idea how he carried me without waking me, but I close my eyes and drift back to sleep, happy in the embrace of someone who makes me feel more treasured than anyone on this earth ever has.

My last thought before I lose my battle with content-edness is as reassuring as it is unsettling. *How did we deny ourselves this connection for so long? It's more right than anything I've ever known. And how the fuck will I survive if it doesn't work out?*

CHAPTER FIFTEEN

STEFANO

TWO WEEKS LATER...

While I'd rather have her safe in my home, I can't deny how much I'm enjoying staying with Katerina. I've never had a desire to live with anyone before, but the little habits and routines we've started engaging together make it impossible to deny how much I enjoy it. We've fallen into a myriad of domestic routines—ones I've never been particularly interested in experiencing with any partner before.

Her shifts make it difficult, but no matter what time she starts, I get up while she's showering and make her breakfast to make sure she's starting her day properly. When she'll let me, I've even been known to pack her a lunch on days when I know I won't be able to meet her.

There's been no more little gifts sent, which only

supports her original argument that I'm overreacting. She may be right, but I'm not about to admit that to her. I can't describe how protective of her I am. It's like a thread that runs through the centre of me, constantly pulling me towards her, demanding to know that she's safe.

It's not just the author of the creepy notes that has me worried. Since Enzo was discharged, tensions are only increasing between the Bianchis and the De Lucas. It's only a matter of time before it escalates and in the meantime, knowing I can protect her myself is the only thing keeping me sane.

When it comes to the hospital, Danny-boy seems to have finally taken the hint. The notes have stopped. Also, word on the hospital grapevine is that he met someone at the wedding, which has me hoping rather than assuming, that he's given up his infatuation. Looks like I had her swap shifts for nothing. A fact Katerina is keen to keep reminding me of. I'm not complaining about her new rota though; the hours seem to work out better for us. It seems whether it's long surgeries or organised crime, we both get home around the same time. Who knew the schedule of a surgeon and consigliere would be so compatible?

I've been at Inferno working. There's a capo meeting with Aurora tomorrow, and I needed to make sure I was fully prepared. As I walk through the front door of her house, my hackles raise as Katerina's raised voice booms with anger, but laced ever so slightly with a note of fear.

I'm down the hallway, hanging off the doorframe as I scan each room. It takes me a minute to track her down, finally finding her in her study, pacing around the desk, and shouting directly into the phone she's holding in front of her face.

"I don't know who the fuck you think you are, but I promise you've picked the wrong woman to fuck with."

I snatch the phone out of her hand, ignoring the spluttering protests and the not so gentle slaps against my back. "Give that back right now," she shouts.

I turn, my free hand darting out and covering her mouth. "Don't test my patience." The strain in my voice makes my words come out too harshly. Her temper flares in response, her eyes narrowing as her jaw clenches under my touch. "Settle down. Let me do this. Please." I let out a relieved sigh when her expression softens, just a fraction.

Turning my focus back to the phone in my other hand, I bring it back to my ear. "Anything you have to say, you can say to me," I bark, the words so loud they scrape against my larynx.

The caller doesn't speak for the longest time, but I can hear his breath grating against the speaker. The rasp is jarring and every exhale rakes through the hairs on the back of my neck, making them stand to attention. Finally, there's a sinister crackle over the line, followed by an emotionless robotic voice. "She'll pay for letting you touch what's mine."

The line goes dead before I have the chance to roar my response. The idea that anyone would harm her makes me want to retch. Our gazes collide, and I'm struck by how scared she looks. All the colour has drained from her face and I swear I can see her lip trembling.

In that moment, I understand that what he said to me pales in comparison to whatever he said to her. I release her jaw, wrap my arms around her, pick her up, and walk her back towards her desk. As I reach for the chair and take a seat in front of her, she starts shouting. "How is you yelling at him any more productive than me yelling at him?' Her eyes bore a hole into my chest where she refuses to make eye contact.

I take her hands in mine and dip my head as I bring them to my lips. I press a gentle kiss to her knuckles, the gesture as much an attempt to soothe the racing pulse that hammers against my thumb as it is a distraction. "I won't apologise for wanting to protect you, Katerina," I say, turning over her hands and laying a heavy palm in hers. My fingers wander as I continue, tickling an affectionate path around her palm and trailing it up her arm and along her collarbone until I can hook a gentle touch under her chin and tip it until she flicks her eyes to mine. "What did he say before I came in?"

A lone tear beads on her lashes. That one tiny drop torments me as it spills over and streaks down her cheek. "Don't make me say it," she whispers.

I rise from the chair and wrap her in a tight embrace, tucking her head into the crook of my neck and trying to use the subtle hint of black cherry that wafts up from her silky hair to subdue the rage coursing through me. To anyone who doesn't know her, her reactions might seem like she's taking this in her stride. But for her to show anything, for there to be the slightest crack in her armour, I know that she's rattled, and that has my imagination running wild.

"It's okay, baby girl. You can tell me."

"I can't. You'll kill him," she says with a sniff.

"I've killed a lot of people, Katerina. But I won't simply kill him. I'll slaughter the man who made you cry." She surprises me when she simply nods her head. Like she's accepting the seriousness of the situation and that as long as she's still breathing, she's mine to protect.

I pick her up bridal style and carry her out of the office, into the living room. She lets out an adorable little squeak as I lower myself to the couch and settle her on my lap. "Tell me."

There are a few huffs of frustration before she speaks. "I hate that this asshole has made me feel so fucking vulnerable." Tears well in her eyes again and it breaks my heart. I remain quiet, stroking a hand down her back while the other grips tightly to her hip, holding her tight to me.

"He said he was disappointed in me and that I'd pay for 'betraying his devotion'." Her face twists in disgust as she quotes him. "He said that I was always meant to be his and that he'd punish me for whoring myself out to another man. I was so angry at being spoken to like that, that I didn't even think to hang up." She pauses and I don't say a word. The last thing I want to do is interrupt or reinforce the idea that she's done anything wrong. "He said that he was done waiting for me to 'see the light' and that it was time to take what was his."

My rage simmers and bubbles under the surface as I comfort her. My fingers squeeze her hip, and she leans into my chest, resting her head against my shoulder. Her posture sags with exhaustion, while my body is more tightly wound than it ever has been.

"Is this the first time he's called?" I ask, my heart sinking when she doesn't answer right away.

She clears her throat and lets the silence hang in the air until it becomes painful. "It's the first time they've spoken."

My temper frays at the edges. I move her off my lap and rise to my feet before pacing the length of the room in a frenetic march as I try to compose myself. A string of expletives burst from my lips, half in English, half in Italian. I can't look at Katerina for fear that I'll direct my frustration at her, but there's a part of me that wants to turn her over my knee and spank her ass red raw for keeping this from me.

"How long has he been calling?" I grind out and I chastise myself internally that my words make her startle.

"A week maybe," she replies, rubbing her arms for comfort. Blood rushes in my ears, roaring like river rapids and drowning out her profuse apologies.

"Don't you dare say you're sorry when you know damn well you're not," I snap.

"That's not fair. I didn't realise how serious it was," she protests.

"How? When I've been telling you for weeks! How are you this stubborn, woman?" I shout, still pacing, unable to calm myself down.

"I just didn't think Danny would ever harm me," she says, her voice raising and her words sounding surer.

She's not backing down, despite my unbridled anger. If anything, the more anger I show, the more she claws her way out of the fear that was gripping her and the more she sounds like herself. "I still don't."

"Then let's find out," I growl. I pull out my phone and dial my second. Marcus picks up within moments. "I want additional men on Costello. He's escalating."

"You want his house wired too?" is his only query. Typical Marcus. Succinct and efficient.

"Start with round-the-clock surveillance." I grind out. "Rotate three teams of two every twenty-four hours, and I want updates on every shift change, Marcus."

As I hang up, my pacing is interrupted by a now furious Katerina blocking my path.

"Don't start with me, Katerina Elena Mancini."

"*Don't you fucking full name me!* This is getting out of hand," she shouts, squaring up against me in a manner that might be intimidating if it wasn't so fucking adorable. I can't help stepping into her personal space and challenging her right back.

"I think you'll find, I'll do whatever it takes when it comes to protecting your safety," I bellow right back at her. "Do you think for one second I'll allow this to continue? I don't give a fuck who his father is or how it affects your career. This isn't just a mild infatuation. He's threatening to hurt you!"

We're both glaring at each other, our chests heaving, emotions a swirling vortex of anger, fear, and frustration. The tension in the air is so thick it feels like it could choke us both. I don't know who moves first but the second her lips touch mine it's like all the oxygen in the room has been consumed and the only way to breathe is with the air we can steal from each other.

I don't know if it takes seconds or minutes for us to burn off our anger with our frenzied kiss but when we come up for air, I lift her into my arms and let the feeling of rightness wash over me as she wraps her legs around my waist. Our eyes are locked together, neither one of us blinking. "Don't ever lie to me again."

"I didn't lie," she protests, but her cheeks flush, betraying her.

"A lie by omission is still a lie. I won't tolerate being disrespected, Katerina. Do I make myself clear?" I try to temper the tone of my voice, but I can't dampen the seriousness of my words. No matter how much I care for her, this won't work if she doesn't trust me with the truth.

She nods, but I don't let it go. I move one arm, and wrap my hand around her throat, gripping with enough pressure to draw out the slightest of moans.

"You won't brat your way out of this one, baby girl. Use. Your. Words. Promise me you will tell me everything." I bite out.

She's nodding before the words escape her. "I promise," she says, her tone soft but resolute, and I can see the regret lacing her features at having lied to me before. *Fuck me if contrition doesn't look hot as fuck on her.*

I lean closer, clasping her neck a little tighter as I press a kiss to her lips and whisper in her ear. "Such a good girl for me." I preen when she smiles and releases a contented sigh, before reluctantly releasing my grip, sending her upstairs to bed to wait for me.

I do a sweep of the house, for security but also to give

myself a few minutes to calm down. I replay every hate-filled word she relayed to me from the call and the more I let them spiral through my mind, the more concerned I become.

I don't like that he's escalating. And I sure as fuck don't like that it feels like she's in more danger now than she was before.

One thing I know though. He's going to regret staking any claim on what's mine.

CHAPTER SIXTEEN

KATERINA

It's been a long day filled with nothing but complicated surgeries and bad outcomes. No one likes losing patients, but losing them back-to-back only compounds the failure you feel. It settles in your bones and makes you question every ounce of skill you've spent years honing.

The last surgery was a clusterfuck and not even the self-proclaimed cardio god was able to repair the aortic dissection the patient sprung on us. Doctor Jenkins followed me out of the OR and kept on at me about my lack of focus these days. While a part of me understands that it's his way to blame everyone else in the room when something goes wrong, today is not the day and I am not the one.

I'd turned my back on him, telling him to lodge a complaint with the Chief of Surgery if he was truly questioning my competence. Thankfully, he didn't try to follow me and had given up on his tirade.

I'm currently refusing to budge from under the rather limp, semi-hot spray of the changing room showers. It's doing two-fifths of fuck-all to soothe my screaming muscles, sore from standing elbow-deep in patients for hours on end, but I needed to wash away the day.

I hadn't felt right since last night. I should have told Stefano the moment I'd started receiving the calls, but I was so convinced that he and Nico were overreacting that I'd ignored them. No matter how much I try, I can't shake the feeling I've let him and myself down.

I finally haul myself out of the cubicle and change. It's not only the sudden shift in temperature that has me shivering. I used to feel safe at the hospital, but now it's like I'm looking over my shoulder at every turn. Although the notes have stopped, the phone calls and now text messages aren't slowing down. If anything, they're getting worse. I reach for my phone and find a flurry of notifications obscuring the screen. Dozens of alerts from the same unknown number. Missed calls, voicemails, and texts. Rubbing my hand over my face, I prepare myself for the worst.

They start out almost friendly, yet they're tainted with a manic level of delusion that turns my stomach. Apologies for his 'unkind words' soon turn into unhinged scoldings for ignoring him and venomous insults.

UNKNOWN:

Whores don't deserve mercy. When I get
my hands on you, I'll flay every inch of
skin he's touched from your bones.

Bile rises in my throat, and I run to one of the stalls,
unable to stop myself from emptying the contents of my
stomach. When I'm quite sure I'm done and it's safe to
put some distance between myself and the toilet bowl, I
drag myself up. I find myself staring at my reflection in
the mirrors above the sink as I wash my hands.

There are dark circles under my eyes, and exhaustion
etched into my face that all of a sudden... Pisses. Me. Off.

How fucking dare anyone treat me—Katerina
Mancini—with so little respect? I'm done letting this
delusional asshole get to me. *Who the fuck does he think he
is?* It's insane to me that the Danny, who I've seen
comfort dying patients, is the same asshole sending such
vile things to me. *How did I misjudge him so badly?*

I storm back across to my locker and tug on a pair of
jeans and a blouse that's somehow managed to stay rela-
tively wrinkle-free in my bag today.

By the time I've dressed and made it to the parking
lot, I've managed to work myself up into the healthy
little whirlwind of rage. As I reach my car, my phone
buzzes in my pocket and for a brief moment, I think it
will be yet another message from my not-so-secret
admirer, but a weight lifts when Stefano's name lights up
my screen.

I'm about to tell him about the latest barrage of
messages when he jumps in first. "Are you on your way

home? We need to talk about something." I'm thrown because while those are never the words a woman wants to hear, there's nothing in his tone that suggests it's bad news.

"Okay, that doesn't sound ominous at all. What's wrong?"

"We need to talk to your father about what's going on," he says with absolute conviction.

My heart stutters at his words and even though I'm deliriously happy right now, the idea of telling my father anything about us and bursting my little bubble of bliss has me nervous. "With my stalker or between us?"

"Both," he says after a pregnant pause.

Something in my brain short circuits. I knew we'd have to face him sooner or later I'm just baffled as to why now all of a sudden. "Why the urgency? Don't you think we should, I don't know, date for more than a few weeks before we start adding the metric fuck tonne of pressure that telling my dad will add? Why now?"

"Because the don took me aside today and tore me a new one. She wants us to tell your father about your stalker—"

"Does she know about us?" I interrupt. I'm not sure how I'd feel about Aurora knowing before I've had a chance to tell my father.

"No, but I can't lie to your dad and Aurora is right—your father should be aware of any threat to you," he says softly but resolutely. I'm nodding, but I don't know what to say. "And you're not some dirty little secret. I won't deny us or pretend that it's not real."

I don't say anything.

"Are you still there, Katerina?"

"Uh-huh... I'm nodding." He gives me a moment and I take the opportunity to get into the driver's seat and take a few deep breaths. "So, we're telling my father?"

"We are."

It takes me a few moments for me to notice I'm nodding again, not speaking. "You get this is ridiculous? This relationship is happening all out of order. You've moved into my house without even taking me on a real date yet and now we're telling my father before we've even had the 'where is this going' conversation. Not to mention the weeks of kissing me in the corridors, pretending you were mine, before that." My words run together in a frenzied jumble. My thoughts are disjointed and scattered from having this conversation over the phone and not face to face. If he were here, he would have dragged me into his lap and be kissing my frown away by now.

When we're together and it's just us, everything feels right and like it's happening just as it should be, how it's always meant to be. Maybe I've been foolish, but now we have to tell people and they're going to ask questions I simply don't have answers to because we've never talked about our future, and that will be the first thing my father asks us. I've known Stefano my whole life and loved him for as long as I can remember, but it's not like I can say that out loud. We've been dating for a few weeks, not the years it feels like.

"Breathe, baby girl. I can hear your mind whirring from here." The rumble of his gentle tenor washes over me and settles over my body like a weighted blanket, making me feel treasured. "Come home, now."

We say goodbye, and I do as I'm told. I forget about the messages and the fear that was racing through me only a few minutes ago and instead, I'm swept away by the loving and fierce protection that I've only ever felt with Stefano.

Wholeheartedly and without reservation, I drive straight back home... to him.

THE MOMENT I turn the handle on the front door. Stefano is wrenching it open and pulling me into his arms. I let out a startled cry before dropping everything on the doormat and jumping into his arms.

He kicks the door closed before he turns, pinning me against the hallway wall and I let his embrace soothe all my worries.

"I need to make something clear. I don't care that we're doing everything in the wrong order. Now that you're mine, I can't see there ever being a future that doesn't revolve around how I feel for you."

I gasp. "You can't possibly mean that." It's everything I want to hear, but after waiting and wanting him for so long, there's a part of me that doesn't want to let me believe them.

"Dammit, woman, don't try and tell me how I'm feeling and actually listen to what I'm saying. I'm trying to tell you I love you." His arms tighten around me, like a physical plea, begging me to hear him.

Rolling my eyes, I reply, "Don't be ridiculous. We've been dating for a matter of weeks. You can't say things like that and expect me to take you seriously." My heart thunders, pounding so hard it feels like it's trying to beat out of my chest.

"For the love of God. Are you really this obstinate? I fucking love you. I've loved you since the moment you first kissed me. I just never thought I'd be fortunate enough to get to kiss you again, let alone have a future with you. Now it's all I can think about, and I'll be damned if I allow you to carry on for one moment, not knowing how I feel about you."

Stefano's breath escapes in great heaving exhalations, blowing the fine hairs that frame my face in ragged huffs. It takes a few seconds for his words to permeate my defences, but little by little my expression shifts as my head catches up with my heart. The corners of my mouth tip up slowly until it blooms into a broad smile.

"Well, what's a girl expected to say in response to that?" I say, with nothing but happiness lighting me up from the inside.

"I don't need you to say anything in return. Yes, it's fast, but we've wasted so many years not saying anything, Katerina. I'm forty-eight, and I'll be damned if I waste one more second without you."

He leans into me, letting his hips take the weight of our embrace, freeing one hand to roam along my curves and up my body until he wraps his hand around my throat. The noise it pulls from me is wanton and desperate and only escalates when he flexes his fingers and tightens his grip, demanding my lips meet his. Our tongues collide in a clash of passion and possession.

We burn ourselves out, coming back up for air and locking gazes. "Stop measuring what we have in terms of weeks because we both know that's a false equivalency. What *we* feel has been growing for years, Katerina. I don't care if you can't say it yet, but I can. I love you."

"I—" I start, but Stefano presses a finger to my lips to stop me from saying something I know in my bones I'm not ready to say yet. The first time I say it, I want to feel it in my soul.

"Say it when you mean it, *micetta*."

"There's very little more irritating than a man who tells you how to feel. Even if he's right."

"Wait a minute. Did you just admit that I might be right about something?" he teases, kissing my cheek and touching his forehead to mine.

"Don't let it go to your head, *vecchietto*."

I unfurl my legs and he releases his hold, letting me slide down to the floor. Stefano brushes the curtain of waves back from my face and kisses me softly. "Go get changed into something more comfortable. I'll start on dinner."

I cup his face, raking my fingertips through his sinfully tempting scruff. I smile when he leans into my touch. It's such a small gesture but I can't deny the feeling of pure happiness that overtakes me with every intimate touch we share.

"Give me five minutes," I say before reaching up on tiptoes and kissing the tip of his cheek. I kick off my shoes and head towards the stairs taking a moment to look back. Stefano is half smiling, half rolling his eyes as he tidies up the bundle of chaos discarded haphazardly by the door.

"A hurricane would leave less debris in its wake," he mutters with an adoring smile that has me floating as I head upstairs to change.

CHAPTER SEVENTEEN

STEFANO

Breathtaking. That's the only word that can be used to describe the goddess before me. As she descends from the porch towards our waiting town car, my mouth parts to compliment her, but every eloquent thought I have is silenced by an uncooperative body.

My eyes trace a languid journey starting at the criminally sexy red stilettos and up the slit of scarlet silk that promises to have me murdering anyone who dares to appreciate her legs. As far as I can tell, she must have been sewn into this dress because the corseted bodice looks like a second skin. One I'd happily rip off her right now, just so I could explore every inch of her body with my tongue.

As my gaze stops on her face, I'm instantly humbled by her smile. She exudes a natural confidence laced with a hint of mischief that makes me want to abandon this whole evening and spend the night worshipping the little minx. She knew exactly what she was doing when she chose this dress for the gala. I'm going to be hard all night long.

With every step, her left leg slices through the cascade of silk, exposing the same exquisite thigh I had wrapped around my neck this morning.

"I think you're trying to incite violence tonight, *micetta*?" I say, barely able to string my words together. I'm practically salivating at the thought of diving under the waterfall of fabric and recreating the morning's activities right here on the front steps.

"Whatever do you mean?" Her voice comes out laced with a melodic innocence while her wry smile betrays her intention.

I push off the hood of my car and cross to her, raising a hand to help her down the last few steps. Leaning in, I let the gravel in my voice rake over the shell of her ear. "It will be difficult not to pluck out the eyes of a single person I catch appreciating what's mine."

I don't miss the shiver that flutters through her at my words. Before she has a chance to rail against my posses-siveness, I circle her waist and pull her close, stealing her lips in a kiss. What starts as a delicate touch rapidly esca-lates to a battle between us, one where we both struggle to rein our desire in. When we break away, I lose myself in her eyes as her pupil's flare, glistening like rich beads of obsidian.

She slaps my chest playfully and rolls her eyes. "Now

that you've completely destroyed the make-up I spent the last half an hour applying, you now have the pleasure of waiting on me again while I fix it."

The glare she throws my way is undermined by the soft desperate pants and smile that teases the corner of her mouth. My cock strains against my zipper as I appreciate the crimson smudges around her lips. Before the night is out, I will have this vixen on her knees and smearing that same lipstick along the length of my cock. I can't stop myself from running my thumb along her plump bottom lip and blurring the smudge even more.

Thrusting her purse into my chest, she turns and heads back towards the house, shaking her head. "What is it about men and a bright red lip?" she mutters, stomping her feet just a little harder than necessary. "And you might want to correct your lipstick too, *vecchietto*. I don't think it's your colour."

I smile and make my way to the car, bending over by the side mirror to inspect the damage. A part of me is loathed to wipe it off, but since this is our first proper date and it happens to be her largest work event of the year, I don't think turning up looking like I've just ravaged her in the car is probably the look she's going for.

It's strange. This is the first time in a long time that I've attended anything where it wasn't about me, or my work. I'm entirely out of my comfort zone and while I'm there to protect her, mostly I'm there as Doctor Mancini's partner. There's no situation where I'd feel out of my depth, that's not what I'm feeling, but it is strange to present myself to a world so different from my own.

I have two jobs tonight. Keep her safe and be her arm candy. I stand by her side while she schmoozes the board and the donors and keep Danny away from her if he shows up.

I've had people on him for over a week now, and the only thing he appears to be obsessed with is his new girl-friend. Maybe he's moved on, but the more intel I'm sent on him, the more something doesn't sit right. Yes, he's young and easily infatuated, as is evident from the sheer volume of time he's spending with this new woman, but nothing about his behaviour screams possessive lunatic. Still, I'm keeping my people on him because the last thing I want is to make a stalker another woman's problem.

There have been no more home deliveries, and since blocking the last number to bombard Katerina with messages, it's been quiet. However, just because Danny isn't tripping my spidey senses, doesn't mean that they're not currently convinced Katerina is in danger. With every day that passes, I have a growing sense of dread. It could simply be that after wanting her for so long, I'm wary of anything that could come between us, but it feels like more than that. I just can't put my finger on it right now and in the meantime, I will do whatever it takes to keep her safe.

As we enter the conference suite, I'm impressed with how they've been able to turn what's obviously a corpo-rate-style conference suite into an exceptionally opulent event space. I was dubious when Katerina said it was being held on site, but it's definitely giving fine dining mixed with rich man's playground. One side of the room is set up with a dance floor and tables with more silverware laid out than I've ever seen, and the other is decked out with live jazz music and casino tables.

"So, this is how you fleece the rich? You get them drunk and let them gamble their money away."

A server walks past with a tray of champagne flutes and I take two, passing her one as she nods. "Every one of those chips they're playing with is a minimum of a thousand dollars, and as we know... the house always wins. However, even the few who win donate it all at the end of the night."

"Where's the fun in that?"

"They get their fun in showing every other rich fucker here that they can afford to lose more than the next person."

"Clever," I say with a chuckle. "Who gives the least fucks about how much they can lose."

"Precisely. Two tech bros got into a pissing contest last year, which ended in the worst display of idiocy I've ever seen. One invited the other to 'take it outside' and they tripped over each other on their way down the stairs and ended up in the emergency room. On the plus side, we got another X-ray suite out of it because they were so angry at the wait time for films."

I let out a burst of laughter that draws attention from the craps table. I straighten my spine as I'm scrutinised by a collection of over-educated, under-whelming men giving off so much small dick energy, it's like being rolled over by a wave of inadequacy. They may be sneering at me, but I can see the switches flip in their heads when they swap their gazes from me to Katerina.

Their faces light up with a lecherous flare and if we were anywhere else, they'd already be laid out flat on the floor. My skin crawls when their eyes linger on her and before she can object, I reach out, laying a palm on the small of her back before moving it to her hip. I can't help the firm grip or the way I pull her into my side in an obvious declaration of ownership.

I stare the pricks down, feeling her breath tickle over the top of my collar as she turns into my touch and says, "Pissing on me would be a more effective way of marking your territory."

"So would bending you over the nearest table and fucking you within an inch of your life, but something tells me the board would frown upon that." I retort. She lets out a giggle, and it defuses me a little, but not by much. I let go of my grip and gesture for her to lead the way. This is her show, and I'm merely her window dressing for the night.

As the night goes on, I find myself more and more in awe of the woman by my side. This is her natural habitat. After checking in with several board members, it's like she's been given her mission for the evening, and we weave through the cocktail hour ticking off each and every big spender. She makes her case for improvements that can be made for her department, but when it's clear, she's hitting a brick wall with our current conversationally challenged millionaire—a chauvinist asshole who'd rather stare at her tits than listen to her speak—she introduces him to one of the male heads of departments.

Once he's been successfully deflected to Doctor Hendrix, I whisper in her ear, "You're a better person than me. I was having visions of plucking his eyes out with salad tongs if he spent one more second staring at your cleavage."

"Just wait until after he's signed the cheque," she replies with a shrug and a wink.

There's a clinking of silverware on glass from the other side of the room, which starts a mass exodus to the tables for the dinner.

"Do we get any respite while we eat?"

"Yes. Cocktail hour is on the docs. It's the board's turn to inflate their egos during dinner. Then it's all hands on deck after the speeches." I roll my eyes when she mentions speeches, but I'm only teasing, and her smile says she knows that. My heart beats a little harder as she takes my hand and leads me to the table. I can't deny the thrill I get being claimed by her in any small way.

Any sense of ease and happiness evaporates the second we arrive at our table. Glancing down at the place settings, we've been seated next to Doctor God Complex himself, Dylan Jenkins. I'd hoped to avoid having to listen to him enjoy the sound of his own voice.

"This is going to be fun." I groan, trying to inject some light-heartedness into my voice as I point Katerina's attention towards the place card.

"Just rise above, *vecchietto*. Be a good boy and you can

tear this dress off me later," she purrs, pressing her lips to my cheek and suddenly quashing every instinct I have to teach the good doctor a lesson in humility. I reach for the bottle of wine in the ice bucket in the centre of the table and fill our glasses, knowing it's going to take more than an improperly chilled Chablis to improve my mood.

CHAPTER EIGHTEEN

KATERINA

The white wine turns to vinegar in my mouth when Doctor Jenkins arrives at the table with the most miserable-looking woman I've ever seen. Even as he pulls the chair out for her, it's painfully obvious that she'd rather be anywhere else than next to him. I can't help thinking 'girl, same' and being thankful that Stefano swapped the place cards to ensure that I wouldn't have to sit next to him.

It was a tiny gesture but one that has me running my hand along his thigh under the table and stifling a giggle when he grabs it to hold it still as he listens to Dylan waffle on about the funding he thinks he's already managed to secure for the cardiology department. I sometimes wonder if he knows how mind-numbingly tedious he is. He's got to know, right? No one can be this delusional. He proceeds to waffle on about fuck knows what for a full twenty minutes, not letting anyone get a word in edgeways.

Doctor Hendrix and his wife sit down opposite us, and I can see from the glower on his face, he's about as happy to be on this table with Jenkins as I am. Oddly, despite our recent run-in over Enzo's care, he's the kind of obstinate asshat I can get behind. I have somewhat of a soft spot for him. He's a prick, but he's a highly skilled and no-nonsense prick. Nothing he does will ever be to inflate his ego; it will always be in the name of patient care. Also, he detests Doctor Jenkins with a fiery passion.

The table falls into a series of polite conversations that are swiftly quashed by Doctor Jenkins' constant need to be the centre of attention. As he wanders off on yet another train of thought that should have been an internal monologue, I lean in close to Stefano and whisper, "Do you think he realises he hasn't introduced his date yet?"

Stefano shakes his head before whispering back, "No, and I can't even see her place card from here to pull her into the conversation."

There's a loud clank of cutlery as Doctor Jenkins drops them on his plate. "Sorry if my conversation isn't engaging enough for you, Mr Tiero." His voice is low and overflowing with the energy of a petulant child. The kind you know pulls wings off flies and burns ants with magnifying glasses. There isn't a pair of eyes at the table that doesn't roll at him in response.

"Not at all, Doctor Jenkins. I was just distracted by your date's stunning bracelet." Stefano responds, leaning forward, ignoring him, and offering his hand to the slightly startled-looking woman. I think she gave up on being acknowledged by her date half a glass of wine ago. "I'm Stefano, a pleasure to meet you."

"Oh, thank you," she says with a sheepish smile and a light blush dusting her cheeks. "It was my mother's. Alison Carter, pleased to meet you."

"How did you two meet?" I ask, desperate to encourage anyone other than Doctor Jenkins to speak but she clams up, and he launches into a long and uninteresting story about meeting at a medical equipment conference where he was a keynote speaker which he quickly devolves into yet more self-aggrandising bullshit. I throw an apologetic shrug her way and don't miss the frustration she's trying to hide. There's not enough wine in the world to make this man palatable in a social setting.

Bless her, she makes it another twenty minutes and four attempts by other people at the table to get him to shut up before she gives up. She lasted longer than I would have put money on, but he barely notices when she excuses herself to the bathroom. He's oblivious when she casts an apologetic nod my way and heads straight to the exit. There's nothing I can do other than raise my glass to her.

"Hats off to the girl. She put up with him longer than I would have," Stefano mumbles beside me.

I can see from the quirk of his lips Doctor Hendrix is fully aware that our sixth will not be returning, and I don't miss the moment when he leans over and quietly informs his wife. From that point on, everyone bar Doctor Jenkins enters into an unspoken secret game, wondering how long it will take him to notice she's not coming back. While I'm not usually one to relish other people's misfortune, it can't really be considered misfortune if the person in question is so oblivious to it.

Besides, the man is a twat.

How he hasn't had complaints made against his atrocious bedside manner or unprofessional treatment of the staff under him I'll never understand. I think the only reason I tolerate his behaviour is because I know if he really fucked me off, I could have him killed.

There are perks to being a capo's daughter.

It becomes harder and harder for everyone at the table to keep a straight face. We're barely holding it together when dessert arrives, and he finally notices the chair to his right is still empty.

"If you'll excuse me, I need to see what's keeping..." he falters briefly, and I grit my teeth in disgust at his disinterest in his date.

"Alison," I bite out, only slightly more pointedly than I intend to.

We all stare after him in disbelief. It's only when he's out of earshot that there's a collective collapse of restraint and we burst into laughter. For the first time, I see Doctor Hendrix smile and as he's wiping a small tear from his eye, he turns to his wife and says, "Vicki if I ever behave like that you have my permission to divorce me and take me for every penny." He's still smiling as he kisses her gently on the temple.

"Thanks, honey, but honestly, you're worth more to me dead," she says, barely able to contain her laughter.

"Twisty," Stefano says with a laugh. "I like you two.

Let me buy you a drink," he adds, motioning to the bar. "I don't know about you, but I'd rather not be here when he realises she ran out on him."

Everyone is quick to agree, and we make our escape from the stuffiness of the formal dinner to hit the cock-tails at the bar. Time flies and it's a while before we notice we've missed the speeches, having been too engrossed in the hilarious story of how Vicki and Doctor Hendrix met—or Simon, as he insists I call him now.

We're several martinis in at this point and now that we've escaped from the clutches of Doctor Boring, the evening is turning into one of the most enjoyable evenings I think I've ever had with my colleagues. Once the music starts, the dance floor soon fills up and Stefano drags me out to the floor.

I haven't seen the man dance since Aurora's wedding and that's a damn shame. There's something about the way he moves that's always been a weakness of mine. He doesn't just move his feet; there's a fluidity to him that makes you want to meld yourself to his body. Exactly the way he's dancing now.

Holding my palm against his chest with one hand and resting the other just above my hips, he's commanding me around the floor, interrupting the steps only occasionally to unfurl me in a sensual spin, stealing my breath every time he draws me back and we collide together.

We might as well be here alone for all the awareness I have of my surroundings. Nothing exists outside of the magnetic gaze I'm trapped in. I couldn't tell you how long we dance for, but as he twirls me around the floor, I lean into every touch and hope it lasts forever. At the end of the last song of the night, he says, "One day I'll dance all night with you at our wedding."

I'm speechless, but he doesn't give me time to over-think his words and doesn't let me ruin the moment with whatever flustered and nonsensical reply threatens to spill from my lips. He silences my thoughts with a kiss, and I let myself drift on a cloud of fantasies and half-baked dreams I never thought I'd experience.

There's a gentle tap on my shoulder and I see that Simon and Vicki are calling it a night. I pull Vicki in for a hug but draw back to a handshake to say goodnight to Simon. He laughs, saying, "I get I haven't been the easiest person to get to know at work, but I hope you'll consider me a friend and not a colleague going forward."

"Deal," I reply, shaking his hand firmly and patting his arm. "When you have colleagues like Jenkins, it makes it hard to want to get to know anyone."

"True," he laughs. "Just don't go spreading it around. The last thing I want is pricks like Jenkins thinking I'm approachable."

"Don't go selling me down the river either. It's taken me years to convince everyone I'm a stone-cold bitch."

"I got you. See you next shift," he says with a grin, steering his slightly wobbly and entirely fabulous wife off the dance floor.

We're encouraged off the dance floor by the waitstaff as they start clearing up—the universal sign for 'you can fuck off now' at a party. I really don't want the evening to be over yet so taking Stefano's hand in mine, I lead him towards a door at the back of the room, and after checking the coast is clear, I drag him with me into the maze of corridors.

We're barely through the door when Stefano pushes me back against the wall, sliding his hand along the flare of my waist, around to the curve of my ass. His broad hand squeezes my cheek before moving forward to slip between the folds of the hip-level slit in the silk. He grasps my thigh firmly, hoisting it up, hooking my leg around his waist, and stepping into me, pressing the undeniably hard ridge of his cock against me.

With one hand holding firmly around his neck and shoulder, the other reaches for the tie that hangs nonchalantly around his open collar. I've been salivating over how sinfully hot he looks in a tux, but I think I prefer this slightly dishevelled and unrestrained version of him more. I snatch at the black satin, grasping a handful of his shirt with it and groaning when it pops open another button. The hint of salt and pepper hair reminds me of how the coarseness of his chest teases against my nipples when he pins me down and fucks me like he owns me.

"It's been torture watching you in this dress all evening. Having to hold myself back every time I saw someone undress you with their eyes."

"Have you been getting hot under the collar, *vecchietto*?" I tease, pulling on the tie and kissing him with every ounce of passion he's igniting within me. There's no finesse to the way our lips clash and every frenzied roll of his tongue against mine lets me know he's as desperate for me as I am for him.

Sparks of electricity jolt through my core as he pulls

back the curtain of fabric and feathers his touch over my damp satin panties. I don't bother to stifle the moan that he pulls from me as he finds my clit and taps it delicately. "How wet are you for me right now, baby girl? If I got on my knees for you, would you fall apart for me? Would it turn you on knowing that anyone could find us?"

What sort of questions are these? And how the hell does he expect me to form complete sentences when he's pulling the soft fabric to the side and tracing my entrance in long, languid strokes? The juxtaposition of his soft touch and how tightly he's pulled the lace edge of the panties against my clit has me rocking my hips against the glorious friction, ready to fall apart from simply riding his hand.

"Uh-uh-uh, Katerina. You come when I say you can come." His command rumbles through me, demanding my submission and though I know I'll plead for more, my body wants nothing more than to take what he gives, when he gives it.

"Please," I beg, drawing out the word into a seemingly endless whimper as I scratch my nails along his neck.

I cry out at the loss of his touch, when he suddenly grabs both my wrists and pulls my arms down to my side, forcing my palms flat against the wall. "Keep them here or I'll stop, and you won't come at all." I whine and his expression darkens, his pupils widening into dark pools that have me wanting to dive right into them. "Do I make myself clear?"

The authoritative tone in his voice vibrates against my skin where his lips graze my collarbone. It sends a tingle through me that travels straight to my core. I flex my fingers but my palms remain flat as I use every bit of restraint I have to keep them exactly where he's placed them.

Resting his hand against my throat and flexing his grip against my rampaging pulse, he says, "Such a good girl when you want to be, aren't you?"

He steals a kiss from my lips before releasing my jaw and sinking to his knees before me. I'm entranced as he wraps his hand around my ankle, stroking up slowly moving to cup the back of my calf. When he reaches my thigh, I let out a frantic moan, struggling to stop myself from knotting my fingers in his hair and demanding he bury his tongue in my aching pussy.

I'll behave. I'll be a good girl. Anything if it means I can watch him worship me on his knees where anyone can walk in on us.

He grips the back of my thigh and pulls my leg off the floor, resting it over his shoulder and I cry out when this leaves his hands free to grasp my panties and tear them free. There's a bite of pain where the lace tightens across my hips, followed by complete bliss as he seals his mouth over my clit and buries two fingers in my pussy.

There's no teasing preamble, just the instant pleasure of his insanely skilled tongue circling and his teeth nipping at the swollen bundle of nerves, while his thick digits fuck into me. The stretch is everything I need, and any hope of remaining quiet goes out the window when he curls his fingers, brushing against my G-spot.

The pace he sets is brutal, and exquisite, and transcendent. I don't know whether it's the fear of being caught, but something stops me from letting myself tumble off the edge. As if he knows my body better than I do, Stefano shifts the angle of his hand and alters the pressure of his tongue. The changes are minute, but it's like he's coercing my body into obeying his demands and won't be denied.

My walls clench as my orgasm peaks, but instead of retreating, Stefano doubles down, sealing his lips tight and sucking as he thrusts against my swollen clit. It takes me by surprise, drawing a string of desperate pleas. "Fuck, I can't take it. Holy fucking god."

His free hand holds back the train of satin against the leg I still have firmly planted to the floor, allowing me to see the wicked expression on his face when he pulls back to say, "I'm not stopping till you soak my face and let me drink you down."

He punctuates every other word with the brutal thrust of his fingers before diving back in and increasing the pressure of his tongue as it undulates against me. To say that I shatter would be an understatement. Debauched sounds reverberate off the stark hallway surfaces, amplifying them into a cacophony of sin. My groans synchronise with the unwavering rhythm of his thrusts. My body coils in on itself like a spring before releasing in one monumental crescendo.

It's impossible not to blush when my body gushes, coming straight into his eager mouth. I've never come so hard—or felt so untethered. Stefano sets my leg on the floor and stands, studying my expression with a mix of tenderness and awe. My cum glistens on his lips and it only adds to my bliss when he smiles back at me. His dimple showing just how much he enjoyed devouring me.

I'm desperate to have him come too, but he pulls my arms from the wall and wraps me in his tuxedo jacket before sweeping me off my feet. He kisses my temple, whispering praise like a prayer. "Such a good girl for me. Doing as you were told and letting me worship you."

I gaze into his eyes, oblivious to anything other than the affection staring back at me. Nestling into his hold, I rest my head on his shoulder, letting out a contented sigh and closing my eyes. Just for a moment.

CHAPTER NINETEEN

STEFANO

Nothing will ever feel as good as loving her. Though I can't deny that making her fall apart and still tasting her on my tongue ranks pretty highly. Her breathing is soft and flutters across my collar as I carry her towards the service elevator at the end of the corridor. From my weeks navigating this place, I know it's the least public route out of the hospital and I'll be damned if I take her out the main entrance looking freshly fucked and half unravelled.

Seeing her like this is a privilege that's only mine to treasure.

She doesn't stir as the elevator car descends, or when I step out into the cold night air on the way to the parking lot, however when I stop in my tracks as we approach my car, my abrupt halt jolts her awake.

"What's wrong?" she says. I don't look down at her, but she gasps as she realises what I'm staring at.

I gently lower her to the ground, unsure how to temper the fury that's building in the pit of my stomach. It's not the smashed windows or the tyres that have been shredded that have me clenching my jaw so hard I can hear my teeth squeaking as they grind together. No, it's the dozens, if not tens of dozens, of white roses that have been torn to pieces and strewn over the hood. A hood that's also streaked with what I hope is red paint and not blood.

We both take a step forward and as she reaches out to touch the petals, I drag her towards me. "Don't touch," I snap and she tenses in my arms.

"Don't tell me what to do." Her tone is firm but there's an obvious wobble to it. I don't argue with her, I just hold her a little tighter before letting her go again.

"I thought he'd calmed down," she says with a sigh, wrapping her arm around herself and shrinking into my jacket. That one gesture of vulnerability makes me feel like a failure. I haven't done a good enough job of protecting her.

I'm dialling Marcus before I comprehend that my phone is in my hand. "Bring in Costello. Now," I bark out. Silence stretches out on the other end of the line, which only serves to piss me off further. "Is there a fucking problem, Marcus?"

There's a nervous cough before he finally answers. "I can tell that now is not the time to question you, but that might be a little tricky."

"Tricky, how?" I shout, my words bouncing off the walls of the parking structure so loudly they ring in my ears, and I see Katerina flinch out of the corner of my eye.

"Well, it's just that he's currently balls deep in his girlfriend and has been—on and off—for the last few hours. If I go in and get him, we're going to have witnesses."

"Fuck..." I say in a low growl and start to pace along the length of the car. How could I have been so blind?

"I mean, we could wait till they're asleep and..." Marcus suggests.

"It's not Danny, but whoever it is has made a pretty public statement here that needs clearing up. I need you and your team at the hospital. You'll need to tow my car and have Sin see if he can tap into on-site surveillance."

It doesn't take long for me to relay all the information, all the while staring at the frayed petals. I've never thought of flowers as particularly threatening, but seeing them torn to pieces and doused in red paint has that low-level dread I've always felt when it came to this guy building into something that feels much more sinister.

Katerina is in far more danger than she realises—and I will do *anything* to keep her safe.

SHE'S BEEN ARGUING with me for the last hour about our new living arrangements, but quite frankly if she thinks she's staying at her house after tonight's little display, then she's delusional.

"I don't care if it's not who we thought it was. Why do I need to leave my home? How is your home any more or less safe than mine? All he'd have to do is follow me home from the hospital to find this place, so why not use my place to draw the fucker out?"

"Because I'm not using the woman I love as fucking bait," I bellow. There's a brief pause, where I try to catch my breath and cool my temper. "Please, can you just trust me? You're safer here. This place can accommodate a full on-site security detail."

Her eyes are fixed on mine and the set of her jaw is firm. She's quiet for so long that I'm tempted to throw her over my shoulder, take her upstairs and tie her to the bed until she sees sense.

"You're going to put a full twenty-four-hour security detail on me, aren't you?" Her tone is resigned but laced with resistance. I try not to poke the bear, so I just nod. I don't miss the soft grunt of frustration or clenching of her fists. I stare back at her, softening my features in some kind of silent plea for her to see reason and let me keep her safe.

She knows I'm right, but I get it. It doesn't mean she has to be happy about her life being spun on its axis. It's difficult to know exactly what to do right now. Every cell in my body is screaming at me to wrap her in my arms and never let her go, but Katerina has never needed a saviour. That woman needs a partner in crime, not a knight in shining armour.

So, I wait. Wait for her to process that because of the actions of one asshole, she's going to have to turn her life upside down in the name of her own safety. To understand that it isn't me making her life more difficult, it's him. Whoever he is.

I hand her a glass of red wine and perch on the stool, letting her pace back and forth along the length of the kitchen, taking the occasional sip.

"This is ridiculous," she mutters. "One unhinged man with boundary issues and I've got to leave my own home. A home I worked fucking hard for."

I know better than to derail her mid-rant, so I simply nod and sip my whiskey. I catch every other word of her now muted venting. The gist being 'fucking stalkers', not having had a security detail since she was a teenager, and 'asshole men'. If the situation wasn't so serious, her mutterings would be almost adorable.

"I'll try to make sure the detail Marcus puts on you is as non-intrusive as possible, *micetta*," I say, trying to placate her.

"That's not the point and you know it." I bite my lip to stop myself from laughing as she turns and stamps her foot at me. The clack of her red stilettos on the tile floor must surprise her, as it snaps her out of her rage and pulls the smallest giggle from her lips.

"Am I really throwing a tantrum like a child... at being treated like a child? Fuck, I'm too old for this shit," she says with a sigh.

Holding my arm out to her, she takes the palm I offer her in mine, and I pull her into me, putting down my glass and embracing her waist.

"No, baby girl. You're having an entirely reasonable reaction to having your life fucked with by an asshole." I kiss her cheek softly. "I should probably point out though, you are dating the Bianchi consigliere." She gives me a 'yeah, and?' glare and I grin at her petulance. Brushing her hair off her slender shoulders as I say, "And since I don't plan on letting you go anytime soon, there was never a timeline in this relationship where my woman wouldn't have her own full time security detail. It's just happening a little sooner than expected."

There's a flash of understanding in her expression. "Holy shit. I'm dating the Bianchi consigliere."

"You're only just realising this?" I say with a smirk.

She drains what's left of her wine before placing the glass on the counter behind me. Taking my cheeks in her hands, she locks gazes with me. "I've spent my whole adult life living two lives, and I don't think I recognised until right this second how completely unsustainable that is."

I reach for one of her hands and wrap mine around it. "I'll do everything I can to make sure that my work doesn't interfere with yours."

Her face softens with a smile. "It's not your job, it's your life. Our life." She pauses to move the hand still cupping my face and runs her thumb over my eyebrow delicately as she explores me with her touch. "Maybe I need to stop trying to straddle two worlds and actually try to live the life I have, now that I have the love I want."

My heart stops when those words pass her lips, and she restarts it when she presses her lips to mine. It's soft and tentative, but no less earth-shattering. Her lips part and we fall into an unhurried kiss, that ebbs and flows with promises of a hundred different futures we might live together. I'm not going to push her, that's as close as

I think she can get to telling me she loves me right now. And I'll take it.

Lifting her in my arms, I take her upstairs, knowing that now I have this woman in my bed, I'm never letting her go.

CHAPTER TWENTY

KATERINA

I'm not sure what's more disturbing. Having a stalker or being disappointed because you don't know who it is anymore?

When I thought it was Danny, the notes and the flowers never felt particularly threatening. I could write them off as some kind of misguided infatuation. I was never truly terrified before because I couldn't reconcile that a man as caring in his work at the hospital would ever be a real threat to me. Now Marcus has confirmed that this latest stunt wasn't Danny, suddenly I'm looking at every note and text in a far more unsettling light.

For the first time since this started, I'm genuinely worried.

I woke up this morning to a barrage of threatening messages. I'd only managed to read the first few before Stefano took it from me. With every swipe of the screen, his expression darkened, only adding to the growing unease settling in my bones.

Fear is like a poison. It infiltrates your system. It's insidious, slowly interfering with everything until it incapacitates its victim.

Never in my life have I allowed anyone or anything to control me, but when I think about leaving the house, there's this feeling of anxiousness that gives me pause—and I hate it. It's like an ill-fitting bra. I can ignore the discomfort, but it makes life uncomfortable.

As the morning continues, it's like witnessing every bubble I've constructed in my life burst. Suitcases and boxes arrive, delivered by Stefano's men. It's not like he's arranged for everything to be delivered to me, but it's hard to escape the very literal representation of my life being decompartmentalised for me. There's a constant stream of people in and out of the house. If they're not delivering my things, they're reinforcing Stefano's security.

Things start to feel like too much when I go to open the front door and there's now a security detail stationed by the front gate. Stefano's turning his, up till now, very private sanctuary into a fortress. For me.

I can't deny the way that realisation washes over me, soothing me like a balm. I turn back into the house and go in search of him. It feels slightly intrusive to have all these people in his house with us. Before now, we've existed in an almost private bubble, and it feels odd to share the time we have together with the people who work for him. But as he said last night, he's the Bianchi consigliere, and it's not like I haven't known this my whole damn life.

However, if one more of his crew asks me if there's anything they can do for me, like they haven't known *me* my whole damn life, I'm going to stab them with something sharp. They're treating me like some sort of delicate flower and not the doctor who pulls bullets out of them when they do something stupid.

I'm about to open the door to Stefano's office when the front door bursts open and a familiar voice booms through the foyer. *"Katerina Elena Mancini. You come out here this instant and explain why I'm only finding out today that my only daughter is in danger."*

Shit.

A sheepish-looking Stefano steps out of his office and I don't waste any time jabbing my nail into his shoulder, punctuating each word with a sharp jab. "You fucking told him over the phone."

"No... He went to your house and found Marcus packing up your things," he says with a grimace. This is less than ideal, and Dad is going to be livid at being kept in the dark.

"Oh, that's just fucking great," I whisper shout. "Well, under the circumstances, I'm holding you to our deal. I tell him about the stalker, but you're on your own when it comes to us."

His face lights up the moment I utter the word 'us' which makes it really hard to maintain my angry face. I reach up on the tips of my toes and steal a kiss before taking his hand without thinking and pulling him to the front door. As we round the corner to greet my father in the entryway, I fully comprehend my mistake. I drop Stefano's hand, but it's too late. He catches the motion and his expression flits from one of shock as he meets my gaze, to one of pure fury when it moves to Stefano.

It takes three strides for my world to implode.

"Mother. Fucker." My father shouts with the first step forward. He draws back his fist with the second, and after the third, he punches his best friend so hard his knuckles crack, and Stefano's nose breaks.

There's a part of me that wants to jump in and put a stop to it. However, they're both grown-ass men and they're big enough to fight their own battles. I step backwards, giving them room to hash it out. There's a slightly comical moment when several of Stefano's men run in to deal with the threat against their boss, but when they realise the threat is my father, you can see the struggle as they try to figure out if they should intervene. When they look to me for guidance, all I can do is shrug because what can you do? Although technically Stefano outranks my father, not one of the men here is going to try and tell a capo they don't have every right to punch the man that's fucking his daughter.

It's almost comical when you think about it.

My father lurches at Stefano, who is cradling his nose, and knocks him to the floor. Dad wastes no time straddling Stefano's chest, gripping him by the front of his shirt, and hoisting him off the floor. Stefano doesn't struggle, seemingly accepting of whatever wrath my father wants to unleash on him.

"How could you? I trusted you!" he screams into

Stefano's unflinching face. "She's my fucking daughter. You watched me raise her."

My father glares down at him, disgust etched in the lines on his face. The weight of his disappointment in his best friend shatters something inside me. "I love him, Dad."

Two sets of eyes snap to mine, one filled with joy, the other shock, but both are filled with love.

I turn to the audience we gathered for this live-action soap opera and raise an eyebrow before waving them off. "I'm sure you've all got jobs to be getting on with," I say, channelling my inner mafia wife. There's a brief pause where they look to Stefano, who simply dips his head once, dismissing them. My father's grip tightens before shoving Stefano back to the ground and hauling himself off of him.

My heart sinks when my father refuses to meet either of our eyes and walks towards the living room muttering, "I need a fucking drink for this conversation."

I hold out a hand to Stefano, who takes it and flashes me a roguish smile. It's difficult to pull off 'dishevelled yet sexy' with blood dripping out of your nose, but he somehow manages it.

"You love me," he whispers.

"That's not how I wanted to say that for the first time," I reply, glaring at him.

"I don't care how or why you said it, *micetta*. Just that you said it." He tries to kiss me, forgetting his nose is broken and letting out a grunt of pain when it bumps against mine.

"You go and talk to my father. I'll be back in a minute

with supplies to set your nose," I order, patting him on the shoulder and feeling like I'm sending a lamb for the slaughter.

It's been over an hour of explaining exactly when I started getting notes, why I thought it wasn't serious, and how it escalated. The whole time my father has given me the same look. One that's starting to pierce my resolve. I've never seen that look on his face, not directed towards me at least. It's disappointment.

"How could you keep this from me?" It doesn't seem to matter how many times I explain that I assumed it was someone else, he's taking my silence as a betrayal.

"I made a mistake." I hardly recognise the sound of my own voice. I feel so small and the longer I meet his eyes, the more I know he's right. Not just that I should have told him, but that I should have taken it more seriously from the start. My hubris has put me, and those I love, at risk.

I finish placing the last butterfly strip over the cut on the bridge of Stefano's nose and pack away my kit.

"Come here, Katerina," my father says, pushing himself out of the armchair and holding out his arm to me. I walk over to him on autopilot, letting out a contented sigh when he squeezes me tightly against him. Before I even know what's happened, tears are flowing and I'm sobbing into my father's chest.

I can't remember the last time he held me like this. It must have been when I was a child. It's been so long since I've fallen apart in front of anyone, it takes me by surprise and draws out every feeling I've been bottling up for so long.

He doesn't say anything, simply strokes my hair and holds me firmly until I'm cried out. Holding my head in his hands, he pulls my focus back to him and runs his thumbs across my cheeks, drying my eyes.

"No one's denying that you're more than capable of looking out for yourself. But my darling, when it comes to your safety, your family has the right to protect you. It's not a sign of weakness to rely on those who love you," he says firmly but laced with more care and consideration than I deserve from him right now.

"I swear I didn't know how serious it was," I try to explain, but my excuses sound weak even to me.

"That's not an excuse. You're an intelligent woman, and you know better than to underestimate the threat of a situation like this. Or are you so jaded by my world that you underestimate the dangers in yours?"

His words are harsh, but the more I consider them, the more I appreciate the full scale of my mistake. By comparison to what Aurora went through, what Enzo endured, the death any family member faces on a daily basis my problem seemed so insignificant.

"I'm sorry, Dad."

I should feel like a failure, but when my father pulls me to hug me again, it's like a weight has been lifted. I'm safe in his arms and he's still here for me. Even if he does want to kill his best friend right now.

"I'm sorry too, Dante. I should have come to you the

minute Nico told me." Stefano's tone is grave as he holds my father's stony glare.

"I don't even know where to start with you," my father spits out. "How could you touch my daughter?"

I pull back from my father's embrace and now it's my turn to voice my disapproval. "I accept that I've handled this whole thing badly, but don't for one minute think I'll stand here and let you reduce the feelings I have for Stefano to something cheap and tawdry. We've avoided each other for years, trying to deny our feelings for each other. Because of our love and loyalty to you."

I don't intend for my words to wound my father, but I can see the force they land with when he recoils under the weight of them.

"It's true, Dante."

"Is it supposed to reassure me that you've wanted her for years? How many years? Exactly how old was she when you stopped thinking of her as your best friend's little girl and started thinking of her as a piece of ass?" My father's outburst is vicious, slicing into me like a dagger to the heart. It's cruel and filled with unbridled rage and while I know deep down he's coming from a place of shock, it's too much.

"Get out," I say, pushing my father away from me. "Until you can speak to him with the same respect you show me, I will not have you here." It takes every ounce of energy I have in my body to hold myself strong when inside, I'm about to crumble into pieces.

"You're kicking me out of his house?"

"She's kicking you out of *her* house," Stefano says,

moving to stand behind me and squeezing my arm in support.

"I love you, Dad, and we didn't plan this, but I can't and wouldn't want to un-ring this bell. I won't spend another decade pretending I'm not in love with him to protect your feelings." Truths tumble out of me like rapids over rocks. "I will never be able to apologise enough for disappointing you. But don't you dare stand there and question the intentions of a man who's closer to you than a brother ever could be."

My father takes a step back, flicking his gaze between me and his oldest friend.

"I love her, Dante. But I won't give her up, not even for you."

It's impossible not to see the conflict in my father's eyes. I don't know what I expect to happen, but it's not him turning and walking away. When he reaches the door, he places and hand against the frame and pauses, looking back.

"I love you, Katerina. You could never disappoint me, but I'm going to need some time." I'm nodding when he focusses his stony gaze on Stefano. "If you hurt her, I'll kill you myself."

CHAPTER TWENTY-ONE

KATERINA

While I haven't admitted it to Stefano yet, moving in with him has its perks. The hot tub is an excellent example. Plus, his coffee machine is vastly superior to mine, and don't get me started on his home gym. Who has a fully air-conditioned basement gym?

Over the last few days, Stefano's gone out of his way to make me feel at home, not just having his people bring my clothes and personal effects, but also my furniture. Going so far as to turn one of his guest rooms into a library and den for me. Ever since we saw my dad, it's like Stefano is doing anything he can to put me at ease and give me my own space.

My father has been checking in with me every day for updates, not that I have any for him. It's been quiet since the gala. No threatening messages, nothing left at my house, which leaves us discussing everything but the elephant in the room. He refuses to speak Stefano's name, which only reminds me that it's me driving a wedge between him and his closest friend. I hate it.

It was a relief to be back on shift this morning. Even if people are acting strangely. I look up from my chart to see a welcome face heading my way. "Doctor Hendrix," I say with a smile.

"Doctor Mancini," he says warmly. "I hear congratulations are in order." I stare back at him, baffled for a moment. "On your engagement?"

"I'm sorry, my what now?"

"Your engagement. The whole hospital is talking about it," he says, reaching over the counter to grab his next chart. "Anyway, I've got a consult on three. I'll come find you later. My wife has told me in no uncertain terms that you and Stefano are our new 'couple friends', whatever that means, and I need to arrange a dinner to celebrate."

He's gone before I have a chance to correct him, heading off down the hallway, oblivious to the bombshell he's just dropped. Although it's beginning to make a lot more sense why the interns have been smiling at me so much this morning. They normally cower in my presence, and I was beginning to think I was losing my touch.

"Hey, Doctor Mancini," I can't help but startle a little when a familiar voice calls out from behind me. "Nurse Costello."

"I really wish you'd call me Danny. I know it's weird because of that date, but I think we can both agree it was the most awkward evening in history." My relief at his words is almost palpable and I feel like an idiot for assuming the notes were coming from him. As I look at his broad smile, it's so fucking obvious that he was only ever trying to be friendly. That and the multi-page report Marcus submitted summarising the last few weeks' surveillance on him. He really is just a nice guy, and I'm pleased that he's found someone.

"Agreed," I say, holding out my hand. "Friends?"

He shakes my hand eagerly before adding. "Oh, and congratulations, Doctor Mancini."

"If I'm calling you Danny, then I think you'd better call me Katerina, but first you need to tell me why everyone thinks I'm engaged?"

"Shit, sorry, was it meant to be a secret? My dad overheard your fiancé talking about your wedding at the gala." There's a brief moment of confusion until I remember Stefano's promise on the dance floor. "Wait a minute. Please don't tell me he misunderstood?" He pulls me to the side and lowers his voice to a near-comical, dramatic whisper. "Because he's literally told the entire board and all the department heads. The nurses have arranged a collection for your engagement present."

I can't help but laugh. I try to muffle my outburst, but I still get several odd looks from the nurse's station and a glare from a passing patient. I don't know what to say and before I'm forced to deny it, alarms sound from a monitor in recovery, and Danny's pulled in to assist.

I can't resist retrieving my phone from my pocket and sending a message to my *fiancé*.

> Apparently, you've been upgraded to fake fiancé according to the hospital gossips.

STEFANO:

???

> A member of the board overheard you talking about our wedding at the gala.

STEFANO:

Well, we are already living together.

> WORST. PROPOSAL. EVER

STEFANO:

Could've been worse.

> I don't see how. Just so you know, this fiancée likes her diamonds cushion cut and big enough to see where the Titanic hit.

Stefano: Noted.

This playful banter is new, and I have to admit I revel in it. Since the gala, it's like I've unlocked this new side of Stefano that he only shows me. It's relaxed and fun and entirely mine to enjoy.

> I'm heading into surgery, but I should be home before midnight.

STEFANO:

See you soon, baby girl

I may love it when he calls me kitten, but holy fuck does it turn me on when he calls me baby girl. I should probably be concerned about that, but it's not like I have daddy issues—I mean, he has issues with my daddy, but I have no overwhelming desire to be infantilised. The problem is when those words pass his lips, his tone drops into some kind of sinful growl that has my pulse racing and my temperature rising. And apparently, it has the same effect when he sends it over text.

I shake off my growing arousal and stuff my phone back in my pocket. I don't have the time to allow myself to be distracted right now. but you can be damn sure I'm going to let him distract the fuck out of me later when I get home. Preferably naked and bent over the back of his couch.

By the time I arrive home, I'm exhausted. And more than a little irritated. There was entirely too much peopling required today. Putting aside the fact that everyone I've ever interacted with went out of their way to congratulate me on my fictitious engagement, but I also had a consult with Doctor Jenkins, who was on particularly obnoxious form today. He made everyone's jobs ten times more difficult and in the end, we lost the patient and were subjected to a tirade of abuse from him afterwards.

It was so bad that I made an appointment with the Chief of Surgery to lodge a formal complaint on behalf of the team. The entire OR worked diligently and did everything they could, and I couldn't give a fuck how fucking talented the man is, I will not be spoken to like that in my OR and definitely won't have my team berated like that.

I spent most of the drive home wondering if I should call up Nico Verardi and have the Bianchi's most brutal enforcer have a little chat with the good doctor. Admittedly, that would be an abuse of my connections, but someone needs to teach that cunt a lesson. Something tells me a rap on the knuckles from the Chief is unlikely to achieve anything.

I love my job. I love the thrill of saving a life. But honest to God, if I could do it without having to deal with men like Dylan Jenkins, it would be paradise.

The incident has left me with a sense of unease itching under the surface of my skin. It wasn't just his complete lack of respect, but every word was laced with venom. I don't know what the fuck crawled up his ass and died, but no one speaks to a Mancini like that and gets away with it.

As I pull into the driveway, the guards nod and the gate closes behind me. I don't miss the car that drives on past the turning. Two men in the front. My tail for the afternoon shift. It should make me uneasy to know that I'm being watched whenever I leave the house, but it feels oddly soothing. There's been a low-grade buzzing of discontent running through me since I left this morning and only now is it starting to leech out of my bones.

That feeling is short-lived, however.

The minute I open the door, my father's voice hollers out from the kitchen.

"She's fourteen years your junior. You watched her

grow up!" I flinch at my father's words, disappointed that he can think so poorly of a man he claimed to love like a brother.

"Don't try and turn this into something it's not. I never once thought about her like that back then."

"So why the fuck are you thinking about her like that now?"

I close the front door as quietly as I can, keen to keep their conversation from the men outside. I stop dead in the hallway, having no idea if this is a fight I want to insert myself into. They're going to have to hash it out sooner or later. It might as well be now.

"Because she's the most impressive woman I've ever known. I didn't fall in love with some fantasy of youthful perfection. I fell in love with a strong and talented woman, a doctor who's the top of her fucking field. Someone who understands the world we live in and does everything she can to support the family you and I would sacrifice our lives for."

"She's a child," my father shouts. I flinch at his words, knowing he doesn't really mean them, but hating that no matter what I do, there's a part of him that will always see me that way. "She's *my* child," he stutters, correcting himself.

"She's thirty-four, for fuck's sake."

"And you're forty-eight. What do you think you can offer her? You'll have one foot in the grave before she's even had a chance to build a life with you."

"I'll give her whatever life she wants with me. For however long she wants it." Stefano's words wrap around me like a warm blanket. They're everything I didn't know I needed to hear.

Let my father rant and rave. I know eventually he'll come around; this is just part of his process. The man may be stubborn, but he loves me. The silence is almost painful, only interrupted by the subtle clinks of ice against a glass.

"You can come in now, Katerina," Stefano says, announcing me to my father.

Busted.

As I round the corner my father casts his eyes downwards, a flush of embarrassment colouring his cheeks. "I'm sorry you had to hear that."

I cross the room and bring him in for a hug. "Honestly, I'd rather know what's being said about me than be kept in the dark."

He starts to object but I shush him. "Dad, I'm going to need you to listen to me now. You're talking about this like I've made some rash and reckless decision. Falling for Stefano is one of the most rational things I've ever done. It doesn't need to make sense to you. It makes sense to me. I have no clue what the future holds for us, but Dad, quite frankly that's none of your business. He's a grown-ass man, and I'm a grown-ass woman. The only person acting like a child here is you."

I don't miss the tick of his jaw as he grinds his teeth together. I don't know if it's because he's mad at me or himself, but I'm relieved when my words appear to get through to him. His face softens, and he dips down to kiss my temple.

"I thought I was ready to discuss this but obviously I'm not, Katerina."

"You can take all the time you need, Dad. But you can't walk in here and insult the consigliere in his own damn house." I'm careful with my tone, trying not to push my luck but setting a clear boundary. "I love you," I add, pulling him into a hug.

"Love you too," he replies with an even tighter squeeze.

When we break apart, I move around the kitchen island to stand at Stefano's side. I can't stop myself from tucking myself into his side and letting him wrap his arm around my waist. My father averts his gaze, and I feel guilty, but equally, there's no way I'm going to sacrifice my comfort for my father's. Not after the day I've had.

Stefano lowers his arm to rub the small of my back in soothing circles, trying to find a balance between comforting me and not flaunting our closeness in my father's face. It's a fine line and the tension in the room is so thick you can taste it in the air. I'm a little disappointed when my father says his goodbyes and shows himself out, but on the bright side, at least this visit didn't end with threats.

That's progress, right?

CHAPTER TWENTY-TWO

STEFANO

"**I** have a surprise for you," I say, revelling in the way her face lights up with excitement. It's as though her presence expels the tension that hung so heavy only moments before. I don't think I'll ever get used to how right it feels having her here. This house has felt so incomplete for so long, but now it feels like I can finally finish it.

Taking her hand in mine, I lead her towards the stairs to the basement. And smirk when she lets out a little whine of complaint. "Exercise is not a fun surprise."

I gently smack the curve of her ass and whisper in her ear. "Don't be a brat. I promise this is a surprise you're going to like."

I had my men bring over more of her things while she was at work today, but this, I went and retrieved myself. When I open the door to the gym, she scans the room. I watch her like a hawk waiting for the moment she spots it. She looks baffled and doing a terrible job of faking interest when she notices I've added her weights and cardio machines along the back wall.

There's an awkward nod and a half-hearted smile. "That's great, thank you."

I let out a chuckle before hooking a finger under her chin and moving her face to look at the opposite wall. Her entire demeanour shifts, and she starts bouncing on the balls of her feet.

"You installed a pole?" she says, clapping her hands and running over to inspect it.

"Well, I installed *your* pole. And your mirrors. I hope you don't mind. I can have them moved back if you want." Suddenly, I'm nervous that I've overstepped. Why didn't I install a new one? Is there such a thing as pole preference? I just figured she'd want the one she already picked.

"No, it's fine. I mean, it's perfect." She trails a delicate finger down the metallic surface, throwing me a seductive smile. When she bites down on her plump bottom lip, she dips her chin before locking gazes with me from under her long lashes. "Although I think I should take it for a test drive, check your people installed it properly."

"If you think I let another man touch this pole you underestimate how reasonable I can be when it comes to you."

She lets out a little giggle as she starts a slow and sensual stroll around the pole. I've been fascinated by this woman for such a long time and while I thought I knew so much about her, it turns out there's this whole side of her I've never seen. One that's playful with her sexuality in ways I never expected. I fell in love with a strong woman and discovered a secret siren.

Katerina pauses and leans against the metal, her back flush with the gleaming column, and raises an arm before arching her back and sinking down, exposing the delicate slope of her neck to me. It's not an overtly sexual move bearing in mind she's still fully clothed, but the way she presents her body has my cock straining against my zipper. She's simultaneously dominant—presenting her body as an untouchable prize—but also gloriously submissive in her movements.

Dropping low, she sinks into a crouch and uses the stability of the poses to release the pole and slip her finger under her shirt. As she lifts it, she rises out of the position, tossing the shirt to the ground, and turns to face the pole.

She pops the button of her jeans before hooking her thumbs into the belt loops and drags the trousers down. Rocking on the balls of her feet, hypnotising me with the sway of her hips as she bends herself over. I'm too busy studying the curve of her ass to see her step out of her jeans, but there's a soft scrape of fabric as she kicks them to the side.

Her body is a sight to behold. Impossibly long lines with a beautiful landscape of curves, perfect whether they're wrapped around this pole or my hips. As she takes a firm hold, high above her head, she swings herself up, legs gripping the metal firmly enough to allow her to let go, arcing her torso back until she's bared to me.

She's been at work all day so it's not like she's

putting on a show, where every movement is choreographed, and she's outfitted in barely there lingerie. She's wearing a sports bra and a pair of Lycra shorts, hair thrown into a high ponytail. Yet she's the sexiest I've ever seen her. Completely at ease with her body and dancing for me as though I'm not here. Her confidence rolls off her in waves and with every undulation and spin, I find myself falling deeper and deeper for her.

As she continues, it feels like the world melts away and I begin to feel restless standing, so I ease a little nearer and drop to the floor, careful not to interrupt her focus by getting too close. I'm in awe of every switch in position. She casts the most exquisite shapes with each pose, displaying her body proudly.

The only sound that fills the room is her subtle exertions as she moves while I'm stunned into silent appreciation. The strength she displays is intoxicating. I've always thought of her as one of the toughest women I know, but I underestimated her. Her power and physicality are magnificent.

She takes her final spin and swings her legs down, landing on her knees at the base of the pole. I crook a finger at her, and I smirk when she shakes her head, deliberately ignoring my request.

"You've been such a good girl; don't you want your reward?" I say, my voice raspy, giving away exactly how much she's affected me. All she gives me in response is a defiantly raised brow and a 'fuck you' grin.

I crook my index finger one more time. "Crawl to me, baby girl."

I don't miss the shiver that chases itself along her

spine or the way she draws her knees together and squeezes her thighs in response. The florescent lights overhead reflect off the dewy sheen of sweat that covers her bare skin. With the slightest of movements, she shakes her head.

"Crawl or be punished." I swear she lets out the quietest little moan of satisfaction and that's all it takes for me to snap. I can tell from her shocked expression she isn't expecting me to move as quickly as I do. Her eyes light up, her smile broadening as she jumps to her feet and starts to run towards the door. She's not quick enough though.

I catch up to her within a few strides, snaking my arm around her waist and hauling her back towards me. My smile broadens when she gives out a shriek of surprise. She's kicking her feet, wriggling in my hold, and the more she squirms, the more she giggles. It's too tempting, I can't resist tickling her a little too.

"No fair, that's cheating," she cries out between bursts of laughter.

"All's fair in love and war, *micetta*."

"War. When did we declare war? I think I missed that part."

"You didn't do as you were told, Katerina," I chastise her playfully.

I sit on the weights bench and wrestle her over my knee, slipping my fingers under the waistband of her shorts and pulling them down.

"What the hell are you doing?" Katerina yelps.

I stroke one hand over the curve of her cheek while my other lies heavy across her back, pinning her across my legs. "Oh, I think you can guess. You can tap out at any time. Just say red."

Lifting my palm high, I pause, in case I've read her playfulness incorrectly, but she doesn't say a word. Instead, she tenses her stomach muscles against my thighs, bracing herself for the first contact. When I land the first smack, I can't tell what turns me on more, the sharp sound reverberating off the walls, the gasp she lets out or the reddening mark that blooms nearly instantly. From the way she wriggles under my arm, rubbing against my hard cock, I don't think she knows either.

"You like that, don't you?" She moans out a garbled response that has me peppering a consistent rhythm on her backside, never hitting the same place twice. I've never done this before, but as I pause, giving Katerina a moment to steady herself, I rub the rose-coloured blushes. Her skin is hot under my palm, and I stroke each mark gently, savouring the sensation as they warm my hand. When I increase the pressure, Katerina lets out an adorable little hum, like she's being lulled into a trance-like state.

My hand wanders lower, slipping between the apex of her thighs. Now it's my turn to let out a groan. She's soaked, her folds slick and her pussy begging for something to fill it. It's my pleasure to oblige, so I curve my hand to cup her sex, dragging my two middle fingers over her swollen clit and back to tease her entrance. Without warning I thrust them into her, and stretching her eager little cunt around them.

I turn my hand over, which, while a little awkward for me, gives me the perfect angle to gently curl my fingers against her G-spot. Her body relaxes against me, her desperate cries settling into a melody of ecstatic whimpers. I move my arm from her back and trace it up her spine and around to cup her cheek, turning her face to mine.

"Eyes on me. I want to watch you fall apart for me." She whimpers in response, and I increase the pace of my thrusts, rotating back so I add another finger. Her walls spasm around them, betraying how close she is to coming for me, and I nearly come in my pants when her eyes roll back in her head and she cries out my name.

I don't give her time to recover. Dragging her shorts off, I then lift her off me and head towards the wall of mirrors. Holding her back to my front, I face us towards our reflection. She's stunning. Eyes hooded, lips parted and panting, breasts heaving, contained in their tight tank bra. I lift her arms and place them against the cold surface, bending her forwards and nudging her legs apart.

I run my hands over her body, loving the moans each squeeze and pinch elicits from her. When I pull away to unbutton my shirt, she makes a move to stand up, but I lay my hand on the back of her neck and encourage her back down.

"Be a good girl and stay where I put you," I whisper in her ear.

"Whatever you say, Daddy," she sighs out dreamily. My heart races while my cock stiffens, liking that moniker a little too much. I wrestle my shirt off and unbutton my pants, shucking them down my thighs along with my underwear.

My cock springs forward, falling against the swell of her ass. Placing a firm hand on her hip, I pull her back, moaning when she arches her spine and presses her wet pussy against the length of my dick.

I stroke my cock from root to tip before dragging the swollen head over her clit, loving the strangled cry she lets out in response.

"Holy fuck. That feels so good." I've never heard her voice so raspy, and from now on I'm going to make it my mission to make sure she always sounds this debauched.

I ease back, notching myself at her entrance and running my free hand up her spine. I stop at her neck, gripping her throat with the lightest pressure. I angle my wrist so I can force her gaze to meet mine in the mirror. As I sink into her, we let out harmonising moans, but I stop the moment her eyes flutter shut.

"Eyes open, baby girl. I want you to see the look on my face when I fuck you full," I grind out, before rolling my hips and thrusting every inch into her tight cunt.

I note every gasp—every flutter of her lashes—as I pound into her, hypnotised by the euphoria etched on her face. I could spend days losing myself in her body, but the way she clenches around me has me barrelling into an orgasm I can't stave off.

Releasing her hip, I pull one of her wrists from the mirror and drag it down, placing her fingers on her clit. "Be a good girl and make yourself come on my cock. Use your tight little cunt to steal my cum."

She wastes absolutely no time, and I lean forward a little, watching in the mirror as she toys with her clit. What I'm not expecting is for her to slide her fingers down and spread them around the base of my dick, squeezing around my hard-on as I fuck her.

Her orgasm rips through her and I have to steady her, taking care that she doesn't collide with the mirror as she presses her face against the cool surface.

"I love the way you take me. Whether I fuck you hard or take you slow, you make me come so hard, *mia dea perfetta*." I tighten my grip on her hip, pulling her back into each brutal thrust and crying out when her vice-like grip pulls rope after rope of cum from me.

Her body goes limp as I fall forwards, bracing my hands on the glass either side of her, careful not to crush her. When my softening cock slips out of her, I kiss the side of her neck, whispering a string of promises. "*Ti amerò per sempre.*"

When I turn her to face me, it's obvious she's exhausted, barely able to keep her eyes open, but as I sweep her into my arms, she whispers back. "I'll hold you to that, *vecchietto.*"

"Be sure that you do, because I'm never letting you go."

(*QR CODE FOR BONUS ARTWORK OF THIS SCENE*)

CHAPTER TWENTY-THREE

T he surgical floor is always quieter at night. No visitors and far fewer staff. I always prefer it this way, no one stopping to talk, boring me with their banal existences, or asking me for patient updates. The last thing I want to do right now is chat with anyone.

Every imbecile in the hospital is gossiping about their engagement. It's all they can talk about. How happy they are for Doctor Mancini. What a charming man her fiancé is. Every time I'm forced to listen to another platitude of simpering congratulations, it makes me want to bury a surgical scalpel in his chest.

This is his fault.

Stefano Tiero. The walking cliché. The criminal in the tailored suit. I knew what he was the first time I saw him. He's a predator, hidden behind a veneer of respectability. I'm done waiting for her and I refuse to allow trash like him to keep on touching what's mine.

He was all over her at the gala. Every lingering touch and

longing gaze made my skin crawl. But it doesn't matter. She'll find out who she belongs to soon enough.

As I turn the corner, I come face to face with my second least favourite person. That pathetic excuse for a man who thought he was good enough for my doctor. Nurse Costello.

Another man who's not worthy of the air she breathes. The pathetic little man-child who only got this job because his daddy was on the board. Everything about him makes my blood boil. The affable pretty boy. A vapid little prick with the intelligence of an amoeba.

I dismiss his muttered apologies, shoving the cart he's pushing out of my way and storming off down the corridor. I try to calm myself, yet every time I think of him on a date with my Katerina, my temper flares. I can practically hear the rage thundering in my ears.

By the time I reach the doctors' lounge, I know exactly what my next step is. She doesn't realise the depth of my devotion to her. But I'll show her. I'll make her see.

I'm done waiting for her to accept that she's always been mine.

CHAPTER TWENTY-FOUR

KATERINA

THREE WEEKS LATER...

I'm jolted awake by the sharp tug of the drapes and a blinding light carving its beams through the bedroom.

"What kind of monster wakes their girlfriend up by blinding them?" I mutter, throwing my forearm over my eyes to block the offending light.

"The kind that needed to give you a present before he leaves for his meeting with his boss," comes his smooth response.

"I'm not accepting anything from you until you apologise," I huff. We may be in the middle of a minor disagreement. One where I'm right and he's entirely in the wrong.

"I'm not apologising for doing my job, *micetta*." His

voice is laced with an air of frustration. I push myself up and throw the full weight of my glare at him.

"I don't want you to apologise for doing your fucking job. I want you to apologise for me not being the first person you called when you were fucking injured," I scream at him, suddenly wide awake and bristling with the anger that lay dormant while I slept. He flinches and I'm glad because he fucking should. He should be sorry. I should have been the first damn person to know and I sure as shit shouldn't have found out after the fact. "And because you should have come straight to the hospital to get checked out, you stubborn fucking asshole."

The last few weeks have been absolute chaos, and yet again made my wannabe stalker seem like a cheap imitation of true danger in the grand scheme of things. Aurora was able to take down her husband. Max De Luca is dead and his organisation has been decimated but the cost was almost too high, and I could easily have lost a man that I've spent years waiting for.

"I was fine. It was only a concussion."

"Are you a doctor? Did you spend years in training?"

"No, but I've been cracked over the head before, and I was fine."

"You were unconscious for fuck-knows how long. And aside from that, you should have called your fucking girlfriend to tell her you were okay." My words start to run together into an angry, garbled mess until I find myself panting and struggling to calm myself down. "You could have fucking died. And I wouldn't have known. No one knew to tell me because as far as they're concerned, I'm nothing to you."

I cast my eyes up to his and catch the moment of realisation as it settles in his chest. He crosses the room and takes a seat on the bed, taking my hands in his and pulling me towards him. I pull back, too angry to be comforted, but he ignores my protests and drags me onto his lap.

I turn my head and struggle, trying to wriggle away, but he's having none of it, gripping my hips, pinning me as I straddle his thigh.

"Stay still dammit. You're right," he growls, and I stop straining against his hold, letting out a frustrated breath.

"Go on," I say, arching a brow before crossing my arms in front of me.

"We've done all this backwards, and I made a mistake when I didn't tell you I was injured. In my defence, you needed to focus on saving Benedict at the time. It's—"

"This doesn't sound like an apology, Tiero. This sounds like an excuse," I interrupt.

He runs a hand over his face, a remorseful expression fluttering over his features, and for a second, guilt washes over me. Then I remember how worried I was when I found out he was injured and hold my ground. He leans in, cupping my cheeks and resting his forehead to mine.

"I hate that everyone doesn't know that you're mine. But that's what you are. Entirely mine." He kisses me softly and it becomes almost impossible to stay mad at him while he's touching me with such reverence, but I manage to hold on to at least a little of the anger that's fuelling me.

"I'm fed up with *playing* at being yours, Stefano. All day at the hospital I have people that mean nothing to me congratulating me on a relationship that no one I love knows about. Not one of the *family* knows. And my father doesn't count because it's not like he's shouting his support from the rooftops." My words catch in my throat when I mention my father. It still hurts that he won't discuss Stefano with me.

"You want *everyone* to know you're mine?"

"Yes," I let out on the barest of whispers.

I can feel my emotions swelling in my chest and I find it more than a little frustrating that these feelings have me blinking back tears. I've never felt so emotional. I've spent most of my life bottling up my feelings and now that I have the man I always wanted, I hate that my body betrays me to him at every turn. It's impossible for Stefano not to see how deeply I care for him, whether I want him to or not.

"Firstly, *micetta*. If they didn't know before, I'm pretty sure everyone knows there's something going on between us. You basically shouted at the don until she called me in to the hospital to get checked out," he says with a smirk. "And secondly—" he pauses to pull a small box out of his pocket and presents it on his palm. "I want absolutely everybody to know that not only are you mine, but that I'm yours too."

My gaze oscillates between his deep blue eyes and the red velvet box.

"What are you doing? We're fake engaged, not real

engaged." The second the words are out of my mouth I want to take them back. He must see the sheer panic in my face because all of a sudden I'm annoyed at the chuckle he lets out.

"Katerina Mancini. This is not a fake engagement ring. It's a very real promise. I'm not asking you to marry me; I'm telling you that you will be my wife," he says with absolute conviction, pulling open the lid and exposing the most beautiful ring I've ever seen. An exquisite emerald-cut diamond with a halo of smaller stones cushioning it. The central stone so large, you can, in fact, see where the Titanic hit it.

It's breathtaking, but it's his words that almost leave me speechless. Almost. "You don't like to follow conventions, do you?"

"I'm too old to waste another minute without you by my side. Tell me I've got this wrong. That ever since I first kissed you, this isn't everything you've ever wanted?"

"I can't do that."

"No. And I can't pretend you're not meant to be mine." As he speaks, I'm so lost in his words that I haven't noticed he's taken the ring out of the box, poised to place it on my finger. He locks his gaze with mine, and a thousand promises of what's to come pass between us as he slides the ring on.

"I love you, Katerina. Now and forever," he says, his voice rough and filled with emotion.

"I love you too."

I slide my hands to cup the back of his neck and pull him into a kiss. The type of kiss that you can get lost in and never want to come up for air from. I let out a little moan of complaint when my pager goes off, releasing him far sooner than I'd have liked.

"I'll see you tonight, baby girl."

His phone buzzes as I reach for my pager. When I check, I see I've been called in for an emergency on one of my patients. "I might be late back, depends on how much this derails my service."

After checking his message, he says, "My day is pretty light after I meet with Aurora, but I've got a late meeting at Inferno. Marcus is on your security detail today. Contact him if you need anything and can't get hold of me."

"Isn't it overkill having your second following me around the hospital all day?"

"No," he says firmly, brooking no argument, even when I glare at his protectiveness.

After another gentle kiss, he heads off to work leaving me to get ready. I may joke that he's overprotective, but the messages are getting out of hand. I reach for my phone to see what today's wake up text says, and a shiver rakes itself through my body.

UNKNOWN NUMBER:

I'm tired of playing this game with you.

Your heart doesn't belong to him.

I let you have your fun, but now it's time to take what's mine.

If you won't rid yourself of the distractions in your life. I will.

My pulse throbs in my neck as I swallow down the

sense of dread and screenshot the messages. I know Stefano and Sinclair have cloned my phone so they can monitor the content, but I'm not sure if Marcus has a view of them so I forward them to him too.

> Make sure any protection working with the Consigliere takes this threat seriously.

MARCUS:

Yes, Ma'am.

> I swear to God if you ever call me Ma'am again the next time you need medical assistance I will forget where the good drugs are.

MARCUS:

Understood…

Mrs Tiero?

> Doc Em.

MARCUS:

That's going to be really confusing when you change your last name. Doc "Tee" doesn't have the same ring to it.

> Fuck all the way off, Marcus.

MARCUS:

Yes, Ma'am.

I throw the phone on the bed, but I let out a soft laugh. I like that even though he's now fully aware our relationship isn't fake, he's not treating me any differently. The last thing I want is to suddenly be treated like some precious little flower, like the mob girlfriends of old. The ones that sat on the sidelines and did as they were told. My father brought me up to carve out a purpose for myself and I'll be damned if I let that be undermined based on who I love.

Stefano's role in the organisation is vitally important, and so is mine. In fact, these last few months have taught me a few things that surprised me. I've worked my ass off to be at the top of my field, the chief of my specialty, I'm respected by my peers, but that's not what's given me the most fulfilment recently. Being there for the don, stepping in when the *family* needs me. Nothing compares to the feeling of being able to save them. I've spent years leading two separate lives, and now I'm beginning to wonder if I want to keep doing that. There's no reason why I couldn't set up my own practice and dedicate more of my time to the family.

As I step into the shower and let the hot water chase away the chill those messages gave me, I let my mind wander and consider the possibility that maybe now would be the perfect time for a change.

CHAPTER TWENTY-FIVE

KATERINA

"What do you mean, he didn't turn up for his shift? I need him in here now. There's no way I'm letting you touch this patient again," I bark at Nurse Henshaw, who's screwed up yet another one of my charts. The first thing I did when we realised that Danny wasn't my stalker, was swap him back on to my service. Not for any other reason than he's a phenomenal nurse, but unlike Nurse Henshaw, he rarely fucks up my entire day by letting me resuscitate a DNR by switching the charts on my patients.

This day has gone downhill from the minute I stepped onto the surgical floor.

"I'm so sorry, Doctor Mancini. I don't know what happened."

"What happened is you spent more time discussing the age difference between me and my fiancé than you did focussing on your fucking job." She blanches at the harshness of my words, but as fuck-ups go, this is a big one.

"That's not tru—"

"If you think your judgemental-as-fuck voice doesn't carry, then you are sorely mistaken, Nurse Henshaw. Had you been doing your job and not telling everyone who'd listen that I'm 'too busy fucking an old man these days', then this would never have happened." I raise my voice and don't miss the growing audience or the way their eyebrows climb higher and higher with each cutting barb I throw out.

"What the hell is going on in here?" the Chief of Surgery bellows, his voice carrying into the room before he enters. "Both of you. In my office. *Now.*"

THE MEETING with the chief went about as well as I'd expected and resulted in my spending most of the afternoon with our legal department, assessing our liability. The long and the short of it was Nurse Henshaw being fired and my being put on administrative leave until a settlement could be reached with the next of kin.

I'm not upset. It's the right thing to do, but there's a part of me that wants five minutes alone with Nurse Henshaw for putting patient care at risk. I'm more than happy to own up to my mistakes, but it sits like a bag of rocks in my gut knowing that my error is as a result of her incompetence.

This never would have happened if Danny had been running my service. That realisation stirs feelings of guilt for ever having suspected him of being capable of sending me all those notes. Maybe I would have taken them more seriously if I hadn't assumed they were from him. How big is my ego that I thought his friendliness equated to an unhinged stalker?

I head straight to my locker after getting the standard spiel from our lawyer. *Don't talk to the next of kin, don't discuss this with your colleagues, and go home until they clear me to come back to work.* It doesn't take me long to grab my stuff, but it's still bugging me that Danny hasn't turned up for his shift. It's not like him, so I dig out my phone and sift through my contacts until I find him. There's another twinge of remorse when I remember he's blocked.

The call rings off to voicemail but I don't leave a message. I have no idea what I want to say anyway, I just want to make sure he's okay and it's not like I have any right to know. However, there is someone else who might have an idea, and they pick up on the second ring.

"I thought you were in surgery?" Marcus questions, like it's personally offending him that my plans have changed.

"Long story but I'm about to head home. Anyway, that's not why I'm calling."

"Really, because that would be super helpful. You know, being informed of a change relating to the person you're supposed to be watching. If you're going to ban us from the surgical floor then we need to be kept informed, Doc." There's a lightness to his voice, so I know he's teasing me, but he's not wrong.

"Fine, I've been put on administrative leave for the

next few days so watching me just got a whole lot easier. I'll be sitting on the couch with a good book for the foreseeable future," I say with equal flippancy.

"What happened?" he asks, his voice now gruff and hard, like he's about to march into the hospital and go to bat for me.

"Down boy. There was a patient error, not my fault but it needs to be investigated. That's not why I'm calling you." There's a begrudging grunt on the other end of the line and I smile a little at the idea that Marcus would be upset on my behalf. "Danny Costello?" I prompt.

"What about him?"

"He's MIA." I reply.

"I'm gonna need more than that Doc."

"He hasn't turned up for his shift. Please tell me *we* haven't done anything to him?"

"Of course we haven't. We dropped surveillance on him weeks ago." There's a pause before he continues. "But it is odd. I followed the guy for weeks and if there's one thing I know about him is that his routine is everything. Like obsessively so. Skipping out on work doesn't sound like him."

"That's what I thought."

"I don't have anyone free right now," he's quick to reply. Trying to shut down the suggestion he knows is coming.

"I'm literally on my way home. Can't you go and check it out?"

"No. Stefano would gut me."

"He'd also gut you if you didn't look into this." My

counter is weak at best. True, but still weak. "What if I agreed to stay here at the hospital until you got back?"

"The answer is no, Doc," he snaps, but he quickly offers me a compromise. "Once you're home safe, then I'll check it out."

"Deal."

A sense of relief washes over me and I end the call so I can gather my stuff to leave. As I make my way through the hospital, it's obvious word has spread about the mix-up. I'm greeted with half a dozen platitudes, telling me I'll be back in no time, and how the suspension is just a formality, but it strikes me that I'm not sure I care.

I'm entirely unbothered. Which I know I probably should be. Shouldn't the Chief of General Surgery be at the very least a little angry at being suspended? Even if it is only temporary.

But I'm not. I'd even go so far as to say I'm glad to be leaving. If the last few months have taught me anything, it's that it's not what I do that brings me joy, it's helping the people I love. And after everything the Bianchi organisation has been through, we're all owed a break. I'm looking forward to curling up on the sofa with a glass of wine and formulating a plan to jump Stefano the minute he steps through the door.

I wait patiently for the elevator to the parking garage and when the doors finally open there's just enough room to squeeze in at the front.

Pulling out my necklace from under my collar, I unhook my new ring and place it on my finger. I hold out my hand and inspect it, like a magpie distracted by shiny things, and smile as the fluorescent lights reflect off the facets. I'm too caught up in its beauty to pay attention as the people get off the elevator on each floor.

The first time I realise there's something wrong is a shuffle and scrape of shoes behind me. It's sudden and startles me. I've barely had time to turn my head when there's a sharp prick in my neck. It pinches for a second before a warm sensation spreads over me. I feel like a TV screen about to go into standby, only I can't find the remote to press a button and stop it from happening. I don't want to shut down. But as my eyelids grow heavy, I can't seem to fight it.

As I fall back into someone's arms, I struggle to make sense of what I'm seeing. My head lolls to the side and my vision is obscured by a swath of green fabric. I try to lift my head and the last thing I see before darkness takes me is a pleated surgical mask and a pair of familiar dark eyes, brimming with a terrifying and malevolent joy.

CHAPTER TWENTY-SIX

STEFANO

"**W**hat the fuck do you mean you don't know where she is?" I roar down the line at him. My heart is pounding against my rib cage with such force I swear I can hear the beat.

"I have no excuse, consigliere. We can't find her and her cell phone has been switched off." Marcus's words are strained, but I don't have the capacity to cut him any slack right now. I clench my jaw hard enough for him to hear my teeth grinding over the phone.

"How the fuck did this happen?" I say, barely recognising the sound of my own voice, fury permeating every word.

"We were waiting in the parking garage for her to shower and change after she finished her shift"—there's a brief pause and I swear I can hear him audibly swallow —"only she never came down to her car."

"How long has she been missing?" I bark.

"We last had contact with her half an hour ago."

"You start a sweep of the hospital, call in everyone. I'm going to call Sinclair, see if he still has a backdoor into the hospital security feeds." I don't wait for a reply, hanging up and already scrolling for Sinclair's contact.

He picks up on the seventh ring, and my words are such a garbled mess of fast-paced demands that it takes a few moments for me to register that he's asking me to slow down.

There's a pregnant pause before I blurt out. "Doc Em is missing; I need your help."

SINCLAIR PROMISES to call me back, and by the time he does, I'm already halfway to the hospital. "What have you got for me? Tell me you found her?"

"No,"—my heart drops into the pit of my stomach— "but I don't think she left the hospital," Sinclair replies. I can tell from his tone that he's managing me. Trying to keep me calm, but it's having the opposite effect. Although I can't honestly say my blood pressure would be any lower either way.

"How can you be sure?" I ask. The lights ahead of me flick to red and I ignore them, putting my foot to the floor and not giving a fuck as I swerve through the junction while tyres screech and horns blare.

"I found footage of her getting on the elevator to the parking garage, but she never made it to her car according to Marcus. They had eyes on her vehicle. When I went back to check the footage, I couldn't find her getting off the elevator or going back to the hospital either. However, there was this porter with a wheelchair that exited with a patient a few minutes later."

"What's that got to do with anything?" I bark.

"The earlier footage showed that the wheelchair was empty when he got on the elevator. Listen, I could be wrong. The patient is under a blanket and wearing a mask, but it could be her."

"Fuck. Were you able to track them on the security cameras?"

"No, I lost them in the ER, but I'm working on it. I've got Marcus and his guys focussing on searching from there."

"He could have taken her right out the front door," I shout down the phone.

"No, he didn't. I've checked the feeds. If the patient in that chair is her, she hasn't left that hospital."

I try to speak, but nothing comes out. *What the fuck is going on? Who the hell has taken her and why? How?* And then an even worse thought occurs to me.

"Why didn't she get out of the chair?" I rasp.

The pause on the other end of the line answers the question, but Sin puts my greatest fear into words. "It looks like the person in the chair is unconscious."

The noise that erupts from my throat is somewhere between a growl and a desperate yell. It feels alien as it scrapes against my vocal cords and burns when I try to swallow the rising bile back down.

"We're going to find her. Nico is on his way and I'm going to coordinate you all from here," Sinclair says, his tone even and clear, trying to reassure me in a way I've seen him use on occasion. It's assertive with enough deference not to piss off whoever he's trying to calm down. "Breathe."

I've been in situations like this before, and I've always been able to tamp down my emotions, to think clearly and focus, no matter the risks. But Katerina means more to me than any other person on this earth, and the thought of her being in danger has my heart pounding and my mind racing with endless questions.

Where has he taken her?

What does he want from her?

What if he's hurting her?

What if I'm too late?

I take a long, slow inhale, and it helps lift the haze of fear-laced rage that's trying to suffocate me.

"Good," he says before adding, "We'll find her Stefano. The doc is made of stronger stuff than half the men we have."

His words only serve to remind me that my beautiful, fierce Katerina wouldn't need to be strong if I had protected her like I was supposed to. Guilt hangs heavy like a weight around my neck, but I can't let it stop me now.

She needs me and I won't fail her. I can't. Not again. Never again. I'll be everything she needs.

Her rescuer, her protector, her wrath.

I'm going to slaughter the man who took her from me and enjoy every second as I squeeze the life out of him.

CHAPTER TWENTY-SEVEN

KATERINA

I startle awake, my eyes flaring wide only to burn my retinas when I look straight up into the bright white lights above me. Squinting does two-fifths of fuck-all to relieve the glare, but as my eyes adjust, I recognise the shape of the surgical lights and the familiar cantilevered arm they hang off. I can just about make out my surroundings as the imprints of the lightbulbs fade from my vision.

The unease shifts to dread as I take in the rest of the room. I'm in an operating room, but it's not one I recognise. It's dated and sparse, not containing half of the supplies and equipment I would expect in a functional OR. Even the monitor beside me looks like it's seen better days.

I crane my neck but I can't see the screen from here, though I can hear the unsteady beep of my heart rate. I catch sight of a surgical pole out of the corner of my eye, and I panic when I notice the tube that trails down and across towards me.

I try to roll off the gurney but only succeed in turning my head to the side. My pulse races as my anxiety builds. This doesn't feel right. I try to move again, but this time, I only succeed in lifting my head a few inches off the bed, and I let out a startled scream when I catch a glimpse of green surgical draping across my torso.

I struggle to hold my head up, crying out when the back of my skull lands with a dull thud on the cold surface of the trolley beneath me. I attempt to calm my thoughts, telling myself everything will be fine, Stefano will find me, but when I try to focus long enough to make sense of my situation, my thoughts are clouded with the aftereffects of whatever I was injected with earlier. I flick my gaze across to the wall and spot the clock.

I look at the time, noting that I haven't been out for too long, maybe an hour at most, but that's not what I want to concentrate on. I need something to centre me, so I watch the second hand slowly revolving around the clock face and time my breathing to the seconds passing by. *In-two-three-four, out-two-three-four, in-two-three-four, out-two-three-four.* Box breathing until I wrangle my rapid pulse back under control and my thoughts become clearer.

I cycle through what I can and cannot do. I can move my head. I can feel the draft of the room as it glides across my cheek. But I'm struggling to feel anything else and when I lift my head again and try to sit up, I notice the restraints. Well, I see them, but I don't feel them. *In-two-three-four, out-two-three-four.*

I'm completely disconnected from my body. The thick leather straps are wrapped around my wrists, across my hip bones, and as I stretch my neck as far as I can, there's a hint of the same leather binding my legs to the gurney as well. I urge my body to move but it's like the wires are crossed, I can see the slightest movement against the tight binds, but I can't feel it.

It can only mean one thing. I've been given a spinal block, and whatever sedatives I was probably dosed with in the elevator are wearing off. Technically, I can move; I'm just numb and have no sensation from the neck down. My heart rate begins to run away with itself, the beeps from the monitor only intensifying the danger. I can't seem to cut through the torrent of emotions to be able to make sense of why I'm here. *In-two-three-four, out-two-three-four.*

A single tear escapes the corner of my eye, searing a trail into my hairline. I've never felt so alone or so vulnerable. *Please let Stefano come for me. Please let him find me.*

In-two-three-four, out-two-three-four.

Pull it together, woman. Now is not the time to fall apart. I can fall apart later. *Fuck* there had better be a later. I only just got to experience my happily ever after and if it's cut short, I'm going to come back and haunt whoever the fuck thinks they can turn my dream into a nightmare. I didn't spend all those years pining for Stefano to be robbed at the eleventh hour. How fucking dare someone do this to me.

In-two-three-four, out-two-three-four.

I'm alone in the room, but judging by the tray of surgical instruments laid out beside the bed, that won't be the case for long. There's something familiar about the way they're positioned, but my mind is still muddled, and I can't figure out what. The door in the corner opens with a loud bang that reverberates off the stark walls, and my head snaps to see who's coming into the room.

I shift my gaze and struggle to focus, my vision still blurry from the drugs in my system. There's a figure standing in the muted shadows at the edge of the room. I can't tell much from the shapeless blue scrubs and the generic surgical cap and mask, but the moment he steps into the light my heart drops into my stomach as soon as those cold eyes lock on mine.

I know those eyes.

Doctor Dylan Jenkins. All this time, it was him...

I don't look away, trapped by his cruel, malevolent stare. His cheeks perk up behind the surgical mask, hinting at a smile.

"It's about time you came back to the land of the living, Katerina," he says scornfully. As if my resilience against the drugs he's pumped into me, is in any way under my control.

My mouth is dry as I spit out my response. "Fuck you, asshole." I'm aiming for angry and incensed with a hint of disdain, but if I can hear the tremor in my voice, I'm sure that he can too.

I can't tell whether it's the coarseness of my words or the obvious hatred I have for him that bothers him more, but I don't miss the way he baulks at my outburst, a veil of anger falling over his eyes. The shift in his demeanour is instant, like a switch being flipped deciding my fate.

The beeps on the monitor kick up even more, betraying my fear, and I hate myself for showing weakness to him.

"Such a filthy mouth for such a talented woman," he says offhandedly as he moves across the room and picks up a scalpel in his gloved hand, inspecting the blade. "I should punish you for that. Sullying your perfect mouth with such poisonous words. Tell me, should I wash out your mouth or simply cut out your tongue?"

I'm still processing what he said when his hand grips my jaw so tight I know he's leaving marks, but that's not what scares me. It's the scalpel he's holding millimetres from my lips. He forces my mouth open, wringing a strangled shriek from me when he moves the blade forward.

I've never felt fear like this, even if I could move I don't think I'd be able to. His gaze holds mine and I see nothing but a malevolent pleasure reflected there. He's enjoying every second of control he exerts over me.

Seemingly satisfied at having scared me into submission, he withdraws the blade and releases my jaw. "That's better. You just need a firm hand."

His words make me want to retch, but I shove every feeling of disgust as far down as I can, knowing that my only option is to keep him talking if I want to buy myself some time.

"Why are you doing this?" I ask, trying hard to stifle my pleading tone, loathing that he has power over me.

"Why? Because you're mine, Doctor Mancini. From the very beginning, I've known your heart was always meant to be mine," he croons, flicking his gaze to my draped chest and staring with something that looks like unhinged obsession. While my chest isn't fully bare, he's staring down at me as if it were, when in fact it's laid out only to expose a five-inch-wide gap between my breasts, from my collarbone to my belly button.

I'm beyond disappointed in myself. Not that he took me. Not that I'm at his mercy. But that in all the years I worked with Doctor Jenkins, I mistook his sociopathy for narcissism, and I never recognised how dangerous he truly was. He's the type of man I should be able to spot at twenty paces. He's always been a threat.

How did I not see it? I'm Cosa Nostra, born and bred, for fuck's sake.

"I've spent years waiting for you, Doctor Mancini. Waiting for you to grow into a surgeon worthy of my attention; to grow out of your youthful petulance and become a respected colleague. I knew the minute you started your residency here that you were special, that you'd blossom into so much more. And yet, now you're finally exceptional, you waste yourself on idiots. Do you really think that nurse was worthy of you? Or that wannabe thug in the designer suit?" He pauses, raising his eyebrows questioningly, but any response escapes me. What the fuck am I meant to say to this level of rampant delusion?

Lining the tip of the scalpel with the opening in the surgical draping across my chest, he nicks the skin. I can't feel it, but when I crane my neck to follow his movements, I see it. A droplet of blood swells under the knife before it chooses its path towards my shoulder.

When I glance up at him, he's laser-focussed on the incision, crow's feet appearing at the edges of his eyes as a malicious joy seems to take over him. He leans over, blocking the bright lights and casting a shadow over me, causing him to curse in frustration and reach for the headlamp beside him.

"Tell me, when I open you up, do you think I'll be able to tell that your heart belongs to me?" Even if he waited for a response, I wouldn't be able to give him one. The callousness of his words freezing me in terror. "I've seen so many hearts on my table, but I've always believed that when I find 'the one', I'll know that it's meant for me."

His wrists flex and strain, digging the scalpel in a little further and dragging it down between the valley of my breasts, stopping a hands-width above my belly button. I want to scream and rage and fight against my restraints, but I know any movement will only make his incision less precise and could cause more damage than it already is. Though I can't feel the bite of the blade, it doesn't make it any less horrifying as the incision pulls further apart.

He lets out a satisfied groan that has me wanting to claw the skin from my bones.

"I can't wait to watch your heart beat for me, Doctor Mancini. To hold it in my hands and know it's mine."

I strangle the scream that wants to tear from my lips, muffling it through clenched teeth.

"Don't cry, my exquisite little rose. I just need to know..." his voice trails off and he turns towards the instrument tray and lays down the scalpel. "I need to know that I've been right all along. That you have been worth the wait."

In-two-three-four, out-two-three-four.

"What are you going to do to me?" My voice is barely a whisper as I'm terrified to hear his response.

"I need to see with my own eyes that your heart is worthy of mine, of course," he says as he picks up the bone saw.

I scream. Long and loud, until there's no air left in my lungs. He scrambles to pick up a syringe, stabbing it into the port in the IV. Spots cloud my eyes and darkness creeps in like a vignette around the edges. My vision tunnels as he leans over and fixes his deranged gaze on mine.

"Night, night, Katerina. Sleep tight." His smile is detached and unhinged, filling me with dread. A shiver chases itself down my neck, only to fade into my anesthetised spine.

Whatever he injected me with overpowers my consciousness, pulling me into darkness. Closing my eyes, I shut out the image of the twisted lunatic above me and summon one of Stefano. I'm safe in his arms, wrapped in his familiar, rich scent. He's stroking my hair and telling me I'm his and he's mine.

My last thought as I drift away brings me solace.

No matter what happens to me now, whether I survive or not, Stefano Tiero will keep his promise—he'll slaughter the man who made me cry.

CHAPTER TWENTY-EIGHT

STEFANO

A scream reverberates through the darkened basement corridor, and I break out into a run, Marcus right behind me. The soles of our shoes slap against the linoleum floor as we chase after her cries. They cease as suddenly as they started and my heart lurches in my chest.

The corridor intersects with another and leaves us with a fifty-fifty choice. I hesitate, second guessing myself, trying to pinpoint what direction her screams came from, as without them, I may go the wrong way— waste precious seconds getting to her. My mind chases itself round in circles, not knowing whether the silence means she's no longer in pain, or worse that she's dead.

She can't be dead. I'd feel it. I'd know.

I need to bury the fear that's threatening to paralyse me because time isn't a privilege I have right now.

She needs me.

"You go left, I'll take right," I bark, pushing his shoulder, spurring him into action.

I pitch forward down the hallway and start hurling open the doors. For every door that clatters open, there's an echo along the corridor as Marcus matches my frantic pace as we scan each room. Nothing but rooms full of filing cabinets and surplus medical supplies.

As I reach the last door, I hear it. An incessant buzzing, like the sound my reciprocating saw makes. It's so out of place in this darkened basement that I know immediately that that's where I need to be.

"Marcus, over here," I yell, before pulling my gun out of its holster and slamming the door open wide. I blink away the darkness, trying to get my eyes to adjust to the low light. My pulse races as the saw's steady whirr increases, getting suddenly more aggressive as if it's being ground against something. Its ominous whine leaves a knot of tension in my chest. I follow the noise to the back of the room, where a sliver of light seeps out from underneath a set of double doors.

Running towards it, I waste no time in shouldering my way through them, gun drawn and raised, readying myself for whatever is on the other side. Marcus's footsteps thunder behind me, and his voice booms in the corridor as he makes a call, ordering our men searching the other floors to come to our location.

The scene before me has my brain short-circuiting. I can't possibly be seeing what I think I'm seeing. There's a doctor in the room who flinches at my interruption, tightening his grip on the scalpel in his hand.

My beautiful Katerina is laid out on a surgical table,

strapped down and covered with bright green surgical sheets that are saturated in blood. Her blood. I blink, but the image of the gaping wound in her chest is burned into my brain—a sight I will never be able to unsee. When my eyes open a fraction of a second later, I focus them on anything that will tell me if she's still alive.

There's a slow, steady beep of a heart monitor and a series of clunks from the pump on the ventilator that's breathing for her. If it wasn't for these two sounds, I'd be convinced from the glassy grey pallor of her skin that I'd already lost her.

But that's simply not a thought that I'm willing to concede.

I didn't spend a lifetime waiting for her, only to lose her now.

Lasering my attention in on the doctor hunched over her body, I catalogue the blood-covered gloved hands and the tip of the scalpel hovering over Katerina's still beating heart, stopping me from taking even one step closer.

A single flick of that knife and he could end her.

A near-volcanic fury chases a path through my bloodstream when I look up and see the sadistic pleasure shining in his eyes at the torture he's putting her through. It's in that moment that I understand my enemy. See him for who he truly is, both literally and figuratively.

I recognise the callous stare of Doctor Jenkins, and while I can't fathom how I never saw it before, I see it now. The cold, soulless eyes of a monster.

Both he and I flinch as Marcus crashes through the

swinging doors behind me, prompting the doctor to move the blade, holding it closer to Katerina's heart as I hold out an arm and shout for Marcus to hold his fire.

"Stay exactly where you are," Doctor Jenkins orders, flicking his gaze between Marcus and me, the panic in his eyes displaying his realisation: he's outmanned and outgunned.

"You ruined everything. She was always meant to be mine." Jenkins looks half crazed, like a wild animal, eyes wide and pupils the size of pinpricks. He drops his focus to the beating heart beneath his blade. "Just look at it. Her heart was always meant for me. It's perfect." Some delusional imitation of emotion overtakes him, causing a hitch in his voice as he casts his gaze to her open chest.

I keep my focus on Doctor Jenkins, forcing myself to block out the horror he's so entranced by. His expression shifts, suddenly darker somehow, like he's lost touch with what little reality he had a grip on. He's more dangerous now than he was only seconds ago.

Firming up my grip on my gun, I aim between Jenkins' eyes. "Step away from her," I roar, my voice cracking under the weight of the anguish I feel.

My world stops when he lowers his hand, the edge of the blade almost touching her exposed heart, making my next decision both the easiest and hardest choice of my life.

I squeeze the trigger, aiming the muzzle squarely at his chest, hoping and praying that the force of the bullet will be enough to push him away from Katerina. The bullet hits on target and he falls backwards. The relief that consumes me when the scalpel clatters onto the floor is greater than any I've experienced.

I yell at Marcus to get help with no real comprehension of the words I'm saying as stalk around the table, fall to my knees, and seize Doctor Jenkins around the throat.

He's not dead yet, but he's clutching his chest where the bullet ripped through his scrubs and left a small wound that's now surrounded by an ever-increasing patch of blood as his heart continues to pump. I stare down at him, making sure that the last thing he sees as the light fades from his eyes, is me.

His executioner.

"I made a promise to the woman I love that I'd kill the man who made her cry with my bare hands. And it's a promise I intend to keep," I bite out with a vicious grin.

My fingers tighten around his neck, and he gapes like a fish out of water, fighting for breath and staring back at me pleadingly, although we both know I'm never going to allow him out of this room alive. The light fades from his eyes and the second I know he's gone, I release my hold on him and scramble to my feet.

It's impossible not to be affected by the carnage that fucking psychopath has wrought on her body. I'm as horrified as I am transfixed staring down at the woman I love. Her heart exposed and vulnerable. I can't reconcile this reality, bearing witness to something I never should have seen, but I can't look away. I hear the steady beep of the monitor beside me, but it's the staggered pulsing of the chambers of her heart that tells me she's still alive and give me some small hope.

As devastating as it is to witness, I have to stand by her side but I can't fathom how she'll ever forgive me for not protecting her.

She was mine to protect. And I failed her.

When people begin to flood into the room, Marcus tries to drag me away from Katerina. I'm surrounded by a hurried mob of people in scrubs shouting out things I don't understand, and all I want to do is kill anyone who dares touch her. More hands wrap around me, and I struggle against them as I'm pulled out of the room. The last thing I hear as the door closes is, *"What the hell did he do to her?"*

I lurch to try to get back to her, only for Marcus to wrench me around to face him and take my head in his hands, forcing my focus onto him. "You have to let them help her. There's nothing you can do." His voice is harried, begging as much as he's ordering.

I'm hit with the reality of the situation. There's truly nothing I can do now. Her life is in their hands, and I'm helpless. I want time to stop. I'm petrified that any second now, the rhythmic beat I can hear through the doors will descend into a continuous monotone and take her away from me.

Marcus rests his forehead to mine as he whispers, "I need you to breathe for me, Stefano. They're doing everything they can." The genuine care in his tone drags me back to my senses and I nod, closing my eyes and letting my lungs take their first full breath for what feels like an eternity.

"I'm going to need to take your gun, consigliere. The

police will be here soon and you need to be without a weapon by the time they get here."

I glance at him in confusion, as he reaches into my jacket to take the gun from the shoulder holster. I don't even remember placing it back there. He wipes my fingerprints off it with his shirt and hands it to Vito, one of our most trusted men, who pockets it immediately and excuses himself. He'll make sure the weapon is never found.

"Whether you were saving her life or not, they'll still take you in for questioning," Marco says, his voice pained. "And charging the Bianchi consigliere will be too tempting for the DAs to pass up. It's not a risk we can take right now, and you need to be here for her when she wakes up." He rests his hand on my shoulder and squeezes.

All I can do is nod and be grateful that someone's thinking straight right now.

There's a commotion in the room behind us and the doors open and the gurney is wheeled through. Katerina is covered and I'm finally lucid enough to start to recognise the faces of the doctors and nurses currently surrounding her.

"Where are you taking her? Is she going to be okay?" I scream as I trail after them out into the hall.

I stop dead in my tracks when Danny turns around, his face as white as ash, and holds out a hand towards me, stopping me from following.

"I'm sorry, Mr Tiero, but you can't go with her. They need to get her upstairs to a sterile OR and close her up. I'm so sorry. She's stable right now, but you have to let the doctors work." He makes a move to follow the gurney but stops himself and adds. "Give my thanks to whoever dealt with Doctor Jenkins. He deserved much worse." The callousness in his voice is by no means unwarranted, but I can't deny that it surprises me and has him climbing far higher in my estimation.

I dip my chin, acknowledging his words before he runs after Katerina.

As she's rolled away my heart stutters, like it needs to be close to her in order for it to function properly. And all I can think is *please don't go.*

CHAPTER TWENTY-NINE

KATERINA

"Please wake up, *micetta*," Stefano whispers, his mouth pressed to my knuckles and his head resting against my thigh. Just to hear his voice is heaven, but to feel him next to me is a joy I was scared I'd never get to experience again.

It makes me worry that he's not real and that this is just a dream. Some drug-induced world of make believe and that I'll never get to feel his touch again. My pulse races as scattered memories assault my mind: how the lights reflected off the scalpel blade and the look in Doctor Jenkins' eyes as he sliced into my flesh.

What if this isn't real?

What if I wake up and I'm still there, trapped on his table and being carved open?

"Please, baby girl. Open your eyes for me. I need to know you're okay," he pleads, anguish lacing every word. I want to open my eyes. Confirm that this is real. That

Stefano is here, and that he came for me. That I'm not at the mercy of a madman. But they're so heavy.

The steady background beep of a heart monitor picks up its pace as my pulse races. I'm groggy and half awake, and although I'm willing my body to move for Stefano, I don't think it's obeying me. I want to squeeze his hand and pull him to me. I want him to hold me and never let go.

At last, my eyelids obey and flutter open.

"Stefano," I croak. His head pops up and our eyes lock. The relief that washes over me is profound and overwhelming. I expect to see him return my smile but instead, it's like a damn breaks inside him and he drops his head to my hand and heaves huge sobs of relief. His tears cut like a knife, telling me exactly how close I came to never waking up again.

"Shh, it's okay. I'm here. I'm okay, Stefano," I say, my voice cracking as I try to soothe him. He lifts his head, wiping away his tears and leaning into my touch.

I reach across with my other arm to rest my hand on the back of his head and gasp as pain lances through my chest. More bursts of memory flash up. Doctor Jenkins' cutting into me, the drugs in my IV, but I don't know what happened after that.

"What happened while I was out? Tell me, please," I whisper. "What did he do to me?"

Stefano sits back, carefully running his fingers along my temple before cupping my cheek in his palm. "You're going to be fine, Katerina," he promises, his voice full of care and concern yet concealing so much.

I throw the slightest scowl his way and arch a brow.

That's the sum total of brattiness I can conjure in my current state. "That's not what I asked."

He drops his eyes, pain evident in his expression, but he obeys. "When I found you, he'd already"—he squeezes his eyes shut tight, like he's forcing himself to say the words—"he'd already cut you open."

I remember the incision, but as I look down at my chest and assess the throbbing ache and slices of pain that twinge with every breath, I know he must have cracked my chest. I stare at the corner of the dressing that's peeking out above the neckline of my hospital gown, and I'm completely overwhelmed with emotion.

I might never have woken up. I could have died.

A heaviness settles in my heart when I think that I might never have seen Stefano's face again. Never held his hand. Never kissed his lips. Just the idea of missing out on our forever has me feeling like my soul is tearing itself in two, but in spite of that, I still need to know how close I came to losing everything.

"Tell me everything, please," I say as a tear I didn't feel myself shedding tickles a trail down my cheek.

"The doctor said that Doctor Jen—" I flinch involuntarily at the mention of his name."—that *he* performed a sternotomy, I think he called it. They had to close you up." Stefano swallows, like the words are choking him.

"Were there any complications?" I ask, my voice calm, years of medical training drowning out the terrified woman inside me who just wants to close her eyes and wish that this isn't true.

"No. It took them a little while to figure out how to anaesthetise you because they didn't know what he'd given you, but they said they were able to close without any problems." His thumb strokes gently up into my hairline and I lean into his touch.

"What about Doctor..." I try to say his name, but it dies on my lips, and I shake my head, hating myself. Hating that I was so ignorant of the danger I'd been in for so long. "What about *him*?"

"He's dead, baby girl." His words are absolute and devoid of all remorse, and I can't stop the relief that overtakes me or the smile that bursts forth.

Stefano came for me. He kept his promise.

"Thank fuck," I reply, releasing a long sigh. It's a ridiculous notion that Stefano would allow him to live for a minute longer than was necessary. "Can you tell me how it happened?"

"I dealt with him, Katerina." He doesn't elaborate.

"I'm going to make you tell me one day. You know I won't let you leave it at that." I reply, before taking his hand in mine and adding, "But if you need time? I understand." What else do you say to a man who's slayed a demon for you? *Thank you* seems so pathetic a sentiment. Instead, I say the only thing I can. "I love you, *vecchietto*."

"*Ti amo per sempre, Katerina.*"

"Forever," I whisper back.

"Sleep now, baby girl. You're safe now."

CHAPTER THIRTY

STEFANO

"Thank you for your cooperation, Mr Tiero. We'll be in touch if we have any further questions," Detective Holloway mumbles, not even having the courtesy of looking up from his notebook as he speaks to me. "Make sure you don't leave town," he adds with a nervous squeak.

Based on how he stuttered and stumbled his way through this interview, he obviously knows exactly who I am, which should mean he knows exactly why he shouldn't piss me off. A task he failed spectacularly at.

He doesn't even shake my hand before he turns to leave, instilling a lifelong place on my permanent shit-list. Youth and inexperience are no excuse. If he wants to survive for long on this city's police force, then he's going to need to learn his place a lot quicker.

In his defence, this was merely a witness statement since, as far as he knows, Vito is the one who shot Doctor

Jenkins and he's currently sitting in an interrogation room on the other side of town explaining exactly that. With what we pay our lawyers, he won't spend a single night in jail and will be compensated handsomely for the inconvenience. Vito knows the drill and volunteered for the task. For that, I'll be indebted and forever grateful to him.

I haven't been more than fifty feet from Katerina's recovery room since she came out of surgery. Given the position this has put the hospital in—an attack on an employee by an employee—they're bending over backwards for Katerina. It's a publicity nightmare and neither they nor us want the situation to garner any more attention than is necessary. As such, we've all been moved to their VIP secure ward for the duration of her recovery.

It's an area of the hospital I'm becoming more than familiar with at this point. The Cosa Nostra are frequent flyers here by now.

I let a few minutes pass, making sure Detective Holloway has time to make himself scarce before heading towards the waiting room door. The detective commandeered it for our little chat, but as I step out into the hallway, I find Nico and Marcus in the hallway, making a beeline towards me. I can tell from the sombre looks on their faces they found something on the little excursion I sent them on.

I'm momentarily taken aback when Nico steps into the room and immediately pulls me in for a brief but heartfelt hug, tapping me on the back with more feeling than I've come to expect from him. Given what's happened, I understand. He's closer to Katerina in many ways than he is to me. She's responsible for saving the lives of the people he loves.

I lay my hand on his shoulder when he pulls away and grip him firmly. "She's going to be okay. She's resting now, but I'm about to head back to sit with her."

They both nod, relief obvious on their faces.

"What did you find?" I'd sent Marcus to check out Jenkins' home as soon they'd taken Katerina up for surgery. I needed to know exactly how I'd managed to miss the threat that was right in front of me.

Looking back, Jenkins' behaviour was off from the start, but I'd underestimated him, pegging him as a narcissist with a god complex and not the monster he was.

"The man is... was, next level looney tunes. When we searched his house, we found diaries, letters, photos of her on every surface of his office. The man was obsessed. I'm amazed he didn't go after her sooner." He pauses and pulls out a black leather journal, handing it to me.

I flick through it to find page after page of nonsensical ramblings about her being made for him, about her heart being true, and how one day, he would hold her heart in his hands. The more I read, the more I feel like I've failed her. I spend my life dealing with some of the most heinous criminals on this earth, yet I didn't see the one that walked the halls of this hospital with her every day.

"Please tell me you left enough for the cops for this to be an open and shut case?" I growl, closing the book with a sharp thwack and arching a brow in their direction.

"What is this, my first day?" Marcus retorts. "We

only took what we thought you'd want to see and left the rest for the cops," he reassures me.

"We took his laptop for Sin to analyse. Thought you'd want to check that he didn't have any surveillance or digital files on Katerina," Nico adds matter-of-factly.

"Good thinking," I say before clearing my throat and adding, "Listen, I need to thank you for having my... *our* backs today."

They both shake their heads in tandem.

"Nothing to thank us for, Consigliere," Nico replies gruffly but with affection. "You're family. She's family. You never have to say thank you."

"I know. But I'm thanking you anyway because that woman in there means more to me than anyone else in the world, and I will always thank the men who stand by my side to protect her." They both bow their heads. "Now, fuck off home. Nico, please update the don and tell her I'll check in with her first thing, and Marcus, set up a rotating security detail on the floor and then you can piss off too."

I reach out, shaking Nico's and then Marcus' hand, sending them on their way for the evening before heading straight back to Katerina's room and taking up my sentry on the chair beside her bed. Content to watch the gentle rise and fall of her chest until she wakes.

CHAPTER THIRTY-ONE

KATERINA

Everything is a hell of a lot louder the next time I wake up. My father and Stefano are standing toe to toe at the foot of my bed, my father's face red with rage.

"If you'd spent more time investigating the people in her life and not trying to scare off the wrong person, this never would have happened." I wince as my father shouts at Stefano. "I'll never forgive you for not protecting her from this. I should kill you myself."

"I should let you, but I won't leave her. Not even for you," Stefano replies, his tone sombre but defiant.

My father grabs Stefano's collar, pulling him closer, looking like he's about to shove him clear across the room. Stefano keeps his hands at his side, doing nothing to retaliate, letting my father take his frustration out on him. Stefano may be cutting his best friend some slack, but I sure as fuck am not going to let it slide.

"Cut it the fuck out, right now," I instruct as I drag myself into consciousness. Nothing hits you quite as hard as recovering from emergency surgery with fuck knows what holding your ribcage together and nowhere near enough morphine. It sucks balls. I pat the bed by my thigh, searching for the call buttons I know the nurses always leave for patients. I'm going to need someone to up my medication if I'm going to make it through this conversation.

"Katerina!" my father exclaims, pushing Stefano away and racing to my side. He goes to hug me, only for both me and Stefano to shout, "No," at the same time.

"The incision," I say, glancing towards my chest and feeling guilty for denying my dad the hug he so obviously needs. "I'm sorry, Dad." His shoulders droop and an expression I've never seen overtakes him. It's a blend of concern and disappointment that has me promising myself that I'll hug my father for as long as he needs the minute I'm able.

As Stefano moves to stand opposite him on the other side of the bed, my father's ire returns. "She could have died," he bites out at Stefano through gritted teeth.

"I told you to cut it out. I love you, Dad, but the man saved my fucking life," I chastise, but he doesn't listen.

"He only had to save it, because he couldn't protect you in the first place," my father spits back as he glares at his best friend.

Their bickering fades into the background as I'm hit with a wave of light-headedness. I try to take a steadying breath, but it does nothing to make me feel better.

I'm not a fan of sternotomies. Zero out of ten, do not

recommend. Whatever pain meds they gave me earlier are wearing off, and I'm rapidly tiring of the sharp pain in my ribs every time I inhale.

I tap the call button again and it takes no more than thirty seconds for my nurse to come in through the door, and there's an odd relief when I see it's Danny. I regret ever thinking all those notes, messages, and calls came from him. But I take comfort knowing I was right about him not being capable of stalking.

"Don't make me kick you both out. My patient needs rest and support, not to have to referee whatever bullshit's going on here," Danny snaps at them. He straightens his spine, like he's trying not to balk against their withering glares.

A full rich laugh bursts out of my mouth, followed by a sharp hiss as my body protests at my sudden outburst. Danny may be my new favourite person. Only he would put a patient's needs above their own self-preservation and chastise two of the highest-ranking members of the Cosa Nostra... and he's not wrong. They can both wind their necks in. At least until someone's upped my pain meds.

When they both make a move to confront Danny, I raise a hand, halting them in their tracks. "I swear if you harm a hair on that man's head I will call the d—" I catch myself, before continuing, "Aurora on you both. He's the best nurse in the hospital." I drop my hand, exhaustion taking over.

"Damn straight, Doctor Mancini. I'm going to check your vitals and ask about your post-op pain," he says with a reassuring smile before turning a judgemental brow towards my visitors. "Not act as a referee between two men who are old enough to know better than to cause my patient any further stress."

"Please, we agreed. You're supposed to call me Katerina," I say, wincing as I try to prop myself up.

"Uh-uh. You know better than that. Sit back and use the damn buttons," he admonishes, placing the remote for the bed into my hand. I smile at his bedside manner and how it's put me instantly at ease, but also how he's taken the wind out of both my father and Stefano's sails and they've stopped focussing on shit that really doesn't fucking matter. "Is she okay?" my father asks, worry seeping out of every word.

"*She* is perfectly capable of answering that question herself, Dad." I don't mean to snap, but I'm right here, and I'm the one with the medical degree.

"But *he* is your father, and he's been pacing the halls, waiting for you to get out of recovery for the best part of the day," Danny says, throwing the same chastising brow lift my way this time. After checking on my pain levels, he tinkers with the morphine drip release rate, upping the dose, before turning to all of us and pointing an accusatory finger my way. "I'll be at the nurse's station. If you need anything, you push the button, Katerina. If I catch you trying to do anything for yourself, I'll make sure you get the worst flavours of Jello come dinner time," he declares before he leaves.

I'd forgotten how much of a no-nonsense nurse Danny was with stubborn patients, but smile, realising his brand of care is exactly what I need right now.

I don't give either my father or my lover time to start

in on each other again before I say, "I know you have a lot to work out, but I'm going to tell you both now. I'm not putting up with any more of that bullshit. I don't want to hear it. Work it out on your own time because I'm not listening to it."

I wiggle the fingers on both hands, and it has the desired effect. They each take one of my hands in theirs. "I'm sorry, Dad, but I'm in love with your best friend. I know that's gotta be so fucking weird for you, but I'm not giving him up."

My father holds my gaze, and while he doesn't say anything out loud, I see the precise moment he concedes defeat. His stony face softens, his resistance faltering as he nods and a small reassuring smile brightens his face. My father looks across to Stefano and bows his head.

I'm too exhausted to analyse the micro expressions settling whatever silent truce they're agreeing, but I am relieved they're not shouting at each other anymore.

When I fail to stifle my yawn, my father places a kiss to my cheek before turning to Stefano. "You look after her, you hear me?"

"I promise, Dante," Stefano replies like he's swearing an oath, and it's all I need to hear to know I'm safe and that he'll be here when I wake.

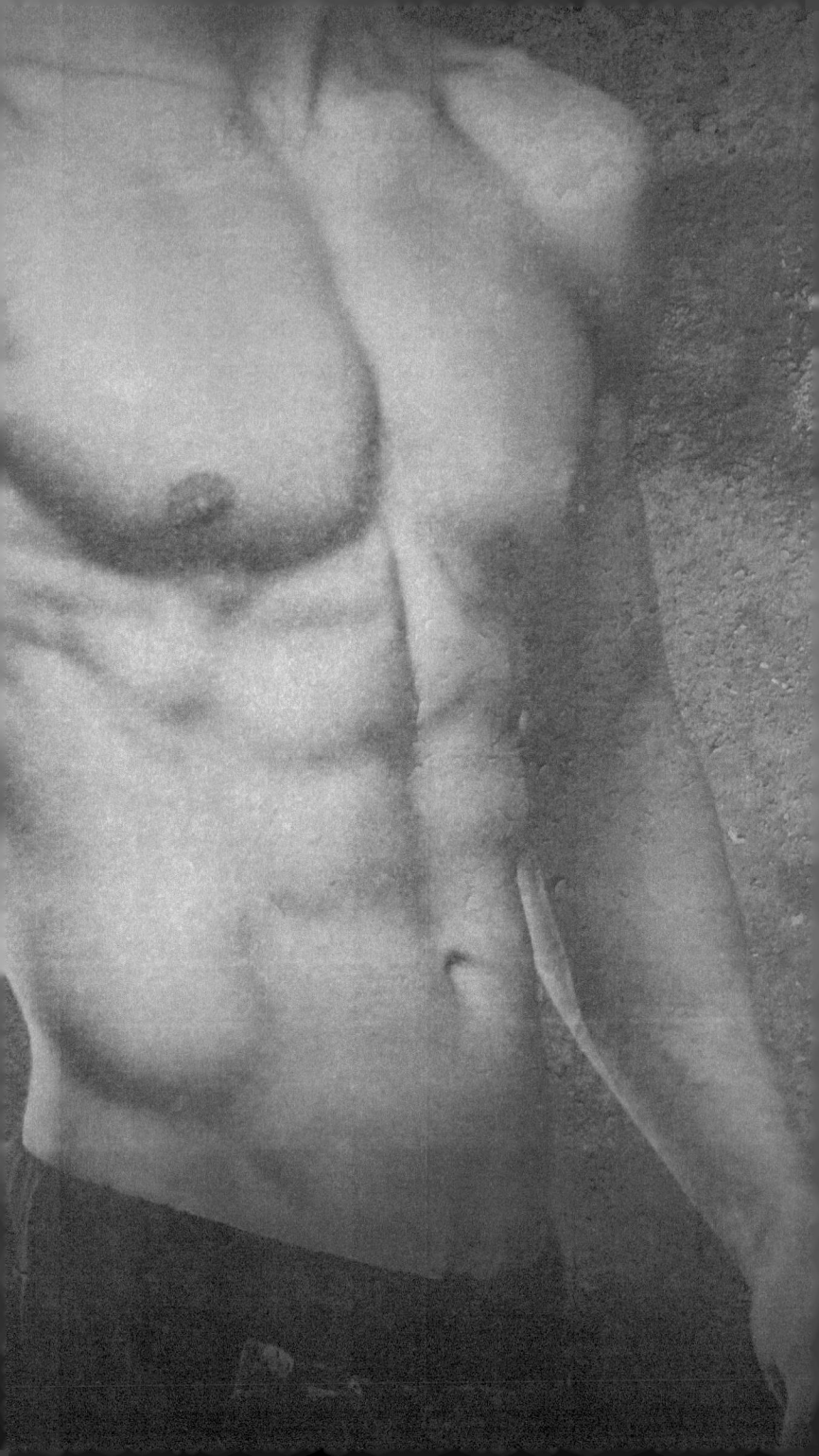

CHAPTER THIRTY-TWO

TEN DAYS LATER...

"I don't think you ever officially asked me to move in with you, you know?" Katerina says with a wry smile as I help her out of the car. She's still recovering, but her doctor gave her the all clear to be discharged this morning. If she could have, she'd have sprinted out of there. She's been climbing the walls for the last ten days. She hates being idle.

"I promised I'd marry you, that's the same thing," I say, kissing her forehead as she reaches her full height.

"It is-fucking-not." Her tone is light, and she's not wrong.

I take her hand in mine and bring it to my lips, kissing the back of it. "Katerina Mancini, will you do me the honour of making this house a home by moving in with me?" I tilt my head, a slightly arrogant smile covering my face, knowing that there's only one answer she'll give me. She's already claimed me in front of her father.

"Are you really hitting me with a dimple-laden smoulder right now? What if I want you to move into my house?" Her eyebrow quirks in a playful challenge.

"But all your stuff is here," I say, pulling her towards my—our—front door.

"True, and I do hate moving."

She leans in, claiming a soft kiss, and I moan when her eager tongue swipes against the seam of my lips. We lose ourselves in the moment, tongues tangling, breath ragged, and the taste of her stirring far more than my emotions.

"I would live with you anywhere you wanted, Katerina," I whisper.

"It's a good job I want to live here then, isn't it, *vecchietto?*"

DOCTORS MAKE THE WORST PATIENTS. It doesn't seem to matter that hers gave her a long list of things she could and couldn't do while she was recovering, Katerina seems to be going out of her way to ignore it and test the limits of my patience.

"Sit your ass down and let me fetch you what you need, woman."

She sits back against the cushions and folds her arms in front of her while fixing a glare at me. She can scowl at me all she likes; it's not going to stop me from doing everything I can to look after her.

"I'm perfectly capable of finding my e-reader without assistance." She couldn't sound any more contrary if she tried. Adorable little brat that she is.

"And the doctor said to take it easy and let me do the heavy lifting."

"My e-reader isn't heavy," she snarks back at me.

"No, but the bag it's in is upstairs and heavy as fuck. Keep your ass on that sofa. That's an order." I try to temper my frustration, but with her incision still healing, the last thing I want is for her to cause herself any further injuries.

I still feel guilty every time I catch her glancing at her scar, overcome by waves of shame that I couldn't spare her the pain she's suffered. What if every time she sees it, it reminds her of how I failed her?

"Fine." She punctuates her reluctant submission by dragging the blanket from the back of the couch and flipping it over her outstretched legs.

She isn't able to maintain the scowl when I lean over to kiss her cheek, whispering, "There's my good girl," in her ear. Katerina lets out the slightest of whimpers at my words, drawing out a contented low rumble from me in response.

"You make me happier than anything else in the world, baby girl. I'm going to take care of you for as long as you'll let me."

KATERINA

I just might be the world's worst patient. In my defence, I'm not a woman who's designed to do nothing. However, I could get used to this.

I'm lazing on the sofa reading a book with my legs flung over Stefano's lap, as the last rays of the afternoon sun stream through the windows. He's reclining at the opposite end with a leather-bound book in one hand while the other strokes gentle circles along my calf.

I place my e-reader down and reach for the glass on the coffee table, immediately drawing the attention and wrath of my overprotective nurse.

"I'll get it," he says, dropping his book and handing me the glass.

My face drops. I hate being so fragile, but it will be a while before I feel like myself. There appears to be no damage to my heart, which I'm thankful for, but it's no mean feat recovering from a sternotomy. It's not the foot-long scar that reminds me of my injuries every day, it's the ache in my chest where my bones are literally knitting themselves back together.

I look down at my incision. It's been a few days since the surgical dressing was removed and honestly, it doesn't affect me as much as I expected it to. I think it was scarier when it was fully covered. I worried that it would make me look damaged; that I was in some way broken. But the longer I look at it, the less it bothers me.

It changes a little every day, and while it's currently an angry red line nestled in a bed of mottled bruises, I know from experience that all scars fade.

"Does it upset you?" Stefano asks quietly, like he's scared to hear the answer.

"Do your bullet wounds bother you?" He raises his brows in shock. "Don't think I missed the scars on the back of your inner thigh when I was on my knees for you all those times," I tease.

"I mean, no, not really." He takes a moment, canting his head as he thinks about it. "They hurt like hell at the time, but I hardly notice them these days."

"Well, there's your answer then," I say matter-of-factly, taking a sip before handing it back to him to place on the coffee table.

He strokes my ankle with his palm as he says, "It's hardly the same thing, baby girl."

"No, I guess it's not. And honestly, it's tough to look at it some days, but ultimately all scars heal in time."

Time stretches out as my words hang in the air for longer than feels natural. Stefano casts his eyes down before asking. "Will you ever be able to forgive me for failing you?"

My heart breaks for him. The anguish in his voice is unbearable.

I shuffle across towards him, glaring when his expression shifts to one of panic, like he thinks I'm going to hurt myself. My chest is tender as I stretch and move to my knees, but it's not painful. I lift my leg and carefully straddle his lap, masking a smile when his face blanches with concern and his palms shoot to my hips to steady me. I run my fingers along his jawline and tip his head back, demanding all of his focus.

"You listen here, *vecchietto*. You did not fail me. You saved me, *amore mio*."

"I couldn't protect you," he replies, anguish lacing his words.

"I never asked for you to be my protector, Stefano. I need a partner in crime, not a knight in shining armour. I only ask that you promise to be mine."

It takes a moment, but eventually, he returns my smile, and I get lost in his midnight-blue eyes. They show me everything I need to know.

"*Sempre tuo,* Katerina."

"Always yours."

EPILOGUE

FIVE WEEKS LATER...

While I'm beginning to enjoy my first real time off in... my entire adult life, there's only so long I can be idle for. After ten days in hospital, and weeks recuperating, I'm going more than a little stir crazy. The only thing that's keeping me sane is the constant stream of visitors.

I didn't honestly appreciate that there were so many people in my life who would go out of their way to be there for me when I needed them. There isn't a day that's passed where there hasn't been someone to keep me company or deliver something I need. It's made me think about what I want going forward. And returning to a life divided into two worlds seems more and more untenable.

Nearly every Cosa Nostra member I've helped or healed over the years has dropped by, including half of the capos and on occasion the don. It's been surreal to have Aurora Bianchi stopping by to chat. We've been discussing ideas for the future and how I might be able to help her set up a private clinic that's more exclusive to the Cosa Nostra.

Danny has been visiting too, as often as his clunker of a car will let him. Turns out he nearly missed the most exciting thing ever to happen at St Joseph's because he was stranded on the side of the freeway. He's been keeping me up to date on the hospital gossip and I've been discovering that we make far better friends than we did dates.

I had a call with the hospital administration this morning, and I'm still reeling from it. It's not like I intended to resign, but the minute they started talking about how I was integral to the smooth running of my department and a key part of their vision for the future of the hospital, I understood that the pencil pushers on the screen viewed me as a commodity and not a person. The more they waffled on, the less I wanted to be the Head of General Surgery at St Joseph's Hospital.

Don't get me wrong, I love my job. I wouldn't trade being a doctor for the world. Not only am I fucking good at it, but I worked damn hard for it. It's just that the more time I spend surrounded by the people who truly care about me, the more I know that being Doc Em to the Bianchis means far more to me than being Doctor Katerina Mancini for everyone else.

The more I think about my decision, the happier I am.

I just need to figure out what I want to do now.

I SPENT the afternoon brainstorming ideas for what the hell I was going to do if I wasn't going back to St Joseph's while also streaming the pilot episode of every show I'd missed in the last decade and deciding that, barring a few notable exceptions, I wasn't missing much.

Doodling on my note pad I don't notice Stefano coming into the room until he leans over the back of the sofa and kisses the top of my head, scaring me half to death and making me jump enough for the notebook to clatter to the floor.

"Sorry, baby girl. I didn't mean to scare you," he says, picking it up and handing it back. His smile is warm and lights something up inside me. I don't think I'll ever tire of seeing that dimple pop every evening when he comes home to me.

"Missed you, *vecchietto*," I practically purr as I reach up and grip the buttons of his shirt, pulling him in for a kiss.

"Missed you too." He beams, crouching beside me and resting on his heels. "Give me a minute to get changed and I'll order us some dinner. I've been looking forward to curling up with you all day."

"Rough day?" I ask as I cup his face and stroke my thumb over his cheek.

"Yes, and no. Long, but it always feels longer when I'm away from you."

"Hurry back," I call after him, but as soon as I hear the shower start above me, I kick off my blanket and sneak upstairs.

I know I'm still recovering, but I've waited long enough, and a girl has needs. It doesn't seem to matter how many times either my doctor or I tell him it's perfectly safe to have sex, he still won't fuck me. I even got a doctor's note saying that as long as we avoid positions where I'd bear weight on my arms or chest, we'd be fine. Still nothing.

So now I'm taking the matter into my own hands.

As I enter our bedroom, I strip off. Carefully. Shucking down my sweatpants and underwear and kicking them off before—somewhat more gingerly—removing my hoodie. While I'm healing well it's still a little tender. I plan to exist in a sports bra or no bra universe for the foreseeable future.

I hurry to my bedside table when the shower shuts off, grabbing my favourite little toy, and climbing onto the mattress, walking on my knees to the end of the bed.

I smile when I push the button and the toy bursts to life, humming out its familiar little pulsations. Of all the toys I have, the one that gets me off the hardest and fastest is this little suction device. There's a reason it's the number one best-selling clitoral vibrator.

Bringing the ring of soft silicone to my body, I trail it down to the apex of my thighs, moaning as the halo seals around my clit and the pressure of the suction starts to fluctuate. I don't know why it works so freaking well, I just know that every other clitoral toy I own only gets dug out of the drawer if the batteries in this one die.

The smile on my face broadens as a towel-clad Stefano emerges from the walk-in closet, stopping mid hair tousle to rake his eyes over my body.

"What do you think you're doing, *micetta*?" Any authority he's managed to inject into his words is completely undermined when he clenches his jaw as if he's fighting to stifle a groan.

"If you won't play with me, then a girl's gotta do what a girl's gotta do. You're welcome to join me. Give me a good seeing to."

"You're racking up the mother of all spankings as soon as you've healed enough to go over my knee. You know that, don't you?" His promises only amplify the pleasure currently being demanded by my battery-operated assistant, sending shivers rolling up my spine to tickle the hairs at the back of my neck.

"Promises, promises, *vecchietto*," I purr. "I've waited long enough to feel your tongue between my legs. Are you really going to deny me the pleasure of coming on your face?"

He stalks forwards and stops in front of me, dropping the towel in his hand and unfurling the one around his waist, letting it fall in a heap. I'm so distracted by his half hard cock bobbing in front of me as it starts to stand to attention that I miss the hand moving to wrap around mine. He grips it tightly and pushes the toy more firmly against my swollen clit, wringing a strangled moan from my lips.

"Are you going to be good for me, baby girl?"

I nod enthusiastically because I can't form words while he's flexing his wrist, creating waves of alternating pressures against my oversensitive clit.

"I'm going to lay down in this bed and you're going to ride my face."

"I am so on board with this plan," I say eagerly.

"But..."

"No, no buts. Unless it's my butt and you're fucking it," I plead, unable to hide the pout that plasters itself across my face. "I need this. I need you."

"If you want me, you'll do as you're told. Do you understand me? I won't risk hurting you." His tone is hard but laced with desire.

"I trust you. You won't hurt me."

He lifts his free hand and wraps it around the back of my neck, threading his fingers into the hair at the base of my skull and pulling me towards him, stealing a kiss as he presses the toy harder against my clit. His mouth swallows my moans as he pushes me closer to my peak.

I cry out in frustration when he steps back suddenly, taking his lips and my toy with him.

"No fair, I was so close," I whine, and he simply arches one eyebrow in response. I either take what he gives me, or I get nothing, and I definitely want whatever he's prepared to give me. I love a solo orgasm as much as the next person, but I'll be damned if I'm going to miss out on one from him.

He stalks around the bed, laying on his back in the centre of the mattress and pushing the pillows aside. "Come over here, grab onto the headboard for support, and sit on my face," he demands, while crooking his index finger at me.

He doesn't have to ask me twice.

The second I throw my leg over him, his arms wrap around the tops of my thighs and he pulls me down. I expect him to go straight for my clit, but instead, he flattens his tongue and laps at my slick folds before thrusting into my pussy at the same time as settling the still buzzing toy against the now throbbing bundle of nerves.

"Fuck, yes, Daddy, I needed this," I cry, flexing my fingers and gripping the headboard so hard I wouldn't be surprised if I were leaving indentations in the wood.

He may say something in response but whatever it is, is more growl than anything else and is followed up with the toy being rocked against my clit and his free hand gripping me tighter. His enthusiasm only turns me on more, as his tongue penetrates me, flexing against the front of my pussy, teasing my G-spot mercilessly. The result is an orgasm that doesn't just reach its peak, it rips through me at a cellular level.

His tongue doesn't stop its brutal pace as he fucks me through my release, drinking down every drop of my arousal and wringing desperate, guttural moans from my lips.

I'm still seeing stars when he taps my thigh, but I pull myself up higher, deciding it's probably wise not to allow a man with such talent to suffocate. It's definitely in my best interests.

I'm exhausted, and my limbs feel like they're floating. I giggle as he shuffles down the bed, not expecting me to swing my leg off him to release him. I mean, I would, but right now, all my energy has been sapped from me.

There's rustling as he kneels up, nestling in behind me and trailing kisses from the nape of my neck to my shoulder.

"You're delicious, baby girl. I could eat you for hours," he whispers against my dewy skin.

"I'd let you if I could take it. I think I'm going to need to build my stamina back up," I pant out, a little disappointed with my complete lack of endurance.

"You did such a good job, coming so hard for me." I let his praise wash over me and lean into his hot breath at my neck, revelling in the way his fingers tease and tickle across the rest of my body as he speaks.

"I love you, Stefano."

"I love you too. So much," he replies, voice thick with emotion. "I thought I'd lost you that day. I'm going to drive you nuts, being an overprotective twat for the rest of our lives, you know?"

"Oh, I know. But when that happens, I think I'm just going to use this tactic again; get naked and demand orgasms. It seems to be working out well for me." I let go of my grip on the headboard and turn around to face him, pressing my lips to his before he has a chance to reply.

The kiss isn't soft, it's ardent and full of passion and all the words we want to say to each other. Now and always. It's a promise that I'm his and he's mine.

When I pull back, his hand reaches out, dusting his fingertips from my collarbone, down through the valley of my breasts, and tracing the line of my scar. His touch is delicate, and his expression isn't one of pity, it's nothing but awe. Respect for my strength. I feel seen on every level.

"I'm going to need you to fuck me like you own me," I say with a smile, mirroring his movements, dancing my fingers across his chest and teasing down to his impossibly well-defined abdominal muscles, not stopping until I've wrapped my hand around his dick.

He keens at my touch and the noise he makes is closer to a whimper than a moan when I tighten my grip and begin to pump his length, running my thumb over the slit in his crown and drawing his pre-cum back down his rigid cock.

"I need you inside me. I need you to fuck me and fill me up."

He leans in, letting his warm lips caress my neck, bringing a flurry of goosebumps that chase themselves in circles, only making me more desperate for his touch.

"I'll fuck you. I'll fill you up. But you're going to do exactly as you're told if you want my cum in your hot little cunt. Do you understand?"

"Yes, Daddy." *Oh god yes Daddy, whatever you say.*

My pussy clenches when he quirks his dimple-laden smile at me, showing me just how much he likes it when I call him that. He takes my hand in his and moves me away from his dick, pulling me down onto my back and nudging my legs apart to give him the room to settle himself between them. As soon as the weight of him presses against me, I smile. It feels more right than I can fathom; like I'm exactly where I'm meant to be, about to be worshipped by the man I love.

He's careful to keep his weight off of my chest and leaves my arms free to wrap around his neck, drawing him down into a passionate kiss that's only broken when he rolls his hips, running the tip of his cock along my seam and notching himself at my entrance.

I gasp with pleasure when he thrusts forward, smiling as the bulbous head of his cock rubs against the walls of my pussy, and let out a string of incoherent whimpers when he bottoms out and holds himself inside me.

"Please, fuck me. Please don't stop. Take me, I'm yours."

"Of course you're mine, baby girl. Your pleasure is mine," he says, pulling back only to thrust right back in. "This pussy is mine." He withdraws to the very tip and my pussy flutters, demanding his cock return immediately. He thrusts again and my whine of frustration transforms into a whimper of ecstasy. "This heart is mine," he says, lifting his hand and laying it flat across my chest, obscuring most of the angry red scar and filling my heart to the brim with more emotion than I think my body can handle.

He holds my gaze as he starts to rock into me, setting a pace that has my orgasm cresting quicker than I could have imagined. My pants become pleas, begging for him to come with me. To take me. To own me. To love me.

And he does. Coming with his lips pressed to mine, stealing the air from my lungs. White light flashes behind my eyes as my orgasm rolls through me like thunder before a welcome storm, crackling in the air just before the heavens open.

As I lay beneath him and lean into his touch as he strokes the stray hairs away from my face, I know that whatever happens, he's it for me. Nothing compares to the love I have for him.

He pulls back and I whimper at the loss, but when he rolls on his back and tucks me into his side, I revel in finding my nook. Laying my head against his shoulder and resting my arm across his chest, I tickle the little forest of hairs across his pecs.

"Sometimes when I look at you, saying 'I love you' doesn't feel like enough," I whisper with a love-struck sigh.

Reaching across, he crooks a finger under my chin and pulls my gaze to his. His sapphire blue eyes glisten with emotion as his words settle in my soul.

"*Ti amerò per sempre,* Katerina."

"Until forever," I answer.

I promise.

I vow.

EPILOGUE

STEFANO

FOUR MONTHS LATER...

"You have some fucking nerve, Tiero," Dante says, levelling a glare at me that could wither fresh cut flowers. While he's been far more understanding than I ever thought he would be, things are still more than a little strained between us.

I mean, I can't blame the man. I am in love with his daughter. That was never going to go down well, but he's handling it with more grace than I have a right to expect. He's even started inviting me back to his family dinners. Although that has more to do with Katerina refusing to attend if he didn't than him actually wanting me there. It's progress though.

"I realise that. But I can't imagine not having you there." This is as close to begging as I'm ever likely to get in my life, but I'll do it if it means I can have my best friend stand by my side at my wedding.

The damage to our friendship hurt me almost as much as I expected it to, but I wouldn't sacrifice what I found with Katerina for it, and I think that's what hurt Dante the most. It's an unspoken truth that if it came down to it I'd choose a life with Katerina every time over a lifetime of friendship. That's a hard fact to overcome and it weighs heavy between us, but there's no escaping it.

And it's the way it should be. I love her above anyone or anything else in my life.

"Let me get this straight. You're not asking for my permission to marry my daughter. You're asking me to be your best man? Have you got a death wish, because you are testing the limits of my newfound acceptance of your relationship with my daughter?"

"Katerina doesn't need anyone's permission, Dante. And if she found out I asked, she'd kick both of our asses on principle," I reply, a smirk teasing my lips, imagining her doing just that. Dante lets out a huff of laughter, knowing full well she'd have no qualms giving us a piece of her mind. Reaching a hand out to rest it on his shoulder, I continue, "When I marry your daughter, she wants you to walk her down the aisle, and I want nothing more than for you to stand by my side when I do. I know, believe me, I know that I'm asking a lot. But even if you say no, nothing is going to stop me marrying her." I fold my arms across my chest, preparing to hear the worst.

The silence grows from merely awkward to next-level

painful, but I don't falter, waiting for as long as it will take to hear his response.

"Fine." My brows raise, shooting somewhere close to my hairline in complete shock. I mean, it's hardly an enthusiastic response, but considering the state of our friendship, it's probably more than I could have expected.

I can't contain my happiness, and he grumbles as I pull him in for a brief and heartfelt hug. It's awkward, but it goes a long way to reassuring me that one day we'll be close again.

"So, when is this wedding?" He grinds out as I finally release him and take a step back, knowing my expression must be more than a little sheepish right now. "Stefano?"

"That's the thing... what are you doing this afternoon?"

Want to find out how Aurora Bianchi became don?
Go back to the start and read *Broken Princess & Brutal Queen*, the introduction to the The Bianchi Chronicles

If you enjoyed Katerina & Stefano's story, it would be wonderful if you could help me spread the word.
Whether that's by telling your book besties, sharing on social media or leaving a review on your website of choice, any support would be much appreciated. I'd love for *The Bianchi Chronicles* to find more readers.

THE BIANCHI CHRONICLES

Novels

Broken & Brutal Duet

1. Broken Princess

2. Brutal Queen

Interconnected Standalones

3. Fierce Protector

4. Wicked Guardian

Novellas

0.5. Axe To Grind (Nico & Benedict's First Date)

ABOUT THE AUTHOR

I live in the south of England with my real life book-husband—AKA Mr Bennett—and our two *delightfully* unruly boys. I'm usually found in my writing cave arguing with my characters trying to convince them to follow the outline I spent weeks planning.

For the latest news and to join my mailing list check out my website www.laurabennettauthor.com/links

ACKNOWLEDGEMENTS

Sarah, thank you so much for helping me wrestle this plot into submission. I wouldn't have been able to publish Stefano and Katerina's story without you. You're a fabulous editor but an even better friend. Thank you for your honesty and for falling in love with Stefano.

Sally, there are no words. You keep me sane, and I hope you know just how much I value our friendship. Thank you—for *everything*.

To my amazing beta readers, **Lara, Amanda, Tracy**, I can't thank you enough for your wonderful feedback and for helping me with Fierce Protector. I'm so lucky to have you.

Lara a special thank you for you help with the Italian!

Darcy thank you for all your hard work, I'm so glad I found you.

I need to give a huge shout out to **all my indie author friends**. You go out of your way to support other authors, whether it's creating a community in your Discord servers, 'Waffle Wednesdays' in the WhatsApp group chat or taking the time to engage through your DMs. THANK YOU. You've helped me so much, and I appreciate each and every one of you.

To my wonderful **ARC Team**, thank you for signing

up and for reading *Fierce Protector*. I've been so excited to share it with you and I can't tell you how much your support means to me. The messages you sent me had me feeling every emotion.

My **readers**, your likes, shares, tags and messages fill me with joy. I can't thank you enough for your support.

Mr Bennett... without you I wouldn't have been able to finish this book or be able to do pursue this dream. Your support is more than I deserve.

www.ingramcontent.com/pod-product-compliance
Lightning Source LLC
Chambersburg PA
CBHW020931260626
47169CB00006B/1668